FEAR
FOR HER
LIFE

BOOKS BY D.K. HOOD

DETECTIVES KANE AND ALTON PREQUELS

Lose Your Breath

Don't Look Back

DETECTIVES KANE AND ALTON SERIES

Don't Tell a Soul

Bring Me Flowers

Follow Me Home

The Crying Season

Where Angels Fear

Whisper in the Night

Break the Silence

Her Broken Wings

Her Shallow Grave

Promises in the Dark

Be Mine Forever

Cross My Heart

Fallen Angel

Pray for Mercy

Kiss Her Goodnight

Her Bleeding Heart

Chase Her Shadow

Now You See Me

Their Wicked Games

Where Hidden Souls Lie

A Song for the Dead

Eyes Tight Shut

Their Frozen Bones

Tears on Her Grave

DETECTIVE BETH KATZ SERIES

Wildflower Girls

Shadow Angels

Dark Hearts

Forgotten Girls

D.K. HOOD

FEAR FOR HER LIFE

bookouture

Published by Bookouture in 2025

An imprint of Storyfire Ltd.
Carmelite House
50 Victoria Embankment
London EC4Y 0DZ

www.bookouture.com

The authorised representative in the EEA is Hachette Ireland
8 Castlecourt Centre
Dublin 15 D15 XTP3
Ireland
(email: info@hbgi.ie)

ISBN: 978-1-83618-225-2
eBook ISBN: 978-1-83618-224-5

This book is for people suffering from a disability, illness, depression, or loneliness. I hope my stories can offer you a few hours of escapism like they do me.

PROLOGUE
DEER LODGE, MONTANA

Sunday

We're all going to die. Another explosion rocked the prison, and Amy Clark ran out of the observation deck to join the other prison guards. Choking thick black smoke filled the passageways and heat from a raging fire rushed over her, burning her nostrils. Sirens screamed and she couldn't hear the warden's instructions over the loudspeakers. As fire rushed through maximum security, guards worked frantically to escort notorious and dangerous prisoners to safety. Eyes stinging and throat raw, she followed the others from her section along a passageway. They rushed through a door and came face-to-face with the warden. He issued orders to everyone but left her standing alone. She glanced at her watch. If only she'd left at the end of her shift, she'd be home by now, but her replacement hadn't showed.

"You're Amy Clark?" The warden scanned a list in his hand.

Wondering what task he had for her, Amy coughed. The smoke was everywhere. "Yes, sir."

"The fire is contained to one area and will be under control shortly. I'm moving four prisoners from the damaged area to Black Rock Falls County. I'll need you to accompany the driver of the prison bus." His stern gaze settled on her face. "I know you're at the end of your shift, but with the staff shortages, I'll need all hands on deck. Go home and get everything you need for an overnight stay and be back within the hour. Once the prisoners are delivered, you'll be staying in town and returning in the morning. I'll have someone message you with the accommodation details. Be fully aware that these are maximum security prisoners. Wear your riot gear and stay alert at all times."

Uneasy, Amy nodded. "Yes, sir." Being five-two and skinny, she'd chosen not to work in maximum security, and although she'd trained in every aspect of her job, her heart raced at the idea of being in such close proximity to the never-to-be-released violent criminals.

"Collect the paperwork before you leave." The warden sighed. "There will be prison guards to assist with unloading when you arrive. Do not attempt to try this alone. Not one of these men would think twice about killing you if given the chance."

One hour later, Amy headed toward Black Rock Falls County with four notorious criminals chained together in the back of the prison bus. She glanced at the clipboard and scanned the hastily put-together transfer documents. A wave of fear rushed over her at the list of names: Eduardo Souza, a mob kingpin; "Ice Pick" Mason Margos, a serial killer of more than twenty people; the Silent Strangler, Sebastian Callahan, another serial killer, with a body count of fifteen victims that they knew about; and the Blue Man, Carl Romero, a sadistic serial killer, who preyed on women in the guise of a handyman. She glanced at Bob, the driver. A prison guard in his sixties who spent his time in admissions or driving the prison bus. "Had any problems with transporting maximum security prisoners?"

"Strange as it may seem, they're usually the quietest." Bob gave her a smile. "Most times, they don't say anything at all, but then they're not usually transferred together. The thing is, even if they start tearing each other apart in the back there, don't be goaded into opening any of the doors to check them out. Whatever they've done to each other will wait until we get to Black Rock Falls County."

Every time Amy looked around, the prisoners seemed to be just staring out of the windows. Bob wasn't into conversation, so she admired the scenery as they traveled along the open highway. The blacktop wound through mountains and then into endless expanses of green and brown lowlands. It went on forever and ahead of them was miles and miles of miles and miles with not a vehicle in sight. In the endless blue sky above her hovered a helicopter. The next second, a rush of dust and debris hit the windshield like buckshot. Terrified, Amy instinctively put up her hands and looked away. Wind stirred into a tornado as the powerful blades stripped the trees alongside the road. All around the air shimmered. The noise from the engine deafened her as she screamed at the driver. "What's happening?"

"Hold tight." The driver slammed on the brakes and the bus slid sideways.

Hanging on as they bucked and slid. She raised her voice. "Don't stop. It might be an ambush."

The bus increased speed as the powerful machine dropped slowly until it sat above them. The *whoop, whoop, whoop* of the blades so loud it trembled through her seat. Wind buffeted the bus as the chopper swung around and hovered in front of them. Two men sat on the edge of the door, their feet dangling like soldiers. She swallowed hard, horrified at seeing rifles in their hands. "Shooter. Drive. Aim straight for them."

She turned to look at Bob and gasped in horror at the sight of a red dot right in the center of his forehead. She didn't have time to react as the windshield exploded. Wind hit her in a rush of broken glass, and blood splattered her face as Bob slumped forward. Frantically, she grappled with the steering wheel, desperately trying to get her foot on the brake. In his death throes, Bob plunged his foot down hard on the gas and the bus careered out of control along the highway.

Covered in blood, her hands slipped on the wheel as the bus increased speed, swerving from one side of the highway to the other. She'd never driven a bus before and, in desperation, forced the gear stick into neutral. The bus didn't slow, and panic gripped her. Ahead, the mountains loomed. Forest lined the highway, the trees getting closer by the second as she fought to keep the bus on the road. Ahead, she hit a steep incline, and although the bus slowed, she'd never make it around the next tight bend. Above her, the *whoop, whoop, whoop* of the chopper deafened her. Would she be next?

Using all her strength, she guided the speeding bus around the bend. Tires screamed and the bus tilted dangerously and bounced along the rough edge of the highway. The next second, the driver's side wheels mounted the verge alongside the blacktop and bounced into the gully. The world shifted as the bus rolled. Time slowed as she flew through the air, arms and legs flailing. In a scream of torn metal, the bus slid along the blacktop. She could hear the prisoners yelling as the bus slammed into a line of trees and stopped in a screech of metal. Broken glass flew around like confetti, and steam poured from the engine, filling the cab. The bus moaned as if in its death throes, and behind her she could hear the curses of the prisoners.

Dizzy, Amy shook her head and panic gripped her. The chopper made a sweeping turn and was coming back. The engine grew louder and whipped up the dust from the road and tossed it at her through the broken window. She must move—now! Pain shot through her shoulder, taking away her breath. She'd slammed into the partition and then fallen onto Ben. She groaned at the bloody mess under her. Ben's body had taken the full impact. Sickened, she crawled off him. Shaken but with only a few bruises, she scrambled around searching for her backpack and phone. She needed to call for assistance immediately, but just as she'd grabbed her bag, the chopper dropped from the sky and landed in front of the bus. Men wearing balaclavas and carrying assault rifles poured out of the chopper. They ran straight for her, aiming their guns. Pulling her weapon now would be suicide.

"Open the door and we'll let you to live." A man walked up to her, aiming his rifle at her head. "We didn't come here to kill anyone. The driver was collateral damage. Do as we say and everything will be fine."

Amy glanced over her shoulder and through the glass partition at the prisoners. They all hung from their seats attached by the chains. None of them appeared to be badly injured. "What do you want? There's no money on this bus."

"We don't want money." The man barked a laugh in amusement. "You have one of our friends and we want him back. Give him to us and you will walk free. Act the hero and I'll shoot you and blow a hole in the door to take the keys from your dead body. I would rather not get my hands dirty." His black eyes met her gaze. "Do you want me to count to ten?"

Shaking her head, Amy grabbed her backpack, opened the door, and slid out. The moment her feet touched the ground, rough hands grabbed her and searched her. They tossed her weapon, stamped on her phone, and grabbed the keys to unlock the bus and free the prisoners' shackles. One man twisted her arms so high behind her back breathing was difficult. She gaped in horror as the man she recognized as mob boss Eduardo Souza climbed out of the bus with the help of two of his men. Behind him, the three serial killers jumped from the bus and stood watching Souza expectantly.

"You are free, my friends." Souza grinned broadly. He waved a hand toward the forest. "People enter this forest and are never seen again. It's a perfect place to hide." His gaze moved over Amy and, trembling, she held her breath, expecting one of his men to kill her.

"Leave her." Souza's mouth curled into a cruel smile as he turned to walk toward the chopper. "I'm sure my friends will enjoy her company."

ONE

BLACK ROCK FALLS

The last seven years in Sheriff Jenna Alton's life had become a kaleidoscope of events. The incident that changed her life forever came when she testified against cartel boss Viktor Carlos. His reaction to the never-to-be-released sentence was to threaten her openly in court. As undercover DEA Agent Avril Parker, she endured abuse for two years to take down his organization. She should have gotten a promotion, but instead, federal marshals whisked her away into witness protection. Before arriving in Black Rock Falls, her entire identity had been changed, along with her face. Discovering the sheriff of Black Rock Falls was weak and left the townsfolk unprotected, she became a deputy, then ran for sheriff and won.

She'd formed a reliable and expert team around her. Jake Rowley she'd trained as her rookie deputy and now he'd become a loyal and experienced law enforcer. They'd managed alone until the unexpected arrival of Dave Kane, who she believed was an injured ex-cop looking to recuperate in a slow town. Later she discovered she had employed an active government asset who POTUS had placed in her town to watch over her. As a black ops sniper and later Secret Service agent, Kane didn't let the metal plate in his head slow him down. She was instantly attracted to the six-five, two-hundred-sixty-pound fighting machine, but it seemed for the first four years at least, that Kane's only interest in her was protecting her, which drove her crazy.

Her team of Deputies Kane, Rowley, and Zac Rio and K9 unit Johnny Raven worked closely with the medical examiner and Kane's handler, Dr. Shane Wolfe. Together, they'd faced some of the most notorious serial killers in America and brought them to justice.

After marrying, she and Kane had adopted Tauri, a five-year-old Native American boy who was the light of their lives. Now almost eight months pregnant and determined to keep working, Jenna stared at her reflection in the mirror. She'd selected loose-fitting clothes, preferring not to attract attention to her condition. She'd realized as she went through her pregnancy that people treated her differently. When in fact, apart from physically engaging a criminal, she couldn't think of a reason why she couldn't do her job. Taking maternity leave to care for her children was a given, and she'd rely on the team she'd gathered around her over the last seven years to run the store. They could handle just about anything in her absence.

Right now, suffocated by the concern for her well-being, she needed a couple of hours alone just to think. A drive to the next town to buy baby clothes would be wonderful and give her a rare opportunity to drive the sleek black Mustang Kane had given her for her birthday. In another week she wouldn't fit behind the wheel. Having a protective husband was wonderful in some ways but annoying in others. She chewed on her bottom lip thinking through what she would say to him. Right now, he was in the garage with Tauri building a Harley from a pile of what looked like junk. She headed outside, enjoying the sun on her face and the fresh breeze from the mountains in her hair. The sound of tools clinking together came from the garage and she found Kane explaining what he was doing and instructing Tauri how to tighten bolts. Her little boy had an expression of wonder on his face as he listened intently. "Hey, you look like you're busy."

"We're trying to piece together some of the parts that Raven dropped by last weekend." Kane stood and wiped his hands on a rag. He indicated to the purse under her arm. "Going somewhere?"

Nodding, Jenna headed toward her sedan. "I haven't had too much of an opportunity to drive my car. I figured I'd drive over to Louan and check out the baby store."

"Okay, give me five and I'll join you." Kane smiled at her and turned to Tauri. "We can work on this later."

"You said we'd work on it until lunchtime." Tauri's bottom lip turned down and he looked at him with sorrowful eyes. "Do we have to go to look at more baby things with Mommy?"

"If you don't want to come with us, I can always ask Nanny Raya if she will read you some stories." Kane crouched down to look at his son. "We can pick this up again when I get back."

Nanny Raya, Tauri's nanny, lived in a self-contained extension to the house. She cared for Tauri when they were working and would be there to assist Jenna with the new baby. The selection of their nanny had been important due to the security necessary around Kane, as he had a bounty on his head. Even with his new identity and face, Kane was kept on standby by POTUS for important missions. Nanny Raya had passed all the necessary security checks, and as a retired FBI agent, she fit in just fine.

"I want to play motorcycles with you, Daddy." Tauri swiped at his eyes. "Before you go and catch the baddy man again."

Squeezing Kane's shoulder to get his attention, Jenna gave a nonchalant shrug. "How much trouble could I possibly get into just driving to Louan and back? I'm weeks away from delivery, and to be perfectly honest, I wouldn't mind some alone time. I know shopping for baby things is boring, especially when I take so much time making up my mind. I'd really like to go alone so I can just stand there looking at everything in the store and not worry about taking too long."

"That's not a good idea." Kane searched her face. "If anything happened—"

Throwing one hand into the air she stared at him. "What could possibly happen? It's practically a straight stretch of highway from here and I'm a safe driver. It's Sunday and very quiet and that little shop is filled with garments and blankets made by locals. It's only open on weekends. I figure I'll be away two hours max. It's not like I have a mother or grandmother to make things for our baby. This is the next best thing." She sighed. "You'll never miss me. Just like when I take a nap."

"Okay, okay." Kane held both his hands up in surrender. "Go, but call me when you get there so I know you've arrived safely, and do the same when you leave."

Throwing her arms around him to kiss him, Jenna grinned. "Not a problem." She bent and hugged Tauri. "Do you want to stay here and help Daddy fix the motorcycle or come baby shopping with me?"

"I want to fix the motorcycle with Daddy." Tauri grinned and hugged her. "Love you, Mommy."

Waving, Jenna headed for the Mustang. "Love you more." She opened the door and placed her weapon in the glovebox and tossed her purse on the passenger seat.

Driving the new Mustang was like being inside the cockpit of an airplane. The seat hugged her and the design of the steering wheel, with its flat bottom, meant it didn't dig into her belly. The car reminded her of her cat, Pumpkin. When she stroked the gas pedal it purred as if it enjoyed the long straight-aways as much as she did. She didn't drive fast and enjoyed the scenery. Late spring in Black Rock Falls was particularly beautiful. Apart from an endless deep blue sky, the forest and the lowlands were awash with bright colors from the many wild-flowers growing in abundance. She buzzed down her window to inhale the fragrance and loved the way the wind tousled her hair. She stopped outside the little store and climbed with some difficulty out of the vehicle. "I figure this will probably be my last drive for a while."

She bypassed the baby store and went inside the diner to use the bathroom and then grabbed a milkshake on the way out. She browsed the abundant baby goods for sale and found herself turning to ask Kane's opinion on this and that and finding the space beside her empty. She stared out of the window, suddenly wishing that he'd come with her after all. "Oh my, now I'm dependent on him."

"What's that you say, my dear?" An elderly lady behind the counter stared at her.

Gathering the pile of purchases she'd chosen and taking them to the counter, she smiled at her. "Oh, I'm just talking to myself. I'm so used to having my husband with me when we go shopping that I turned to talk to him and he's not there."

"That's nice." The old woman scanned the items and folded them neatly before placing them into bags. "You're not from around here, are you?"

Shaking her head, Jenna paid with her credit card. "No, I'm from Black Rock Falls, but I'm sure glad I dropped by today. This is a great store and I have everything I need now."

"Trust me, when it comes to babies, you never have everything you need." The old woman handed her the bags. "Are you sure you have everything?"

Turning away from the counter, Jenna giggled. She'd had a strange feeling the woman was going to say, "Do you want fries with that?"

She hurried back to the car, dropped her bags into the trunk, and slid inside. She grabbed her phone and called Kane.

"I arrived safely and now I'm leaving. I'm sorry I didn't call before, but I needed to use the bathroom and I forgot."

"Did you get everything you wanted?" The relief in Kane's voice was palpable.

Guilty for not calling him before, Jenna chewed on her bottom lip. "Yeah, I did. It was lovely spending some time alone, but I turned around to ask your opinion more than once when I was in the store."

"I can't wait to see what you've found this time." Kane paused for a beat. "Oh and check the gas. It was getting low when we last went for a drive. It will probably get you home, but it might be a good idea to top it up just in case."

Smiling into the sunshine, Jenna started the engine. "Okay. I'll see you in a little while." She disconnected and headed out of town.

She recalled a gas station along the highway on her side of the road. It was an old run-down and isolated place and not somewhere she would usually stop for gas, but the needle was just above empty and she couldn't risk being out of gas in the middle of nowhere. An old battered truck pulled in behind her and two men climbed out. One went inside and the other pumped gas. Jenna swiped her card at the pump, lifted the nozzle, and filled her tank. She tried to avoid the gaze of the man behind her, but his eyes never left her. He was dressed in filthy jeans and a T-shirt with stains all down the front, and she couldn't miss the festering needle tracks on his arms. Unease rolled through her. She pushed her credit card into her bra and then climbed into the car. She fastened her seatbelt, but before she could start the engine, the man jumped into the passenger seat. A wave of unwashed male and alcohol hit her in a wall of stench. She glared at him. "Get out of my vehicle."

"Nope." The man pulled a knife. "You and me are going for a little ride."

Glad she'd locked the glovebox, and her weapon was safe

from him, Jenna pressed her tracker ring. It would alert Kane and he'd be able to hear everything being said, although needing to be saved by him the first time she'd gone out alone stuck in her craw. As a self-reliant woman, being vulnerable wasn't in her wheelhouse. She'd wanted to prove that even in this late stage of pregnancy, she could do her job. "You're making a big mistake. Get out of my car. Do you know how long you'll spend in prison for waving that knife at me and kidnapping me?"

"I'm not getting out." He pushed the tip of the knife into her arm. "Drive."

If she got out of the car and ran into the store, he wouldn't be able to start the car. She had the smart key safely inside her pocket. She unfastened her seatbelt and reached for the door handle. "Just let me out. You can take the darn car."

"Look at me, lady. You figure I'm fit to drive?" The man's red watery eyes settled on her face as he waved the knife at her. "I can get cash for the Mustang today, but they won't want it all banged up. Drive or I'll stick you."

Unable to stop her hands trembling, Jenna pulled down the harness Kane insisted was safer for the baby and stared him down. "This is a very bad idea. You're bringing down a mountain of trouble on yourself. My husband won't care if you're on drugs. He'll hunt you down and show no mercy."

"You figure I'm gonna let you live that long." He barked a laugh. "Dream on, lady. No one will ever find you and no one is coming after me." The man waved his gloves at her. "See, no fingerprints. Now be a good girl and head along the highway. My friend will be right behind us, and one wrong move, you're dead. He has a shotgun and knows how to use it. Drive or I'll stick you with the knife, and I really don't want to mess up the carpets in this brand-new Mustang."

Trying to remain calm, Jenna stared at him. She'd dealt with many types of criminals over the years, and the way his hands shook, this was an addict desperate for his next fix. In this state, he wouldn't care about the consequences. It chilled her to the bone knowing he regarded her life as a means to an end. She pressed her ring again. Now the alert would go to her entire team and she needed to get as much information to them as possible. "You know I didn't want to stop at that old gas station just outside of Louan but the needle was nearly on empty." She looked at the man. "The next town is Black Rock Falls. I'll drive there but then you must let me out."

"You stupid or something? I'm not going into town." He chuckled deep in his chest and then buzzed down the window, coughed violently, and spat. "Drive to the Triple Z Roadhouse. I'm meeting someone there who'll give me cash for this ride." He buzzed up the window and sat staring at her.

Lifting her chin, Jenna refused to be intimidated by this idiot. She needed to be heading toward Kane as fast as possible. "If you have a problem with drugs, there are places in Black Rock Falls that can help you get clean." She pulled out onto the highway.

"Just drive, lady, before I cut your throat to shut you up." He went through her purse, finding only tissues and lip balm, and then tossed it into the back seat.

Hoping he hadn't noticed the phone between her legs, Jenna formed a plan. The man hadn't clicked in his seatbelt. If she drove fast and then slammed on the brakes, he'd be thrown into the windshield, but what about the baby? Could she risk it? She bit down hard, wanting to growl in frustration. Right now, Kane would be driving toward her. She gripped the steering wheel and accelerated. Immediately, the powerful Mustang ate up the blacktop. She flashed past a few vehicles on the highway, leaving the old truck way behind, but the man beside her didn't seem to notice. She went past a signpost. Time to give Kane another update. "Ten miles to Black Rock Falls."

"I don't need a commentary. Drive or I'll cut you bad and toss you out. Although, you're pretty and you smell real nice."

The man's gaze moved over her and he touched her hair, curling it around his finger.

Swallowing the disgust and building fear, she leaned away. "Get your hands off me."

What if Kane didn't get to her in time? Had he even heard her call for help, or had it been drowned out by the roar of a motorcycle engine?

TWO

BLACK ROCK FALLS

A second buzz came through the speakers when Jenna had activated her tracker for the second time. Kane didn't need to call anyone. Wolfe, Rio, and Rowley would be on the move. All had received Jenna's call for help. Having Nanny Raya living at the ranch was a godsend. Kane rushed Tauri to her, and she'd care for him in her part of the ranch house until they returned. *If they returned.* Trying to fight back the rage boiling to the surface knowing that someone had threatened his wife, Kane slid the Beast onto the highway and slammed his foot down hard on the gas. The others would never catch him but they'd be there as backup very soon. As Jenna's red dot on the map headed toward Black Rock Falls, he could tell she was driving fast. He sent up a silent prayer to keep her safe and then dropped into the zone. It was his mechanism to push away all anger, doubt, or fear. He'd used it in combat and it was as important now as it had been back then. Losing control wasn't an option for a man with his skills. He'd kill without a second thought if under orders or if someone threatened his life. Such was the life of a sniper, but his time in the Secret Service had created a part of him that needed to protect her, and it often suffocated Jenna. He didn't have a problem taking a bullet, for her or anyone else in danger, and had done so more times than he'd like to remember.

He'd driven the new Beast in all situations since it arrived, and it had become an extension of himself like the old truck. During his life in the military and beyond, he'd needed to be able to drive anything. The only skill he lacked was flying, and when or if he found the time, he'd add that too. He pushed the Beast hard, making the engine roar. For once the traffic along the highway was minimal. Lights flashing and siren blaring, he flew past the other vehicles as if they were standing still. He'd keep his flashers on until he got closer to Jenna and then shut them down. To anyone on the highway, the Beast looked like a tricked-out truck and not a law enforcement vehicle. When Jenna's voice came through his speakers, the hairs on the back of his neck stood to attention.

"I said don't touch me. Do it again and I'll run us into a ditch."

"You're some crazy lady." A man slurred his words. *"I'll enjoy watching you bleed out when I stick you."*

An image flashed into his mind of Jenna covered with blood. One mistake now and he'd lose his wife and baby again. Digging deep to keep in the zone, Kane bit down hard on the inside of his cheek and hit the nitro. The front of the Beast rose and the engine roared its appreciation, like a wild stallion set free on the plains. The forest and lowlands blurred as Kane concentrated on following the yellow line. Nothing mattered but Jenna's safety as he threw caution to the wind and aimed the truck into a narrow space between two eighteen-wheelers, ducked out again, and headed through the mountain pass. He must get to Jenna.

The red spot on the map was getting closer and he switched off his siren and the red and blue flashing lights. In the distance, a black vehicle headed his way, its silver stripes catching the sun. *Jenna.* She'd seen him too. Her headlights flicked on and off and she slowed down. Kane kept his foot on the gas, and flew past her, surprised to see her pull onto the grass verge along the side of the highway. He listened as he spun the Beast around, crossed the highway, and headed back in her direction.

"I'm going to spew. I need to get out." Jenna's voice came through loud and clear. *"Tell your friend in the old truck behind us not to kill me. I won't run away."*

Fighting back the need to rip someone's head off, Kane slid to a stop within a few inches of Jenna's Mustang. As Jenna rolled out of the door, he jumped from the Beast. In one stride he'd punched through the window. Glass shattered and sprayed in all directions as he grabbed the hand with the knife, pulled it through the window, and twisted. The man howled like a stuck pig, and the knife dropped to the ground. He grabbed the skinny, filthy man by the shoulders and dragged him kicking and screaming through the window. He tossed him against the Beast and followed with a punch to the kidney. The man buckled and slid to the ground. The next moment an old truck pulled up and a man climbed out brandishing a shotgun.

"Shooter." Jenna ducked down behind the Mustang.

Before the man had time to chamber a round, Kane drew his M18 pistol and shot him in the shoulder. The bullet went straight through and made a hole in the truck's windshield. The shotgun fell from the man's hand. In a scream of abuse and sobs, he grabbed his shoulder and fell to his knees.

"Nice shot." Jenna stood, brushing dirt from her clothes. "Need any help?"

Desperately wanting to go to Jenna, Kane shook his head. His heart raced from the rush of adrenaline and he took a few deep breaths to clear his head. "I'm good. The team is on its way."

"Okay." Jenna indicated to the broken glass. "I'll clean up

the mess so I can drive it, although I'm not sure if I'll ever get the stink out of it."

It was like waiting for the other shoe to drop with Jenna. She acted as if this happened on a daily basis. How long before the shock set in? Troubled, he gave her a long assessing look and shrugged. "I'll fix it when we get home but I'll need to order glass for the window."

He used flexicuffs to secure the men, and after checking the gunshot wound, he dragged them onto the side of the highway. The men moaned, cried, and pleaded with him. He stared at them with disgust. "I wanted to kill you, so you've gotten off easy."

"We'll give you a cut of the Mustang money if you let us go." The man with the knife wiped blood from small cuts on his cheek with his shoulder. "We have a guy waiting with cash at the Triple Z Roadhouse."

Resting one hand on his weapon, Kane stared into space for a second as if considering their offer, but he'd use the information to take down a carjacking organization. "That's good to know." He bent down low and eyeballed them. "Sheriff's department, and that woman you kidnapped is Sheriff Alton—and my wife. You know, I must be getting soft. When someone pulls a weapon on me, I usually take them down. It must be your lucky day." He asked them their names and then read them their rights. As he headed for the Mustang, he turned to look at them over one shoulder. "Move a muscle and I'll shoot off your kneecaps."

Jenna leaned against the door, her face sheet-white, but the smile she gave him made his heart leap. He gathered her in his arms and buried his face in her hair, inhaling her honeysuckle fragrance like a starving man at a smorgasbord. She trembled in his arms, but as she pressed against him, the baby kicked hard, as if sending him a message all was well.

"When I saw your expression, I figured you'd kill them."

Jenna looked up into his face. "When that guy drew the shotgun, my heart stopped." She cupped the back of his neck. "I've never seen you draw so fast."

He'd been in control and the order to shoot to kill hadn't been issued. His training had kicked in, and the men hadn't met the lethal machine; they'd met Deputy Kane. He shrugged. "Drawing fast and firing under pressure is the difference between death and survival. I keep in practice, is all." He tapped his chest. "In here, after hearing that scum running his mouth, I wanted to kill him, but in here"—he tapped his head—"I knew there would be way too much paperwork." He turned to make sure the prisoners were right where he'd left them. "We have the chance of bringing down a carjacking racket. Some guy is waiting to buy your Mustang at the Triple Z Roadhouse. I figure we go and meet him."

"They'll recognize the Beast and us the moment we arrive." Jenna frowned. "I hear sirens, the team is coming. We'll need to work something out real fast. That guy who held the knife on me will need to be in the Mustang or the perp will run."

Three trucks slowed and turned across the highway to stop either side of them, lights flashing. Vehicles going by slowed down to see what was happening, and immediately Rowley sprang into action and waved them on. Wolfe climbed out of his white SUV with Emily and headed his way. Rio climbed out of his sheriff's department truck, went to Jenna's side. Kane smiled at them. "Well, now we know the trackers work. Thanks for coming."

"I'm glad you kept your anger under control." Wolfe took him to one side. "By the way, Jenna is still transmitting. Emily said she'd take Jenna's place, but she wants someone in the back seat in case the drug addict goes postal."

Kane rubbed his chin. "I'll do it, but who do you figure is gonna drive the Beast into town? Jenna is under enough stress already."

"You're driving—and I'm fine, just a little shaken. I'll drive the Mustang." Jenna walked to his side and pressed her ring to disconnect. "We'll stop alongside of the highway before the Triple Z Roadhouse and change vehicles. We'll leave the Beast alongside of the highway. It's not as if anyone can steal it. The buyer will be concentrating on the Mustang, not who is following behind. Wolfe can follow. No one will take notice of him wearing sunglasses. As soon as the guy shows, hit your tracker and we'll all move in."

Nodding, Kane smiled at her. "That sounds like a plan." He glanced over at the prisoners. "Now I just need to convince Don Riley over there to cooperate. I figure he will. He's kinda desperate right now."

"I'll tend to his friend and we'll talk to them." Wolfe nodded slowly. "I'm sure we'll be able to persuade Riley to cooperate."

Twenty minutes later they arrived at the Triple Z Roadhouse and put the plan into action. They would be meeting a man by the name of Tom Little. As Emily pulled the Mustang to the pump Riley buzzed the passenger window down and Kane pressed his pistol into the man's side. "Act normal and complete the transaction. You ready, Em?"

"Yeah, my phone's recording." She turned her head to look at the roadhouse. "Someone is heading this way now."

"Don. Nice to see you, man." A young man, with brown hair wearing a cowboy hat, T-shirt with an obscure band on the front, and Levi's bent to peer in the Mustang's window. "Nice ride. Does the girl come with the car? I'm happy to throw in a few extra bucks."

"No, just give me the money, Tom. I need to be someplace else. The keys are in the console." Riley held out his hand.

"Sure, sure." Little handed a brown paper take-out bag to him. "Five grand. Don't shoot it all up your arm at once."

"Get out of the car." Riley glared at Emily. "I know where you live and I'll kill your family if you open your mouth."

As Riley climbed from the vehicle and Little slipped behind the wheel of the Mustang, Rio's and Rowley's sirens blared as they blocked in the Mustang from front and back. Relieved everything went as planned, Kane sat up from the back seat and pressed the muzzle of his M18 pistol into the back of the man's head. "Big mistake. This vehicle belongs to the sheriff of Black Rock Falls."

THREE

BLACK ROCK FALLS

Monday

After tossing and turning all night, plagued by dreams of knives and blood, Jenna overslept. She'd woken at seven, hurriedly showered, and dressed before heading for the kitchen. The previous day had turned out to be the opposite to the nice restful day out she'd envisaged, but hopefully some good would come out of it. Although all of the men involved in the carjacking would do time, the DA had informed her they'd roll over on another criminal for a deal, likely wanting a lesser sentence and a drug rehabilitation program. She'd be interested in discovering the details when everything was finalized. *If only serial killer cases were as easy.*

Pushing away the cobwebs that came with sleep, Jenna walked into the kitchen. Tauri sat at the table, eager to be heading for kindergarten to finish a project the class was working on. His happy chatter filled the room as he switched between his native tongue and Spanish, as Kane prepared breakfast. "You're up already." She bent to kiss Tauri on the cheek.

"I'm helping Daddy make pancakes." Tauri adjusted the dish towel tied around his neck to protect his clothes. "I added the flour." He grinned.

Jenna noticed the dusting of flour on his gold-streaked hair. "So I see. I'm looking forward to trying them." She sat down and took the cup of decaffeinated coffee Kane slid across the table to her.

"You okay?" Kane's gaze traveled over her. "Bad dreams?"

Nodding, they exchanged a knowing look. "But I'm awake now."

"Hungry?" Kane went back to the stove.

Jenna added the fixings to her coffee. "Starving." She liked that Kane wanted to cook all the meals, mainly because her specialty was burned toast. "I feel kinda useless, sleeping so late. By the time I wake up, all the chores are done."

"The horses maybe. I turned them out to the corral this morning and they're rolling around in the long grass." Kane removed a pile of pancakes from the oven, piled them on plates, and then added crispy strips of bacon from a pan on the stove. "You're always doing chores. You haven't stopped cleaning the house. Every time I turn around, you're polishing something or wiping down counters. Please don't try to wash the windows again. If you fall from the stepladder, you might hurt yourself."

Shaking her head, Jenna took the plate, buttered her pancakes and then Tauri's, before adding maple syrup. "I'm sorry, I was speaking to Nanny Raya and she told me it's called nesting. Many women in their third trimester suddenly get the urge to clean." She smiled. "So I'm just cleaning my nest."

"You don't have a nest, Mommy." Tauri giggled. "Birds have nests."

"Mommy's just being silly." Kane grinned and looked at Jenna. "Just don't start collecting twigs from the yard and putting them in our bed."

Jenna laughed. "I promise."

As she took a sip of her coffee her phone chimed. Jenna frowned. In the last week, she'd diverted calls to Chief Deputy Rio. He was more than capable of handling any situation and would notify her if needs be. "Sheriff Alton."

"This is the warden of the state pen. We had a fire yesterday in the maximum security wing. Due to our current overload of prisoners, it was necessary to transfer four of them to Black Rock Falls County." The warden sucked in a deep breath and blew it out slowly. *"Reports I've received tell me the prison bus made it to just outside Blackwater. The local sheriff found a wreck. The driver was dead, and the prisoners and one prison guard are missing."*

Jenna muted the phone. "Okay, can you give me a second?" She exchanged a meaningful glance with Kane. She never discussed cases in front of her son. As her little boy popped the last piece of pancake into his mouth and drained his glass of milk, she looked at him. "Daddy is going to help you wash up and get ready for kindergarten. Would you like Nanny Raya to take you today?"

"Yes, she's teaching me a song. We could sing all the way to town." He slipped from the chair and headed toward the bathroom with Kane on his heels.

Moving her attention back to the call, Jenna stood and took a notepad and pen from the counter. "Do you have any reason to believe that this was a prison break?"

"Initially no. We didn't have any suspicions until the body of the driver was examined by paramedics. They found a gunshot wound to the head. There's no blood inside the back of the prison bus, so we're assuming the prisoners and the other prison guard got out of the wreck without serious injury. The problem I have, Sheriff"—the warden paused for a beat—*"is that after finding four sets of footprints leading into the forest, the Blackwater Sheriff's Department has been combing the area. They were able to follow the tracks, and the group have moved across the county*

line. *They're heading toward Black Rock Falls, which is your jurisdiction."*

Pushing her hair from her eyes and tucking it behind her ear, Jenna frowned. "You said there were four prisoners in the bus, and a prison guard and yet there are only four sets of footprints. Did you find the body of the other prison guard?"

"No, there were no other bodies and one set of the footprints is small. The others were made by typical footwear we use at the prison. One of the prisoners is unaccounted for and we assume this person was responsible for the breakout. We have no idea who it is or why they didn't take the others with them. I can only imagine it was agreed to prior to the escape. Lately, because of staff shortages, I've been transferring prisoners to Black Rock Falls County. I figure when they planned the escape, they assumed I'd be sending them there."

Stanton Forest was massive, covering her entire county from the mountains to the lowlands. It spread out all over and there were parts of it in the west so dense that no one ventured inside. Anyone who didn't want to be found would be extremely difficult to locate, even with her resources. "Do you have the coordinates of where they were last seen?"

"I do and I will message them to you." The warden cleared his throat. *"Unfortunately, these aren't just general population prisoners. These are maximum security, and the warden who is missing is a young woman by the name of Amy Clark. This is an exemplary young woman. She has never been in contact with any of these men before and we can find no reason why she would collaborate with them in any way. We can only assume they're holding her as a hostage. My hope is that she is of value to them. It might just save her life."*

Prisoners placed in maximum security posed a risk to others, and now she had three of them roaming Stanton Forest. "Who exactly are we talking about?" She placed the phone on the table and fished her earbuds out of her pocket. "Do you have a list at hand?"

"*Eduardo Souza; 'Ice Pick' Mason Margos; the Silent Strangler, Sebastian Callahan; and the Blue Man, Carl Romero.*" He sighed. "*The odd one out in that group is Eduardo Souza, a cartel kingpin. The other three are serial killers.*"

A shiver ran down Jenna's spine at Eduardo Souza's name. The cartel boss had kidnapped Kane and Tauri, and wanted them both dead to prevent Kane testifying against him in court. Left chained to a wall, Kane and Tauri barely escaped an explosion, but Souza and some of his men were spending time in prison... or had been until now. As she wrote down the names, her fingers trembled at the memory. "Yeah, I know him and I've read about the others in Special Agent Jo Wells' book about psychopathic behavior. I believe she's the best behavioral analyst in the country. We're very lucky to have access to her. I believe she interviewed them in prison at one time."

"*She did indeed and we spoke about rehabilitation. Although, I can't imagine anyone rehabilitating these men. Some of them have murdered more than twenty people we know about. Once they get that far gone, there's no coming back.*" The warden sighed. "*I've notified the governor and, as I can't spare any staff to assist with the search, he offered to supply you with resources until we can organize a group of guards from other prisoners to join the search. All you need to do is call. There's the FBI, as well, and state troopers who'll be able to assist. If you locate the prisoners, get County to collect them. Don't put them inside a patrol vehicle. They're too dangerous.*"

He was speaking to her as if she had no experience with serial killers, or maybe he believed being a woman sheriff was a disadvantage. She lifted her chin. "Trust me, Warden, I'm fully aware of what a psychopath can do. They seem to flock to Black Rock Falls. Our town is known locally as Serial Killer Central."

"*Well then, I'm sure you'll have everything under control.*"

I'll have a Department of Corrections command post set up ASAP. The forest warden has suggested the check-in point at Bear Peak, so I'm looking into that now. Keep in touch with them." He disconnected.

Concerned how Kane would react to hearing that Eduardo Souza had escaped, Jenna waited until Nanny Raya collected Tauri to take him to kindergarten before explaining the seriousness of the situation to him. "Four escaped, three apparently took the female prison guard with them. The driver's weapon is missing. The warden figures the fourth prisoner organized the breakout and went with his friends. The others are all serial killers."

"Well, the organizer will be in the wind. My bet he's got the resources to plan something like this." Kane narrowed his gaze. "What about the others? Anyone we put away?"

Jenna's heart missed a beat. She needed time to think. "Only one, I believe." She flicked him a glance. "The warden is sending their files. He mentioned Jo has interviewed them. I'll call her and Agent Carter to help us, and we'll have a better idea of who we're dealing with." She gathered up her things. "If the governor will supply resources, another chopper would be a good idea. We could call in Agents Katz and Styles from Rattlesnake Creek. They all have choppers, so does Wolfe. If we can get another one for Raven, we can have four in the air at one time."

"I agree with calling in the FBI agents, and utilizing the choppers for initial sweeps might be beneficial, but the forest is dense and I doubt they'd be able to distinguish prisoners from hikers or hunters from above." Kane collected the dirty dishes from the table and put them in the dishwasher. "Think about it. If you were trying to escape in the forest and you heard a chopper, what would you do?"

Horrific memories of being lost in the forest flooded Jenna's mind and a shudder went through her. "At this time of the year, with all the lush vegetation, I guess hiding from a chopper would be easy enough. So we're gonna need boots on the ground." Knowing her husband was an expert in tactical maneuvers, she moved to his side. "What do you suggest?"

"We'll need to go in as one unit and track them. Then it depends if they split up or stay together. Either way, the best way forward is in teams." Kane's mouth twitched up at the edges. "Think about it. We have our bloodhound, Duke, and Raven's K9, Ben. Then there's Carter's Zorro and Styles' Bear. I figure all you'll need is a few extra deputies for them to use as backup. They'd be able to move through the forest silently and have a better chance of surrounding the prisoners."

Nodding, Jenna went on tiptoes to kiss him on the cheek. "Thank you. I'll call everyone on the way to the office. We'll work out the teams when we get there." She took a cloth to wipe the table. "You can organize the search."

"Yes, ma'am." He chuckled when she threw the cloth at him. "Ah... I mean, sure thing, Jenna."

FOUR

STANTON FOREST

Terrified, Amy Clark stumbled along root-covered trails. The uneven ground beneath her feet made every step more difficult. Her blood-caked clothes and skin stank like death. Her legs ached and her tongue stuck to the roof of her parched mouth. Even with the thick jacket she'd brought for the trip, overnight had been a horrifying nightmare and so cold. The sun had been up for some time now, and as she walked, sweat trickled between her shoulder blades, soaking the back of her shirt. The prisoners had their own ideas about what they wanted to do to her, and their suggestions terrified her. Her experience with psychopaths was limited to the few shows she'd watched on TV. She understood it was small things that triggered them into an uncontrollable rage. There could be no reasoning with them, so her only chance to stay alive would be to remain as passive as possible and say nothing.

They'd walked all night, only stopping occasionally for a short break. These men had little to do in prison but work out, and all of them were extremely fit. Mason Margos did all the talking. It seemed that he'd earned respect in the world of maximum security prisoners. As they walked, the smell of woodsmoke drifted toward them, and Amy searched the gaps in the pine trees for any sign of a cabin. Fear gripped her belly. The prisoners had been talking about finding a cabin where they could hole up to get some sleep. As they rounded the bend, the trail ended at a dirt road leading to a small cabin. The roof held antennas and two solar panels. A washing line with an assortment of large men's clothing waved in the breeze. The distinctive prison garb worn by the prisoners wouldn't go unnoticed and one glimpse of them would be enough for the homeowner to come out blasting. Beside her, Margos removed the clip from her weapon and handed it to her. She took it and just stared at him.

"Put it in your holster. When the guy comes out, tell him someone crashed into our bus when we were working alongside the highway. It knocked out your communication with the prison and you need assistance." Margos waved Romero forward. "Keep your gun in her back. If she says one wrong word, shoot her."

Realizing the reason they hadn't murdered or raped her, Amy swallowed hard. They wanted to use her as their spokesperson. A distraction to lure people into a false sense of security. If she wanted to stay alive, she must do what they say. Sooner or later, search parties would be out looking for them. If she could just stay alive long enough, help would be on the way. When Romero dug the pistol in her back, she flinched but nodded in agreement. From what she knew about these prisoners, they'd all murdered women. Maybe they would just tie this guy up and be on their way. A knot of worry caught in her throat as the door to the cabin creaked open to reveal the muzzle of a double-barreled shotgun. The gun in her back propelled her forward a couple of steps. "Hello, we've been in a wreck. Do you have a phone I could use? Mine was damaged. I need to get transport for these inmates."

"Why is a young woman like you walking through the forest

with prisoners? Don't you figure that's a might dangerous?" A man's graying head peeked around the door and his eyes widened. "How come you're covered in blood?"

Trying to stop shaking, Amy met the man's inquisitive gaze. "We were collecting garbage alongside the highway and a truck clipped our bus. The driver died on scene. This is his blood. I couldn't just leave the prisoners on the side of the road, could I?" She rested one hand on the handle of her empty weapon. "Do you have a phone I can use or not?"

"No phone, but you can speak to someone on the CB radio. The local sheriff's office has one now. Come along inside. They can wait there." The man opened the door, dropping the shotgun so it pointed to the ground.

Before Amy could take a step forward, the bang from Romero's pistol deafened her. She gaped in horror as red blossomed across the shirt of the man in the doorway. Clutching his chest, he tumbled down the steps, falling flat on his face, arms and legs spread out like a snow angel. Horrified, she stared as the life drained out of him and his eyes stared into nothing.

"Get rid of him. I smell pigs." Margos grinned. "Go and feed them." Two of the prisoners rushed forward, took one arm each, and dragged the dead body away like yesterday's garbage. He turned to Amy, slid out her empty pistol from its holster, and slammed in the clip. He indicated with the gun toward the washing line.

"Collect those clothes. We need to get out of this prison gear, and they look like they're going to fit just fine."

Trying to push the image of the poor man from her mind, Amy complied without uttering a word. As she pulled the clothes from the washing line, her heart thundered at the thought of spending time locked inside the cabin with the men. This might be her last few minutes on earth. She gazed up at the trees and the mountains trying to memorize one last bit of beauty to keep locked in her mind. The washing collected, she dragged her legs toward the cabin and up the steps trying to avoid the blood spatter. She stood in the middle of the small room as the men ransacked the cabin.

"See I told you she'd be useful." Margos smiled at the others and then turned back to her. "Get to work and cook us a meal before I change my mind and feed you to the pigs. On second thought, first go and wash up." His expression changed and cold eyes raked her body. "Washing is a privilege, and you need to earn them—right? Step out of line, complain once, and we'll punish you." He kicked her backpack across the floor to her. "Use the clothes in your backpack." He waved a hand under his nose. "You're stinking up the place."

FIVE

BLACK ROCK FALLS

In the bulletproof, bombproof, tricked-out black truck affectionately known as the Beast, Jenna stared at the list of escaped prisoners. Knowing Eduardo Souza was out there, free to exact vengeance against her and her family, sent shivers down her spine. She hadn't divulged the names on the list of criminals who had escaped the prison bus and, taking a deep breath, turned to look at him. "I have the list of names. One of the missing prisoners is Eduardo Souza."

"What!" The tires screamed as Kane slammed on the brakes and pulled alongside the highway. "We just sent Tauri to the kindergarten. If this happened yesterday, it's possible that Souza was picked up by a chopper. He could have his goons in town by now." He pulled out his phone. "Shane, we have a code red. Eduardo Souza escaped from prison yesterday."

"Copy that. Have you activated the chopper security net?" Footsteps echoed on tile as Wolfe walked through the mortuary and into his office.

"Yeah, it's never off unless we know someone is dropping by." Kane met Jenna's gaze and his eyes widened when he read the list of escaped prisoners. "Souza is likely the organizer and will be in the wind, but the others are in Stanton Forest with a female prison guard. They're all serial killers and tried and convicted scum of the earth, but right now Souza is my worry. You know as well as I do, if we let down our guard for one second, he'll use Jenna and Tauri to get to me."

"*Leave the security to me. You have Nanny Raya to watch over Tauri. It would be very difficult to infiltrate the kindergarten after all the changes we've made since the last attempt on your life.*" He cleared his throat. "*What are y'all planning to do? The DOC should be in charge of the retrieval.*"

Unable to meet Kane's gaze, Jenna swallowed hard. "I'm only guessing the warden has gotten the wheels rolling. He has no men to spare. The fire is taking up all his resources. The Department of Corrections hasn't contacted me yet, but I'd expect them to send officers from the state pen. We have the Blackwater Sheriff's Department on the ground, and I guess we call in Louan and the Montana Highway Patrol to set up roadblocks." She frowned. "There is another resource, the Two Bear Air Rescue. The DOC will need to call them in to assist with air surveillance. The problem is, Shane, right now we're on our own and we can't sit on our hands. We need teams out there searching and we need them moving now."

"*Blackhawk is here today. I'll ask him to supply the horses we'll need and bring along any other trackers available. If you work out what you need, I'll get the supplies together.*" Wolfe sighed. "*Call me when you get a team organized. I have a storeroom filled with survival packs. You don't know when a relief team will arrive. Do you need me to pull some strings?*"

"Okay, thanks, Shane." Kane stared straight ahead. "We need to bring these guys in before they hurt someone."

Concerned by Kane's reaction to knowing that Souza was free, she grabbed the list of the other prisoners to show him. Surely if Souza had arranged the breakout, which was more than likely, he'd be long gone by now and back in a secret family facility. She tapped Kane on the arm to allow her to speak with Wolfe. He gave her a slight nod. "The governor has already offered to call in the local sheriff's departments to join our search parties. All I need to do is call him, Shane. It might be better if you're not seen to be involved."

"*Trust me, Jenna, no one will ever know that I'm involved.*" She could almost see Wolfe smiling. "*You handle the governor and I'll keep you safe in other ways. I'll arrange for someone to monitor the exterior security footage at the ranch and around your office. If he or one of his men takes a step inside your property or work, we'll know about it. We have ID on the majority of Souza's people, so the facial recognition software will be running until he's caught.*"

"That's good to know." Kane looked over one shoulder and moved the truck back onto the highway. "Thanks. We'll need you in the field. These guys need to be captured. Can you make time?"

"*Yeah, not a problem.*" Wolfe's chair squeaked in a familiar way as he pushed away from the desk. "*I'll get my gear ready. Just call when you're organized and I'll load up my truck.*" He disconnected.

"Call Nanny Raya." Kane spoke to the Bluetooth phone connection and in seconds she picked up. "Souza escaped from prison. Take every precaution to protect our son. Leave an hour early today and stay inside the ranch."

"*Okay and I always protect Tauri, but I'll step it up.*" Nanny Raya was inside the kindergarten by the sound of the kids in the background. "*I'll volunteer to help out today and I'll call to confirm when we're home this afternoon. I'll be there by two. Tauri won't leave my sight and I'm armed.*"

Glad they had her to protect Tauri, Jenna ran a hand down her face. "Thank you, Raya. See you tonight." She waited for Kane to disconnect and then looked at him. "I didn't consider Souza as an immediate threat. I figured he'd be more concerned about leaving the state than coming after us again."

"We have no idea what plan he cooked up in prison." Kane flicked her a glance and his hands tightened on the steering wheel. "Never underestimate a cartel boss. Their numbers breed like rats and every member lives in fear of being killed. He pays them well to risk their lives and they'll face any danger to complete their task. We took down most of his henchmen, but others would be coming along to take their place, and all as sadistic and ruthless as him. No matter how many of those vermin we catch, there's always more of them. Now he's back in charge and we're all in danger—again." He ran a hand down his face.

Unable to push away the feeling of emptiness and hopelessness she'd experienced when Souza kidnapped Kane and Tauri, a sudden terrible thought struck her. Her fingers trembled as she looked at the list of escaped prisoners. "You don't figure Souza organized this escape to get us hunting down the prisoners in the forest so we'd be away from the protection of our home and office, do you?"

"It's possible." Kane's mouth turned down. "I wouldn't put it past him to recruit notorious serial killers to do his work for him. He's already broken them out of prison, he'd likely offer them safe refuge once the job was done, a new identity, and money. It would sure beat spending the rest of your life in prison. I mean, killing us would just be sport to them."

A rush of fear sent goosebumps running up Jenna's arms. "Now I guess you're going to tell me that I can't get involved with the search. I might be waddling around, but my brain is working just fine. You know darn well I'll be able to find these men."

"The only way you'd be safe without me around is if I'd locked you in a jail cell." Kane drove into the back entrance to the sheriff's office and parked in his usual spot. "I'm not letting you out of my sight today. Raya's truck has bulletproof glass, and I had the door panels reinforced. She should be fine driving back to the ranch today, but until we catch them, Tauri is staying home where it's safe, and so should you."

Uncomprehending, Jenna stared at him. "I'm not staying at the ranch."

"Yes, you are." He climbed out and opened the back door to lift Duke down from the back seat and gave her a long look. "How do you plan on trekking through the forest at almost eight months pregnant? You understand the conditions out there and we'll be moving fast on horseback." He ran a hand through his hair and then pushed on his black Stetson. "I'm seriously considering locking you in a jail cell." He scratched his cheek slowly and stared at her for a long few seconds as if making up his mind what to say next. "Will you *please* stay home with Tauri and Nanny Raya? You can oversee everything from there."

Anger flared and Jenna slid from the truck, gathered her things, and then whirled around to face him. "Absolutely not."

SIX

STANTON FOREST

Terror shuddered through Serena Lee as two men wearing prison garb dragged her grandfather's blood-soaked body past the chicken coop. As the heels of his boots dug a double trail into the soft ground on the way to the pigpen, she wanted to scream and run to him, but from his fixed blank eyes, he was long past help. When he'd sent her outside to avoid the visitors, the gunshot had startled her and sent chickens scattering in all directions, with some flying into the forest. Familiar with the sound of a shotgun, the single crack of a pistol put her on alert but if it hadn't been for the voices, she'd have walked right into the prisoners ransacking her grandpa's house.

Shocked, the realization of the danger hit her like a hammer. She would be next. Her only hope of escaping to safety would be to remain as quiet as possible. Her mom had told her about bad men and what they could do. The images of Grandpa flashed through her mind. He'd want her to be brave. She tried hard not to cry and pressed her fist into her mouth. The two men would be coming back and they'd hear her sobs for sure. Knees trembling, Serena backed into the coop. Heart thundering in her chest, she hunched down to make herself as small as possible and then duckwalked into the farthest corner of the coop. The men walked past again, laughing and joking as if killing someone were as normal as eating apple pie. As the footsteps disappeared, she stood slowly. If they found her, they'd kill her as well. She must go for help. It would be dark soon and riding was her only chance to survive these lunatics.

Wearing only jeans and a light top, she wouldn't survive a night in the mountains even in late spring. The drop in temperature was substantial overnight. In desperation, she went to the door of the chicken coop, and after making sure no one was around, she dashed across the open ground and into the barn. Heart pounding, she leaned against the door panting. Her legs trembled but Grandpa's words drifted into her mind. *If bad men come here, run and get help.*

Panic gripped her but she nodded. *I can do this.* Inside, a horse her grandpa used to drag fallen logs back to the cabin stood dozing in its stall. The horse wasn't usually ridden as Grandpa had a truck to get into town. She stared at the truck and then shook her head. At ten years old, she couldn't risk driving it, but she could ride and she'd made friends with the horse. Fighting back tears, she took the tack hanging on a peg beside the stall and, speaking quietly to the horse, she pushed the halter over its ears. "Good boy, Thunderbolt."

Listening for voices close by, she grabbed her grandfather's thick jacket from the peg and took two feedbags and filled them with bottled water from the supplies in the barn, a few cans of food, a can opener, a Zippo, and a horse blanket. She tied the tops with a length of twine and attached them to a leading rein. She swallowed hard. Getting to the next cabin would be a problem if Thunderbolt decided he didn't want her to ride him. As a retired rodeo horse, he'd had enough of people riding him and was currently enjoying his retirement. She considered the direction the prisoners had come from and where they might be heading. It would be likely they'd keep heading in the same direction away from the highway.

Holding back sobs of distress, Serena tossed the bags across the horse's neck and led him to a bale of hay. Using it to help her reach his broad back, she climbed on Thunderbolt. She ran her hand down his silky neck and spoke to him softly. She often brought him apples and carrots as a treat, and maybe he'd remember her kindness. "Okay, let's go." She squeezed her legs rather than kicking him in the ribs and to her surprise he moved out of the stall and headed for the forest.

As she rode away as slowly as possible, agonizing screams came from the cabin. She hadn't seen a woman, but there could be no doubt the men had captured one. Men's voices raised and laughter echoed through the night. She urged Thunderbolt on, trying to block out the misery behind her, but images of her grandpa's staring eyes haunted her thoughts. Teeth chattering with shock, the knowledge her grandpa's body would be devoured by the pigs made her sick to her stomach. Trying hard to find her way, she took a trail Grandpa went along to drive to the highway. It followed the edge of the mountain, and dark shadows cut across sunlit paths, playing tricks with her eyes. Without warning, Thunderbolt reared, his ears flat against his head. The horse danced around on his back legs, and then shot off at tremendous speed. She clung to his mane for dear life as the horse dashed through the forest with little regard to who was on his back. Behind her, the sound of a bear roaring came over the noise of thundering hooves. They galloped, skimming around the trees, and shot past the next cabin. Hanging around Thunderbolt's neck, all Serena could do was hold on tight. The horse kept bolting and she could do nothing to stop him. Eventually he slowed and stood, his chest heaving. As the horse scanned the forest, his head high and ears twitching, a tremble went through him. Serena rubbed his neck and spoke in soothing tones. His ears twisted as if listening to her and then he moved off, weaving through trees, until they reached the banks of the river. At a sandy riverbank, Thunderbolt waded into the water and drank his fill.

Unfamiliar with this part of the forest, Serena tried to get her bearings. Her grandpa had told her stories about the early settlers in the area. Most of the people built cabins close to the river. A long time ago, when they erected them, they didn't consider the problems of drinking water from a flowing creek. Nowadays people filtered water or sterilized it by using a simple pill. So to find help, she'd need to follow the river. Tears streamed down her cheeks, but the determination to get to a phone and notify the sheriff burned in her. Serena patted Thunderbolt's neck. He'd allowed her to ride him and saved her life. At no time had he attempted to buck her from his back. The image of her grandpa's empty staring eyes had stuck in her mind. She'd seen what those men had done to him, and there was no way she'd let them get away with it.

SEVEN

At the office Jenna and Kane worked the phones, trying to get everyone on the same page. Getting special agents to drop everything and come at once would be difficult. Katz and Styles had assisted her in the past, and Jo and Carter were close friends, but they'd all agreed in seconds and would be on their way soon. After speaking with the governor, he'd already liaised with the DOC and had the highway patrol setting roadblocks within her county on both sides of the bus wreck. With two of the prisoners potentially armed, they could easily steal a vehicle from one of the local residents in the forest and be heading along the highway. The other local counties would have road-blocks set up on the borders, and help would come as soon as it could be organized.

As she disconnected, she overheard Kane talking on a call to Atohi Blackhawk. A family member via their son, Tauri, Blackhawk was a close friend and a superb tracker. She looked over at Kane. The talk was about horses. He'd just returned from the ranch with the horse trailer.

"Yeah, that sounds fine. I've only brought Warrior. Seagull

gets spooked too easy." Kane smiled across the desk at her. "Thanks. I appreciate you." He disconnected.

Raising her eyebrows, Jenna looked at him. "What was that all about and why didn't you bring Seagull? I'll need to ride her."

"Atohi is bringing along the extra horses and wanted to know how many we'd need." Kane stretched out his long legs. "Seagull is an Arab, who dances and gets spooked by falling leaves. You must admit she's not really suitable for sneaking up on escaped prisoners, is she?" Kane shook his head. "Blackhawk says his horses are bombproof." He gave her a long look. "The other reason I didn't bring her is because you need to stay home and protect our son, Jenna."

Rolling her eyes, she stared at him. "You want me to stay home when we have an FBI agent as a nanny?"

"Yes, I'm sure Wolfe will advise you chasing down serial killers on horseback isn't safe for a pregnant woman in the third trimester. Seagull is a handful at the best of times and I'm concerned about what might happen out there. To be perfectly honest, I don't want you delivering our baby in the forest with three serial killers on the loose." He sighed. "For once, run the case from the office, delegate, and organize. Leave the grunt work to us."

Of course Kane was right, but she'd been coping well with the extra weight, apart from the backache and swollen ankles. She did have the option to sit this one out and stay home with Tauri and Nanny Raya. She clicked her pen and stared at him, seeing only concern in his eyes as she made her decision. "Okay, I'll stay here or at home."

"Good. Blackhawk is bringing along a packhorse as well. I'll spread out the supplies and extra ammo to lighten our load." Kane stood and bent to kiss her on the forehead. "Now everything is planned. Wolfe is bringing extra com packs if we need them. Rowley and Rio have packed everything we need into our backpacks. As soon as the FBI teams arrive, we'll be leaving. Once they're thirty minutes out, I'll get Tauri and drop you home."

Jenna blew hair from her eyes and leaned back in the chair. "Oh goody, you mean I don't get to be locked up in the cells."

"It's not too late." Kane gave her an amused look and then checked his phone. "Jo has uploaded a file to the server. It's profiles on the three prisoners. The warden also sent a file on the female prison guard." He looked at his watch. "We have at least two hours, maybe more before the choppers arrive. Do you want to look over these now?"

Jenna shook her head. "We'll all head to Aunt Betty's and discuss the files over a meal. I figure having a snack before you leave would be good. I'll grab some sandwiches and coffee for later as well. You'll need to keep up your energy if you plan on catching them."

When they arrived at Aunt Betty's Café they headed to the reserved table in the back. Rio, Rowley, Wolfe, and Raven had already arrived. She sat down, opened her tablet, and looked at them. "From the report I received from the Blackwater sheriff, the prisoners were heading north along the river. It's what most people would do if they wanted to avoid getting turned around. So you should be able to pick up their trail if we can estimate how far they've traveled."

"It also gives them access to cabins along the way." Raven frowned. "If they're armed, we might be following a trail of dead bodies. They'll need clothes, food, and weapons."

"Maybe." Kane leaned back in his seat, with one hand wrapped around a cup. "The mountain folk tend to shoot first and ask questions later."

Looking from one to the other, Jenna shrugged. "What if they send in the prison guard? It's what I'd do in their position. They'd have guns aimed at her back, and she'd know they'd kill her if she slipped up."

"That's a valid point." Rio rubbed his chin. "I've been giving this some thought as well. If I were an escaped prisoner, I'd keep walking all night if necessary until I found a safe place to hole up. Raven mentioned the cabins along the river. If they made it there and took down the owner, it's likely they'd rest up for a short time and then keep moving." He looked at Jenna. "We might be out in the forest for days. Rowley packed supplies, but will you be okay to ride for so long?"

"You're not contemplating riding are you, Jenna?" Wolfe raised both eyebrows and his gray eyes flashed concern. "I would certainly advise strongly against it. You could deliver early. Have you thought this through?"

Suddenly the wisdom of Kane's words struck home and her annoyance with him melted. Lifting her chin, she turned to Rio. "I'm staying at the ranch. Maggie will be in the office and I'll be coordinating the teams from there or home. Seeing as Souza is on the loose, I'm not risking my son a second time."

"That's good to know." Rio smiled at her.

"Amen to that." Wolfe blew out a relieved sigh.

EIGHT

After speaking to Nanny Raya, Jenna decided to get a ride home with her and Tauri. Before leaving, she'd pull two M4 carbine semiautomatic rifles from the gun locker and extra clips for the trip. The saferoom at the ranch could be utilized if by chance anyone managed to get through the upgraded security. With its own power supply, backup generators, and solar, the chances of it being breached would be close to impossible. As the group waited for Carter and Jo to arrive, they decided to remain together until they located the prisoners' tracks and then follow Kane's plan to split up and surround them. Luckily, Blackhawk had organized two of his cousins to act as trackers for the other teams.

As everyone headed for their vehicles, a pang of regret hit Jenna at being left behind. She watched Kane slip on his liquid Kevlar vest and then pull on a jacket. She wanted to keep the mood upbeat and normal. He hated leaving her alone and she could see how much it concerned him. "Do you have everything you need?"

"Yeah, even spare batteries for the phones." Kane held her against him and then stared into her eyes. "Call me when you get home. Leave the horses in the corral. They have more grass in there than they can eat in a month. Stay inside the house until I return. I'll call you at ten every morning and seven at night until we catch them." He kissed her. "Stay safe, Jenna." He clicked his fingers. "Come on, Duke."

She hated seeing him go and stood at the top of the stairs watching him head out of the back door. The office fell so quiet and then the lawyer Samuel J. Cross marched into the foyer with the DA. She leaned over the railing before they reached the counter. "Can I help you?"

"I figure we need to talk." Sam Cross led the way to her office with the DA close behind.

Jenna sat down behind her desk and waved them to the chairs. "Has something happened?"

"Yes. As you were required to recuse yourself from the case, I questioned the men involved in the carjacking this morning. Mr. Cross has discussed a deal for his clients." The DA leaned on her desk with his hands clasped in front of him. "What came up in the conversation is something that you need to know. Mr. Cross has spoken to his clients and requested they wave attorney-client privilege as the facts in this case relate specifically to you and your family."

A shiver of uncertainty skittered down Jenna's spine. What could a couple of drug addicts and a carjacking racket have to do with her family? "I think you'd better explain."

"You'd be aware that Eduardo Souza escaped from prison recently?" Sam Cross gave her a direct stare. "Well, according to my clients involved in your abduction and carjacking, they were hired by him to cause a diversion, to ensure your officers were occupied during the escape. They insist they were unaware of the details, but Souza instructed them to stake out your ranch and office to make sure no one headed toward Blackwater, where we now know the escape was planned close to the county line." He cleared his throat. "When they observed you leaving alone in your vehicle, they decided to tag along. They knew if they could do something to you, it would bring all the deputies from town running in the opposite direction of where the escape was due to take place."

Shaken, Jenna looked from one to the other. "They followed me?"

"So they say." The DA let out a long sigh. "They first planned to run you off the road and steal your Mustang, but when you stopped at the gas station, they decided to carjack you. They apparently had an acquaintance in Black Rock Falls who paid cash for stolen vehicles. They called him and arranged to meet him at the Triple Z Roadhouse. I figure you know the rest."

Astounded, Jenna leaned back in her chair and stared at them. "If they hadn't given you the name Eduardo Souza, I wouldn't have believed this in a million years. I can't believe how he managed to persuade these men to do this to me. One thing is for darn sure, they certainly did cause a massive distraction. Every member of my team, including the medical examiner, came running." She turned her attention to the DA. "I know they've admitted to what they did to me but surely you can charge them with something else? They were involved with the prison break and now we have three serial killers running loose in Stanton Forest."

"Oh, yes, indeed." The DA smiled. "I'll make mention on the charge of carjacking and kidnapping as they cooperated, but I will charge them with aiding and abetting. They've admitted that Souza paid them to create a diversion so you wouldn't be around to respond to the escape." His mouth turned up into a satisfied smirk. "Both men who kidnapped you will be charged —as will Souza if he's caught as well. It carries a seven-year sentence."

Jenna nodded. "And the guy who handed over the cash for my car?"

"Right now receiving stolen property is all we have on him." The DA stared at her. "Finding his accomplices might be something you can get your teeth into because you're not directly involved, but Tom Little isn't talking."

"He is prepared to plead guilty and will likely get only a fine." Sam Cross leaned back in his chair and tipped up his cowboy hat. "I know that you're alone here at the moment, Sheriff, so you might want to put that on the back burner for a time. In my experience most of the chop shops are run by biker gangs. It's very rare that a carjacking organization actually sells on the vehicles, unless they can get them across the border. They make more money with less risk by selling parts."

Annoyed by his sudden rush of empathy toward her, Jenna shook her head. "Absolutely not. My team might be out in the forest looking for escaped prisoners but they'll need a case to work when they return. I can do all the preliminary grunt work while they're away."

"It's a lot to cover alone." Cross gave her a pointed look.

"Jenna is not alone." Jo walked into the office, flicked open her creds to display her FBI badge. "I'll be working right along beside her."

Biting back a smile, Jenna looked from the DA to Sam Cross. "I think we'll start with speaking to Mr. Little. I'll keep right away from his involvement with me this morning." She looked at the DA. "Can you arrange for them all to be taken to County this afternoon? I no longer have the manpower to watch over them overnight again."

"Not a problem." The DA looked at his watch. "I'll have them collected by two." He stood. "It was nice speaking to you again, Jenna." He marched out of the door, head held high.

"I apologize if I offended you, Sheriff." Cross removed his hat and ran his fingers around the rim. "It wasn't my intention."

Jenna nodded. "Apology accepted. I will be down to speak to your client directly."

"Give me twenty minutes." Cross met her gaze. "I'll need to run through a few things with him first and explain why you want to speak with him."

As Cross walked out of the door, Jo closed it behind him. Jenna smiled broadly at her. "It's good to see you again. Thanks for backing me up. Sam Cross can be an ass sometimes. What are you doing here? I figured you'd be going with Carter."

"It looks like I arrived just in time." Jo grinned. "I decided I'd be more useful in the office with you going over the profiles of the escaped prisoners so the team knows who they're up against, rather than trekking through the forest, but I see another case has opened up."

Jenna nodded. "Either reason is fine by me. The team has only been gone for five minutes and I'm already getting bored."

"Well then." Jo shrugged out of her jacket and hung it on the peg behind the door. "Let's get at it."

NINE

STANTON FOREST

Tuesday

Serena Lee had kept going until darkness prevented her from seeing the trail ahead of her. A moonless night meant the forest was pitch black and the horse stopped frequently and shied every time an owl or strange noise came close by. Having no other option, Serena found a patch of thick underbrush, tied the horse to a nearby tree, and made camp for the night. The ground was cold and damp, but the horse blanket helped. Images of her grandfather's staring eyes and blood-soaked body flashed through her mind in a never-ending cascade of horror. Overcome with grief, she buried her face in her hands and wept. Tears streamed down her cheeks and dripped off the end of her nose. She cried for the grandpa she had loved and who had cared for her. She loved spending part of her vacations with him. He'd taught her so much about the forest and told her stories about her family that went way back to the old gold-mining towns. Now he was gone. She needed her mom. She must find a way out of the forest and tell her dad what happened. He'll go to the sheriff and she'll catch the men who did this. Her sobs turned into hiccups, and exhausted from crying, she leaned back against a tree and wrapped the blanket around her. Thunderbolt would alert her to danger. She closed her eyes and eventually dozed off.

Waking as sunlight hit her in the face, she ate a few of her meager rations and climbed back on the horse. She'd been following a trail alongside the river for about twenty minutes when voices came on the wind. Thunderbolt's ears stood to attention, turning this way and that listening. Who could be coming? Unsure if she could trust anyone, she moved away from the trail and into the forest as the sound of men arguing sent birds flying into the air in panic. A group of people trudged along the sandy river's edge toward her. She looked all around trying to get her bearings and swallowed hard in dismay. Had she become turned around overnight and was heading back the way she'd come? Could she be walking straight into the group of men who'd killed her grandpa?

Horrified at the thought of running into them again, she scanned the forest desperately searching for a place to hide. Alongside the river, a few cottonwoods grew, but a variety of pine trees covered the forest and combined with the thick underbrush. The men might not notice a black horse. Thank goodness she decided to keep to the trail rather than walk the horse along the sandy bank leaving a trail of hoofprints. She urged Thunderbolt deeper into the zebra-striped shadows, moving as silently as possible before stopping to dismount near a small boulder. She'd be able to use the rock to boost her back onto the horse's back. Heart thundering in her chest, she stroked Thunderbolt's nose as the voices got louder. If he whinnied at the approaching men, she wouldn't stand a chance. She pulled a horse carrot out of the backpack just in case Thunderbolt decided to make a fuss. Leaning against the horse, she waited, terrified of what might happen next.

One man appeared pulling a woman with her hands bound

together behind him. She was dressed in a uniform and had a bruise on one cheek. Her eyes, with dark circles below, appeared lifeless as she moved mechanically, as if forcing one step in front of the other. The man had a gun stuck in his waistband. Two others followed behind and she recognized them as the men who had killed her grandpa. All of them were wearing his clothes. A shiver went through Thunderbolt and he stamped his hoof hard on the ground. Serena broke the carrot in half and offered him a piece to take his mind away from the approaching men. She spoke to the horse in hushed tones, stroking his nose and trying desperately to keep him quiet. As they got closer, Serena held her breath, willing them to pass by without seeing her.

"Where do you figure the kid went?" One of the men waved a gun at the woman urging her to keep walking.

"I didn't find any signs of her apart from in that one room. Maybe she died?" A second man, wearing her grandpa's ball cap, skimmed pebbles across the river as if he were on vacation. "I looked around. I couldn't find any trace of her. There were no plates in the sink or anything like that to say she was living with him and the only washing on the line belonged to the old man."

"I figure she's just a regular visitor." The third man, wearing a green jacket, scanned the forest. "I don't see any cabins along here. You told us there would be cabins all along the riverside."

"I've seen maps of the area. There'll be cabins coming along soon." The first man turned and stared at Green Jacket. "Maybe we'll find ourselves a truck and we can drive for a time. Souza said there were fire roads all over this forest. We don't need to risk traveling along the highway. There will be roadblocks set up by now for sure, but they won't be setting up any on the fire roads. If we keep traveling west, we should come to a bridge across the river. Souza said once we get over to the west, no one will be able to find us. It's a good place to vanish. There are many old gold miners' cabins along the river there as well that are deserted. We can hole up there. The next cabin we come to, we'll collect what we need to survive off the land. The folks out here do it all the time and it sure is better than being on death row."

"And we have the woman to do the chores and keep us company." Green Jacket grinned. "It sounds like a lifelong vacation in paradise."

Knees trembling, Serena fed the last piece of carrot to Thunderbolt. The crunching noise he made sounded like gunshots in the quiet forest, but the men hadn't noticed and kept on walking along the sandy riverbank. She waited for ages, counting down the minutes in her head, and each time she got to sixty, she held up another finger, figuring if she waited for ten minutes, she could go back the way they'd come and find her grandpa's cabin. She'd be able to call for help on the CB radio. Grandpa had shown her how to use it many times, just in case anything happened to him during her stay. He'd told her the call sign to use and how to get in contact with the sheriff's office. She packed her bag, climbed onto the rock, and threw the bag over the horse's back before climbing onto him. Picking up the reins, she urged him forward in the direction the men had come. Her grandpa had taken her fishing, but so far nowhere along the riverbank looked familiar. Many rivers ran through Stanton Forest, and this could be any one of them. She'd just keep moving and hope for the best. Sooner or later she would recognize her surroundings and find her way back to the cabin. She hadn't been traveling for very long when gunshots rang out in the forest. Thunderbolt reacted immediately by trying to bolt. Serena tried to turn him around and kept talking to soothe him, but not before he'd trotted a hundred yards or so in the opposite direction.

A crashing sound came through the trees and she could make out a red baseball cap worn by one of a group of men and they were running toward her. Serena gathered up the reins, turned Thunderbolt around and urged him along a track heading east. Voices were getting closer. In a few moments they would see her. She leaned down over Thunderbolt's neck and kicked him hard in the ribs. The horse bucked and tossed his head around, but Serena hung on for dear life. She had to get away. As Thunderbolt headed deep into the trees, she glanced over one shoulder. The men who had killed her grandpa dashed along the sandy bank but their attention wasn't on her. It was on the bear chasing them. The horse had sensed the bear as well and increased his speed. He ran until sweat coated his flanks. When he finally slowed, Serena looked around in dismay, all she could see were miles and miles of trees. She had no idea which way to go and searched frantically for a landmark. A sob caught in her throat. Without help, she'd die out here all alone. Her family would never know what happened to her. She'd never see her mom again. Swallowing the overwhelming fear, she urged Thunderbolt through the trees. Behind her were murderers and bears. She had no option but to continue on into the unknown.

TEN

BLACK ROCK FALLS

Behavioral analyst and Special Agent Jo Wells had spent the last fifteen years studying the criminal mind. These ranged from petty thieves to gang members influenced by peer pressure to commit crimes they wouldn't normally do if left to their own devices. The next class of criminal behavior was born from greed. These people came from all walks of life and didn't exhibit a typical type, other than the need to improve their lot in life by stealing from somebody else. Many of these started by stealing old women's purses, vehicles, or by holding up convenience stores and ended up running cartels and accumulating great wealth from the suffering of others mainly by fentanyl distribution, sex slavery, or child exploitation.

The next group of criminals she'd studied had been murderers. People killed for a variety of reasons and there was always an excuse for a sane person to murder someone. These motives included jealousy, hate, covering up a crime, greed, self-defense, power, passion, and obsession. This group of people usually had normal upbringings, and the murders usually stopped with one or two.

During her time with the FBI, Jo had dealt with all these

types, but the criminals that intrigued her the most were psychopathic serial killers. These people were in a class of their own. They came from every economic background and both sexes, although men outweighed women by five to one. She discovered a large portion of them had a psychopathic parent, and having a parent with no empathy can trigger psychopathy in a child. Their parent or parents may not have been pushed to murder and managed to live reasonably normal lives, but a parent who raises a child without love and affection causes an instability that can emerge later in life in many different ways. From a child being cruel to animals, to bullies needing to exert power over others, to the quiet withdrawn kid who suddenly explodes into a serial killer. It's not an exact science, as so many variables and different psychoses or personality traits go into the mix to create a serial killer.

After interviewing many convicted serial killers, she'd concluded that once they'd stepped over the line and begun their murderous spree, none of them could be rehabilitated. Even those who had spent a long time in prison began killing again the moment they were released. After interviewing some of the most notorious serial killers at various state prisons, she'd written a series of books on the subject using the actual serial killers as a reference. Surprisingly, all she'd interviewed had been enthusiastic to be listed in her books. All wanted to be remembered for their crimes. Their egos being such as they were, the frightening fact she discovered was that they all wanted to be the best.

Jo grabbed a pen, went to the whiteboard, and turned to Jenna. "Eduardo Souza isn't a psychopath in the normal sense of the word. He kills for power and removes anyone who stands in his way. His fortune is endless, and from our recent investigations, so is the army of people he has behind him. The chances of taking them all down is about as possible as counting the stars in the sky."

"So we will never be free of him?" Jenna ran a hand down her face and sighed. "I can't believe he's gotten out of prison."

Jo fully understood the ramifications of having Eduardo Souza running loose again. "You can be assured the DEA is moving on him as we speak. One thing is for sure, Souza isn't running around Stanton Forest. We detected an unauthorized helicopter in the area around the time of the bus wreck. From the direction of the gunshot wound found in the driver of the prison bus, the shot could only have come from above. This would indicate that Souza escaped in a chopper and he would be long gone by now."

"Okay, so we've got three serial killers wandering around Stanton Forest." Jenna glanced at the notes on her tablet. "The warden gave me the names I sent you. What do you know about them?"

Jo wrote the three names on the whiteboard. "We have Mason Margos, known as Ice Pick. I figure his name is pretty explanatory. He is a good-looking charismatic man, tall and muscular. He picked up women in bars, drove them to a secluded place, and hacked them to death with an ice pick. When I spoke to him, he said the reason he killed them was because he took offense at the way a woman looked at him."

"So how did you manage to conduct the interview? You had to look at him?" Jenna stood, went to the counter, and poured them both a cup of coffee. "Did he become aggressive with you?"

After adding Margos' characteristics to the whiteboard, Jo sat down and sipped her coffee. "As you are aware, psychopaths always need an excuse in their minds for murdering someone. His excuse was that, when he picked them up in bars, they all looked at him with appreciation and chatted as if he were their best friend, but when he got them alone in his vehicle and drove them somewhere to be intimate, they became afraid of him. He didn't like women looking at him as if he'd frightened them."

"So he murdered them with an ice pick?" Jenna turned her cup around in the tips of her fingers. "What a horrible way to die."

Vividly recalling the interview with Margos, Jo shuddered. "The crime scene photographs were gruesome. Because he didn't like the way they were looking at him, he attacked their eyes. Most of them were outside the vehicle at the time, so he managed to convince them to go with him into a secluded place. We discovered the bodies in forests and in parkland, behind buildings and in alleyways." She sucked in a breath and let it out slowly. "We're talking about multiple murders. I believe he murdered well over twenty women that we know about. He is very well respected in the prison by the other psychopaths. It's unusual for psychopaths to follow anyone—all are individuals and they don't like to share kills—but I guess even in a prison someone has to be the boss. So Margos would be in charge of the other two prisoners who are missing, both of whom are equally as dangerous as he is."

"Who else have we got?" Jenna sipped her coffee.

Jo stood and added notes to the whiteboard. "The information that the warden gave you about these men is accurate. Sebastian Callahan, known as the Silent Strangler, is more of a stalker. He puts the blame on the women he kills by saying that they dissed him. Being rejected is a reason many psychopaths will kill. It often stems from childhood, when they were humiliated at one time or had a parent who made a habit of embarrassing them in public." She glanced at Jenna. "Then we have Carl Romero, known as the Blue Man. His excuse was that if a woman invited him into her home, he had the right to rape and murder her. So he showed up at the front door of his victims dressed in blue coveralls and we believe told them there'd been a gas leak in the building." She sat down and lifted her coffee cup and sighed. "When I did a background check on him, I discovered his mother was a sex worker. So he often saw men coming in the house wearing coveralls. For a small child, he probably witnessed things he couldn't understand and it triggered his psychopathy."

"What chance has the prison guard of surviving these men?" Jenna peered at her over the rim of her cup. "She is only small and in her early twenties."

Just the thought of a woman being alone with these three men churned Jo's stomach. "I'd say she has a ten percent chance of survival. It will depend how long she is useful to them and how much power Margos can exert over the other men. Any one of them could flip out and kill her. The good thing is that they've been in prison for a long time and will be in some type of control. In prison, they couldn't just kill anyone at their leisure like they used to. It's as if while in prison they go into some type of remission due to being confined and away from the triggers. The problem is we have no idea how long it will last because usually when psychopaths are released from custody they kill again." She sighed. "Her only hope is that she doesn't cause friction between them or accidently trigger one of them. If she does and they kill her, just witnessing the murder will set them all off. It will be a bloodbath."

ELEVEN

Jenna checked the clock and pushed back her chair. She collected a legal pad from her drawer and looked at Jo. "Do you want to sit in on the interview with Little?"

"Yeah, sure." Jo stood and followed her down to the interview rooms.

After setting up the cameras and going through the usual procedure before taping an interview, Jenna looked at Little across the desk, who stared back at her with a belligerent expression. Sam Cross sat beside him flicking through notes he'd made earlier. It hadn't been the chop shop that interested Jenna. She wanted to know just how deep Souza had infiltrated Black Rock Falls. She placed her legal pad on the table and then looked at Little. "How long have you been involved with Eduardo Souza?"

The prisoner looked taken aback and his eyes grew wide. He moved around restlessly in his chair flicking glances back and forth toward her and his lawyer. Jenna kept her gaze fixed on him. "Well, it's a simple question." She sighed, acting bored. "The two drug addicts who kidnapped me have spilled their guts, so why don't you make it easy on yourself?" She stared him down. "I'm not interested in the kidnapping or the carjacking. In fact, it would be a conflict of interest as it was my car involved. Your friends have both informed the DA that they work for Eduardo Souza. The DA has been in a good mood today and it would be in your best interest if you explained your connection to Souza before we make inquiries and then discovered just how deep you are in his organization."

"I'm not deep in his organization." Little gripped the edge of the table. "You do know that he'll kill us if he discovers we've spoken to you?"

Twirling the pen in her fingertips, Jenna leaned back in her chair nonchalantly. "Then you'll need some type of protection, won't you? Your friends have already given up Souza, and knowing his reputation as I do, he won't give you a pass on this, so maybe you just need to tell us what you know. If we believe your life is in danger for testifying against him, we can place you in witness protection."

"Testifying against him?" Little's eyes almost popped out of his head. "Are you insane? I'd never make it to court. He has people everywhere. You don't honestly believe that he contacted me or the others personally, do you?"

Finally getting somewhere, Jenna shook her head. "No, I don't. He was in prison at the time. Just tell us what you know. Maybe start at the time his organization made contact with you and asked you to create a distraction, and we'll discuss the chop shops later."

"Stop right there." Cross glared at Jenna. "If you continue with this line of questioning, everything my client tells you will be thrown out of court due to a conflict of interest." He leaned forward. "The questioning was to discover how Souza was involved in the chop shops. This is starting to get personal and overlap into your case. I can't allow it."

"For me it isn't." Jo leaned back in her chair and crossed her legs. "I've been requested to take over this case and will conduct the questioning. Start from the beginning. What is really behind everything that happened to Sheriff Alton?" She crossed her arms and drummed her fingers on her forearm and then uncrossed her legs and slammed one hand down on the table. "It's already out that you and your pals have squealed. As an FBI agent, my word that you're willing to testify and need protection goes a long way. We know creating a diversion is only part of the plan. What else do you know?" She eyeballed him. "Think now, what you answer could mean the difference between walking out of here unprotected with a fine, or testifying in court and being protected for the rest of your life." She narrowed her gaze. "It would be nice to start over, wouldn't it?"

"Maybe." Little turned to look at Sam Cross. "Is she just yanking my chain?"

"No, she wouldn't be able to do that in a recorded interview." Cross shook his head. "Everything discussed here is on record. This is why it's recorded and videoed, so it's obvious if anyone is putting you under duress. She is offering you a way for a new life. The witness protection scheme is very safe and it has never been infiltrated."

Biting her bottom lip, Jenna held her breath as Little leaned back in his chair thinking through the proposition. Convinced there must be more to the story than the escape, she willed him to open up. Eduardo Souza didn't do favors for anyone. He must have another angle. Whoever contacted Little must have given up more information to make the pot sweeter. She exchanged a glance with Jo, mentally urging her to continue to push for answers. Keeping quiet was difficult. There were so many questions she wanted to ask him.

"Well, Mr. Little, I haven't got all day." Jo gave a frustrated sigh. "Do you have a story to tell or are we just wasting our time here?"

"I don't have too much to tell you." Little shrugged and cast his eyes down on his clenched hands resting on the table.

"I was given the five thousand to give to Don Riley and I got the car. I would have made big bucks on the Mustang, so for me it was a good deal and worth the risk. What Riley didn't tell you is that this was all organized on the run. It wasn't his idea to carjack you and bring the car to me. His job was to stake out your ranch and then follow you if you left home. When you left the ranch alone, Riley made a call to his contact, who'd already paid him to stake out your place. The plan to carjack you and bring the Mustang to me was planned when you stopped in Louan." He sniggered. "You don't figure Don Riley is smart enough to plan that out on his own, do you?" He brushed the back of one hand under his nose and shook his head. "You're correct, this was planned as a diversion to keep your deputies occupied and away from the county line. What you don't know, is the only reason Souza left the other prisoners behind is so they would keep the deputies occupied and maybe kill them if the opportunity arose."

"What else?" Jo stared at him one eyebrow raised in question.

"He needed insurance, so he wanted to get to her." Little pointed a finger at Jenna. "It hasn't escaped Souza's people that she is pregnant. He figured she'd remain in town during the search for the prisoners. With all her resources used up, she's vulnerable. Putting her in danger, would ensure her husband would come running, just as he did when Riley carjacked her. Souza would have taken him down then, but they didn't have time to organize a chopper." He turned his gaze slowly to Jenna. "As long as Souza is alive, your time on this earth is limited. He has a score to settle and doesn't give up easy."

Needing more information, Jenna leaned into Jo to whisper in her ear. "If this is so personal, does Souza plan to be there when he disposes of Dave?"

"Okay." Jo nodded and turned her attention to Little. "Just

one more question, Mr. Little. Is Souza planning to be there when Deputy Kane is murdered?"

"From what I heard, he'd like to do it himself but he doesn't care as long as he's dead." Little leaned back in the chair with a smug smile on his face. He turned to Jenna. "He won't stop until he's murdered every one of your family."

TWELVE

STANTON FOREST

After estimating the distance the prisoners might have traveled, they headed to the river's edge to find their trail. It was clear from the footprints left in the sand along the riverbank that the woman was still with the prisoners, although from the footprints, she often stumbled and might be injured. Kane decided the best chance of catching them would be if they broke the group into two. He, Atohi, Raven, Wolfe, and Rowley had the fastest horses and would head back to the fire road. By using well-known trails, they'd get in front of the prisoners. Keeping in touch with their coms, they should be able to close in on them in two different directions. Sitting astride Warrior, Kane took Duke from Blackhawk's arms. His dog had become quite familiar riding this way. As he wasn't getting any younger, keeping up with a galloping horse would be difficult. Raven's dog, Ben, wouldn't have any problem at all. Given that Styles and Carter had worked together in the past and having Rio as backup and two of Blackhawk's cousins to guide them, the plan would work well.

They'd traveled approximately three miles ahead of the other team, and were moving along trails running parallel to the river to keep undercover in the forest, when Kane's phone vibrated in his pocket. He listened in astonishment as Jenna brought him up to date. "I'm sure glad that Jo and Beth decided to stay with you."

"*I know, you were concerned about leaving me alone, and this time you were right.*" Jenna's voice sounded strained. "*We'll be leaving for the ranch in a few minutes. I'm going with Nanny Raya and Tauri. Beth and Jo are driving my SUV. Beth figures, being blonde, they won't confuse her with me.*"

Since Souza kidnapped Tauri from their ranch, Kane had spent a great deal of time scoping the area, looking for threats and possible sniper positions. Since they had engaged the laser net around the area, landing a chopper or flying a drone above the house was impossible. The laser net interfered with the onboard computers but unfortunately did nothing to prevent a sniper's bullet. He pressed the earbud tighter into his ear and constantly scanned the immediate area for the prisoners. "You'll need to get inside the house and stay there. Keep everyone there. They'll be fine and we have plenty of spare bedrooms. You can't risk sending anyone to the cottage. The path from the house to the cottage is in a direct line from the hillside, and if there's a sniper up there... well, you know the rest. Suit up for the ride home as well. Just in case."

"*I intend to. We have enough Kevlar vests for everyone, including Tauri. I'll add helmets as well.*" Jenna took a deep breath and blew it out slowly as if trying to keep calm. "*We've made so many new improvements to the security, I'm sure we'll be safe once we're inside the house.*" She paused a beat. "*Any sign of the prisoners?*"

Kane readjusted Duke in front of him. The old dog was prone to falling asleep and sliding off the horse. "No physical signs, no. We found tracks alongside the river and decided to split up into two teams. Rio, Carter, and Styles along with two of Blackhawk's cousins are following the tracks. The rest of us have gone ahead using the fire roads to hopefully get around in front of them. With luck, we can surround them and take them down without too much difficulty."

"I hope so." The familiar squeak of Jenna's office chair came through the earbud as she sat down. "We'll be leaving soon. I'll call you again when we get there. I don't really know Agent Katz, but when Styles assisted me he insisted she was tougher than she looked and fought like a demon. I figure she's going to be an asset if anyone shows."

Kane smiled to himself. "I'm sure if a few of Souza's henchmen manage to get through our security, which I doubt, they won't know what they're up against. Nanny Raya was chosen for a good reason. She might be older than us, but she has a chest full of medals for bravery under fire. Along with Jo and Beth, I'm sure you'll be just fine. Don't forget these men are more than capable of creating a diversion to try and get you out of the house. The horses are safe in the corral. They have plenty of food and water to last them for a week at least. If they set fire to the barn for instance, call the fire department. You know the fire chief by sight. Don't leave the house."

"And the house is covered with fire retardant, I know. Maybe we should have used some on the barn as well?" Jenna cleared her throat as if someone had just come in the room. "I'd better let you go. I'll call you later." She disconnected.

After catching up to the others in his group, Kane brought everyone up to speed. "So this was well planned ahead of time. It seems the moment the prison warden started moving his extra prisoners to Black Rock Falls County to avoid overcrowding, Souza decided to set fire to the maximum security area so there wouldn't be any space for them. All Souza needed to do was to get the plans of his escape to his associates. The moment the fire was lit, it was only a matter of time before the transfer was made."

"I'm impressed how fast someone in maximum security can

get the word out to organize a prison break." Raven moved his horse alongside Kane. "Money talks, huh?"

"So it would seem." Rowley came up behind them. "The women should be safe at the ranch."

Kane nodded. "I sure hope so." He tapped his mic. "Copy. Is there a problem?"

"I believe so." Carter was keeping his voice low. "They've split up. Two are continuing along the riverbank. One is moving in your direction with the prison guard. I figure you'll be running into them soon if they keep heading in the same direction. We figured we would stay on the heels of the two walking along the riverbank." He cleared his throat. "We also found hoofprints, which Blackhawk's cousin insists are fresh. So we have an unknown rider in the mix as well. I've heard a few shots, but I believe they're from the other side of the river. Over."

Shooting a glance at Rowley, Kane raised his eyebrows in question. Rowley knew which areas were designated for hunters. When he gave him a nod, he tapped his com again. "Don't worry about them. They're hunters. They should be moving away from the river. Over."

"That's good to know. Just a second, we've found something. Over."

The others had heard Carter's transmission and they slowed, bunched up in a group along the trail waiting to hear what they had found. Kane waved them on. "Keep moving and stay alert They could be anywhere close by."

A few minutes went by before Carter got back to him.

"We found a cabin with blood on the front stoop and drag marks. We followed them and discovered partial human remains in the pigpen. The cabin has been ransacked. There's evidence there's a female living here. Looking at the clothes hanging in the closet, I would say female around ten to twelve years old. There's no sign of her anywhere and we've found no footprints or any evidence that she's left the premises. We can only hope that she *visited here at one time. Or maybe she died and he's just kept her room as is."* Carter, heaved with the effort of remounting his horse. *"Rio has marked the cabin with crime scene tape. There's nothing we can do for the victim now. So we're going to keep moving. Over."*

"The hoofprints you discovered, do you figure the girl took a horse to escape?" Raven tapped his com. "Maybe you should check out the place and see if there's a stable anywhere. It's pretty easy to see if there's fresh manure or a dirty stall. Over."

"Copy that. Will go. Over and out." Carter disconnected.

Kane wiped a hand down his face. If there was a young girl alone in the forest, that was another problem to add to the list. With serial killers running around, she would be in danger with them or on her own. Now nowhere was safe. He turned as Blackhawk came to his side. "You heard about the girl?"

"Yeah, I know the family. That would be Troy Lee and his granddaughter, Serena. If Carter comes across her, one of my cousins would be able to get her out of the forest safely." Blackhawk met his gaze. "With Jenna out of town, it would be safer to take her to the res. There are trails from the riverbank that no one would be able to find. They look like they're going nowhere but they offer good cover if you're trying to get away."

Nodding, Kane heaved in a deep breath. "Thank you, I figure that's my only option at the moment. We don't want a kid witnessing the takedown of serial killers or running across them in the forest. I just hope she didn't witness the murder."

"If she hightailed it on a horse, there's a good chance she did." Wolfe's horse sidestepped and danced sideways along the trail. "I figured they holed up in the cabin overnight, and maybe found a change of clothes. If they're wearing regular clothes, we won't be able to distinguish them from local hunters."

"Styles here." Styles came through the coms. *"We found signs of a horse and some kid's footprints. The cabin's been ransacked, but from the prison clothes tossed all over, I'd say the*

prisoners are all dressed like regular guys." He paused a beat. *"We have a kid out there alone in danger. I've read their files. These men really love to kill kids. We need to locate her ASAP."*

Kane took two seconds to consider the options. Children in danger took priority over everything. "Follow the tracks of the horse and locate the girl. Send her with one of Blackhawk's cousins to the res. He'll know a safe way through the forest. Right now the res is the closest place, and no one will get in there."

"How can you be sure?" Styles wasn't convinced. *"Blackhawk's people aren't going to be there to stop serial killers getting onto the res."*

"Yes, they will. They are aware of the threat." Blackhawk stared at Kane and his mouth turned down. "The prisoners would need to cross the bridge from this side of the forest. The elders will have people there to stop them. I doubt they'll be able to find the bridge. The trails through the forest and into the res are known by only a few outsiders. Most people who visit come by road."

Kane tapped his mic. "Find the girl. We'll keep moving in from this side. There should be a number of empty cabins along the river. The prisoners might stop to hole up there, so check them out. It would be better for us to do the same. Right now, the escapees don't know we're chasing them. The moment we light a fire in the forest, they'll know—smoke from a cabin they'll ignore. You know the deal: take turns sleeping and stay alert."

"Okay, gotcha." Styles paused for a beat. *"I nearly said, 'yes, sir.' It felt like I was back in uniform. I'll run it back at you. We find the girl, send her off with Blackhawk's cousin. Locate an empty cabin and hunker down for the night."*

Glancing at Wolfe's sudden grin, Kane shrugged. He took charge naturally, and everyone accepted it without comment until now. "Copy that."

"We'll call you with our coordinates when we stop for the night. Over and out." Styles turned off his com.

"Military police." Wolfe continued to ride beside Kane. "I've worked with him on many cases, and he worked alone before Beth Katz joined him at Rattlesnake Creek. He's a maverick and follows his own rules, but he gets the job done. Rattlesnake Creek is a mining town with a sheriff and no deputies. Styles wades into the brawls there and no one gets killed. One look at his revolver and they seem to fall into line."

All he needed was a maverick loose cannon in charge, but Jenna had found him responsible, and as an ex-MP, at least he had the skill set. Kane dismounted and dropped Duke gently on the ground. "As I'm in charge, I figure it's time to take a break. Maybe if we sit here for a time, escaped prisoners will come to us."

"We can live in hope. I'll unpack the supplies." Raven dismounted and led the packhorse to a tree and secured it before opening the saddlebags. "I know this area of the forest down that way." He indicated along the trail with his chin. "There are three cabins in this area owned by the forestry and used as hunting cabins. The first one is about six miles away. There is another closer to the river, so I figure if the prisoners planned to hole up in one, it would be the one close to the river. They wouldn't know about the one inland. None of them have ever lived in this county. I checked that out before we left. These guys are walking around blind."

Kane smiled at him. "I'm starting to like these odds."

"There is only one main problem that I can see if we hole up in the cabin, and that's the horses." Blackhawk's dark gaze moved across Kane's face. "If they steal our horses, they'll take the advantage." He looked from one to the other. "We'll need to take the horses to a safe place. I'll stay with them."

"I'll take first watch." Wolfe took a pack of sandwiches from the bag and sat on a boulder. "I'm used to working late."

Kane glanced at his watch. "We still have three hours of daylight left." He looked at Raven. "It's slow going along these small trails. You sure you can find this cabin?"

"Oh yeah." Raven held up his satellite phone. "I have the coordinates of every cabin I've found. I buy many of the abandoned ones from the council or the forestry. Making them available for vacations is a lucrative business."

Astounded by his ingenuity, Kane poured coffee from a Thermos and reached for the sandwiches. "You never cease to amaze me. Is there nothing you can't do?"

"Not yet but I usually draw the line at killing people." Raven shrugged. "It goes against my Hippocratic oath."

THIRTEEN

The person who created the phrase *living a nightmare* couldn't have possibly imagined what Amy Clark had suffered over the last twenty-four hours or so. How long had it been since the wreck? Time meant nothing to her. She lived between each heartbeat, dragging every breath past a sore throat and into aching lungs. Taken as a hostage, she'd foolishly imagined they would keep her in reasonable condition if they planned to use her as their frontperson to get inside cabins without being shot. That naive impression had stopped the moment they'd entered the cabin where they'd murdered the old man. The memory of what happened next crawled over her skin like maggots on dead flesh. On arrival at the cabin, Margos had sent her to the bathroom to clean up. Covered in blood from the guard shot during the escape, she foolishly believed the foul smell was getting to him. Blood had dried on her face, and brain matter clung to her. The stink of death had gotten worse by the minute and she'd welcomed the chance to get clean. The bathroom had a shower and the water had been deliciously hot, but the moment she stepped out and wrapped her towel around her, her life had changed forever.

The prisoners had been locked up for a long time, and naked and smelling of soap, she quickly became a toy for them to play with, and when she complained, they'd beaten her. The threat to kill was always there. In fact, they wagered which one of them would break first and cut her throat. The episodes of abuse came between the time spent in the small kitchen preparing meals and making endless cups of coffee. Seeing daylight pour through the windows had acted like a signal. Play-time was over. The prisoners acted as if they had a mission, but they discussed nothing in front of her, although she'd caught the name of a place: Louan. She'd been allowed to clean up and dress before cooking breakfast. Apart from a few sideways glances and coarse remarks, they didn't touch her again, each of them intent on moving on.

She'd seen signs of a girl in the cabin, and the men concluded she'd maybe been a visitor, but as they left the cabin, pushing her ahead of them, she'd noticed a yellow ribbon snagged in a pine tree on a trail heading in the opposite direction. If a young girl had been inside, she'd thankfully escaped and would be raising the alarm. Any other time, hiking in a lush green forest with new growth all around and the scent of wildflowers would have been a delight, but not with three serial killers breathing down her neck. They followed the river until they'd spotted a drone. She figured the cops had sent it to find them, but it turned out to be another mystery. When Margos waved as if greeting an old friend, it flew low and dropped a parcel.

Amy stumbled to a halt. With her hands tied behind her and attached to a rope like a dog, escape was impossible. Exhausted from lack of sleep and hurting all over, she tried to keep positive. Hunters roamed the forest, and seeing her tied, they might alert the cops. It was her only hope. Right now, she must be of use to them. The moment that changed, she'd become another name on a long list of victims. They'd all been waiting for the delivery. Although they spoke in hushed tones, excitement was streaked all over their faces. She took a few steps backward as Margos unwrapped the box and tossed the lid to one side. The container carried pistols, ammunition, and satellite phones. Moments later, Margos received a call. He'd made no reply, just listened and disconnected. After distributing the phones and ammo, he told them they should split up and sent the other two prisoners along the riverbank.

"Keep heading north. I'm going inland." Margos waved the others away. "You'll get a message if that changes. We're being tracked, so don't leave the trail."

"I want the woman." Callahan raised his chin and his eyes flashed with anger. "You said, fair shares in everything,"

"No." Margos shook his head. He straightened his burly body and clenched his fists. "Don't mess with me. I need her as a lure. You can have her when we're done here." He pulled on the rope, turned his back on them, and headed into the forest.

As they moved through the trees, terror gripped her. *What were they planning? Dear God, are they planning on killing another innocent soul? Whatever, I'm disposable unless I can find a way to escape.*

"Hold up." Margos pulled on the rope tied to her hands. "Sit there." He pointed to a fallen log.

So thirsty, Amy's tongue stuck to the roof of her mouth, but asking him for anything would be a mistake. The argument the men had over her the previous night had almost come to blows. She'd seen different sides to all of them during the horrific time she'd spent with them, never knowing if the next second would be her last. Her stomach lurched at the memory. She needed to scream, cry, and push the awful memory out of her mind, but it came back in a rush of torment. She closed her eyes as the rerun replayed again. The moment she'd stepped out of the shower, Romero had grabbed her arm and pulled her against him. Roaring like a bull, Margos had pressed his pistol into Romero's temple. Callahan had dragged her away and thrown her to the floor, insisting a woman was a waste of time to argue over. His suggestion was that they all murder her and at least have a thrill out of what was becoming a boring journey, and he'd rather be back in prison with three squares a day. The way they'd looked at her, all of them considering the best way to kill her, had chilled her to the bone. Their demeanor had changed completely, their eyes becoming hard and expressions almost blank. The compromise had been worse. During the ordeal, she wished she could pass out, but they'd kept her awake. Dying would have been better.

Being under Margos' complete control terrified her. It was like being a cow in a slaughterhouse queuing up waiting for the bolt in the head. She sat and waited as he sent a message, waited for a reply, and then checked the GPS coordinates. He glanced at her and then removed his ball cap to scratch his head.

"There are two teams of cops chasing us down." Margos reached into his backpack for a bottle of water. "None are close, and splitting up will make it easier for me to find them." He sipped water and then looked at her. "You look thirsty. Hard to drink with your hands tied together, huh? I figure the split lip wouldn't help either."

Amy didn't want to meet his gaze and stared at the ground, but she nodded slightly. None of the men had held a conversation with her. She'd obeyed their orders and kept as passive as possible rather than risk them losing their temper with her.

"You don't need permission to speak to me." Margos held out the bottle of water and waved it under her nose as if it were a glass of fine wine. "It's been a long time since I've had a conversation with a female. There were the nurses in the infirmary, but they weren't so nice."

Keeping her eyes averted, Amy gathered what courage she had left. "Yes, I'm thirsty. It's difficult to keep going without drinking water."

"Then I'll make you a deal. I figure if we've got drones out, so will the cops. If they see us walking through the forest with you on a tether, they'll know who I am and come running." Margos moved a little closer and she could smell the onions they had for dinner with the elk steaks she'd discovered in the freezer. "I'll untie you, but if we come across someone and you start flapping your lips or screaming, I'll shoot you and them without a second thought. You see, I've got nothing to lose. I was in prison on death row. They don't execute many prisoners, so it means never to be released. So how many more years can they give me? When or if I go back to prison, I'm going to be there until I die."

Cooperating was her only chance of survival. The alternative slipped across her mind. If they came across others in the forest and they recognized him as one of the escaped prisoners, he'd kill them without a second thought. She couldn't allow that to happen. Slowly lifting her head Amy glanced at him and then looked away. Before leaving the prison, she'd hastily scanned the files of the men they were transporting. "Ice Pick" Mason Margos attacked women because they looked at him strange. To him, eyes were an affront. Her hands trembled. This man terrified her, and his arrogant face would probably be the last thing she saw before she died. "Okay, what do you want me to do?"

"Simple, just act as if we're a couple hiking through the forest on a nice sunny day." Margos' gaze ran up and down her and he gave his head a little shake as if pulling himself out of a fantasy. "If we meet anyone, you let me do the talking. With luck, before it gets dark we'll find another cabin. I'm told there are many in this area." He sniggered. "Maybe I'll let you take another shower, but this time I'm going to watch or I might even join you." He leaned forward and untied her wrists. "Have a drink. We'll stop again later but right now we need to keep going."

Horrified by what was to come, Amy's hands shook so bad she could hardly get the water to her parched mouth. The fluid burned the cut on her lip, but she drank it down so fast it spilled out of the corner of her mouth and ran down her shirt. Afraid to empty the bottle, she lowered it from her lips and handed it to him, keeping her lashes low. When he stood up and hoisted his backpack over one shoulder, he gave her a push in the back as she stood. Amy stumbled forward, her feet tangled in the under-brush, and she fell flat on her face into the decaying leaf mold.

"Get up." Margos kicked the sole of her boot. "You rest when I tell you to rest."

Clamping her jaw shut, Amy pushed to her feet and brushed pine needles and dead leaves from her clothes. Nasty kids had bullied her at school as a child and she understood when someone was baiting her. He wanted a reaction and she refused to give him the satisfaction. Desperately afraid, she placed one foot in front of the other and followed the narrow animal track. Behind her, Margos' eyes burned into her back. He made no more verbal threats, but he didn't need to. Just having him behind her was like trying to escape a grizzly.

FOURTEEN

Pretending to play hide-and-seek in the back seat of Nanny Raya's SUV, Jenna snuggled down with Tauri. Jo sat in the front seat and Beth slid onto the back seat beside Jenna. She had removed her hat and her blonde hair spilled over her shoulders. In the front seat Jo had done the same. No one could possibly believe either of them were Jenna. They headed out along Main and Nanny Raya hit the gas the moment they made it onto the highway. Twenty minutes later, they were heading along the driveway to Jenna's ranch. The gates whined open and Nanny Raya drove around the ranch house to the door to her private entrance. The back of the house was well treed, shielding the entrance from the road. They all piled out and went through the extension built exclusively for the nanny and into the main house.

When Tauri took off along the hallway and into his room to play with his toys, Jenna led the way into the kitchen. So far so good. They'd gotten home without any incidents, but they needed to stay alert and that meant posting lookouts overnight. She went about setting up the coffee machines and searching the fridge for something to eat. She smiled seeing the peach pie on the shelf. It seemed that Kane always had a good supply of pie.

"You have a beautiful home." Beth Katz dropped a duffel onto the floor and, after placing a laptop onto the table, scanned the kitchen smiling. "I figured, from the stories that Styles told me, the kitchen would be spectacular. Kane enjoys cooking I hear."

Taking down cups from the cabinet, Jenna nodded. "Yeah, he does all the cooking. I'm not sure if it's by choice or that he can't stand eating my food. I can make scrambled eggs and burned toast but honestly my career doesn't really leave me too much time to experiment with recipes."

"Well, I'm a great cook." Jo searched the freezer. "Dave always has a well-stocked pantry, so one thing's for sure, we won't go hungry while they're away."

Jenna looked from one to the other. "Now we have the food organized, we need to work out who is going to stand guard overnight. We have perimeter alarms, so we should be safe enough, but people have gotten into the ranch before when we believed it was impenetrable."

"I'll take first watch." Beth dropped into a chair. "I usually work on my laptop late into the night, so I won't fall asleep on the job."

"I'll take the second watch." Nanny Raya smiled. "I'll sleep after dinner. The one thing about being an ex-FBI agent is that I can sleep anywhere and at any time."

"I've never been able to do that." Jo heated the pie in the microwave and then slid it onto the table. "Quantico seems a lifetime ago. What made you retire?"

"I wanted to live in a small country town where it was quiet. When the position of nanny came available for Jenna, I couldn't resist it." Nanny Raya chuckled and poured the coffee. "I hadn't realized I would be working in Serial Killer Central."

The sound of a chopper came from overhead. Heart thumping in her chest, Jenna ran along the passageway and into the family room. Along the way, she grabbed one of the semiautomatic rifles they'd taken from the office. She glanced over one shoulder as footsteps came behind her. Following closely, Jo and Beth flanked her. Nanny Raya ran into Tauri's bedroom and shut the door.

"Don't you have a net?" Beth stood to one side of the window scanning the sky.

Stomach clenching, Jenna moved out of the family room and toward the front door. "Yeah, and it's activated." She turned as Jo joined her, rifle in hand. "It will prevent them from landing, but it doesn't stop bullets. If this is Souza, he knows we're here and all our resources are in the forest. I just hope he doesn't have people who can hack our system and bring down the net."

"They don't know about me being here, do they?" Beth's lips curved into a smile. "Anything they can do I can do better and faster."

Keeping her back to the wall, Jenna peered out of the window at the chopper circling high above. It was an indistinct helicopter and she couldn't make out any numbers or distinguishing features. The one that had kidnapped Tauri had a blue flash on one side, but this one was plain gray. One of the doors was open and she could see the legs of a man sitting on the edge like a military sniper, with a rifle across his lap. "We have a shooter. Keep away from the windows."

"I could probably take him out from here." Beth gave her a small smile. "I'm being a little optimistic. I'm great on the rifle range but nothing like Styles. My expertise is in cybercrime, not as a sniper."

"I know how to use a rifle. Carter makes sure I hit the range at least once a week, but I agree, hitting a moving target at that distance would be optimistic." Jo's face was etched with concern. "I figure shooting at them would only start a gunfight. It's better if they believe that we're not here."

A trickle of sweat ran down Jenna's spine. The women, both FBI agents, gave out different vibes. She'd known Jo for a long time, and together they'd taken down serial killers without the help of men. It had been easier then. Being almost eight months pregnant and with a young son to care for, she couldn't go gung ho into danger. Jo had taken in the situation and decided to stand down and wait and see what happened. Beth, on the other hand, was excited and ready to jump in, boots and all. Styles had mentioned she was a little unconventional, even to the point of being eccentric. She had a very dark sense of humor, which popped out in the most inopportune moments, and yet he'd seen her place herself in danger to protect women and children without a second thought.

Undecided about what she should do next, Jenna turned to Beth. "It's likely they have us outgunned. We have no idea how many shooters are in that chopper. I figure we close the shutters and use the camera array to watch what's going on outside. My office has a bank of screens. It's comfortable inside. We'll need to take turns watching the monitors, but for now we can rely on the perimeter alarms. They go straight to my phone. There's not a chance anyone is going to sneak up on us."

"Yeah, that sounds like a plan." Beth looked at Jo. "Help me close the shutters."

"No need." Jo kept her attention on the circling chopper. "Everything is automated."

Keeping low, Jenna dashed to the control panel beside the front door and hit a button. Metal shutters slid down over the windows. The house was safe. She turned to look at the other two. "If they breach the house, head for the safe room. I'll leave the door propped open the entire time we are under threat. Once inside there, even if they set fire to the house, we can escape."

"Unless they drop explosive devices on the roof." Beth frowned. "If what I've read about Eduardo Souza is true, he wouldn't stop at anything. The only chance we have is that he is using you to lure Kane out into the open. It's him he really wants, isn't it?"

Nodding Jenna, turned to look at her. "So it would seem, but why him, when a team of FBI agents were involved in taking him down? It wasn't just Kane who gave evidence."

"Souza needs to be taken down permanently." Beth shrugged. "I hear that Kane doesn't balk when it comes to taking a shot when necessary." She flicked a glance at Jo. "It's a fine line, the one we walk between right and wrong. I've worked out my own set of rules since working alongside Styles. In a fight there's no rules, and if someone draws down on me or tries to stick me with a knife, I aim center mass. I don't get paid enough to be shot or cut up by criminals."

"You've been through many shootings of late." Jo's eyes narrowed as she openly assessed her. "Do you get flashbacks?"

"Nope." Beth returned her gaze, and they stared at each other like two gunslingers in the O.K. Corral. "The only reruns in my head come from seeing abuse of any kind. People I've killed in the line of duty who were trying to end my life don't deserve my thoughts. Yeah, I remember them, but I don't lose any sleep over them." She looked at Jenna. "Kane would be the same, right?"

All Jenna could hear was the chopper overhead and this conversation was going nowhere. She never discussed Kane's past life or his feelings. "In my team, we prefer to incapacitate than kill. It's not an order, but we've discovered the perps usually have information we can use. They can't do that when they're dead." She sighed, suddenly needing to sit down and rest her aching back. "Would I shoot to kill if those men circling my home came through the door? Yeah, without hesitation.

Now, can we figure a way of getting that chopper off our backs?"

"Sure." Beth headed for the kitchen. "I'll try and hack the computer onboard the chopper. I did notice a registration number on the side when it turned around. If I can get in, they'll suddenly be out of fuel."

Jenna pushed her hair from her eyes and followed her. "Anything to get them away from here." She walked into the kitchen and placed her rifle on top of the refrigerator. "We can't forget we have a child in the house. Carry your pistols, by all means, but keep the rifles locked up for now. I have a gun safe in my office and in the safe room. If you want to take them into your bedroom, that's your choice, but they need to be on top of the closet not out in the open."

"You don't need to talk to me about gun safety." Beth rolled her eyes toward the ceiling. "My partner is ex-military police, and although he's known as a maverick in the FBI, trust me, the MP is never far away." She sat down at the table and opened her laptop. She cracked her knuckles and went to work.

As the chopper circled in never-ending loops above the house, Jenna took a deep breath to steady her nerves and went to Tauri's room. "We have pie. Do you want a slice? I have ice cream as well."

"I like pie." Tauri looked up from the book he was reading to Nanny Raya. "Is that Uncle Ty flying around?"

Keeping her expression neutral, Jenna sat beside him. "Not this time. They'll be gone soon, but you'll see Uncle Ty very soon. He's with Daddy chasing bad men. He'll be back in a few days."

"Okay." Tauri licked his lips. "Can I have his slice of pie too?"

Smiling, Jenna ruffled his hair. "Maybe after dinner. Okay?"

"Okay." Tauri closed the book and took off along the passageway to the kitchen.

As Jenna followed him, chatting with Nanny Raya and trying to keep everything normal, the sound of the chopper moved into the distance. In the kitchen, Beth was sitting back in her chair sipping coffee. She raised one eyebrow and looked at her. "The chopper is leaving."

"Yeah, I found a nice little back door into their computer system." Beth chuckled. "They'll have so many warnings flashing, I don't figure they'll be back for a time."

Shaking her head in amazement, Jenna sunk into a chair and turned to her. "When we met Bobby Kalo, the computer black hat hacker, I figured he was the best, but you have skills I've never heard of before."

"Never underestimate Kalo." Beth reached for a slice of the pie Jo was pushing onto plates. "He's evolving faster than I ever imagined. We've worked together on many cases and he's darn good. You're lucky to have him on your team." She chuckled. "I guess me and Styles are on your team now."

The woman was smart—there was no denying that—but did she take orders? Could she trust her to have her back? There were so many questions that needed answering and Jenna's sixth sense insisted she act with caution around Beth. She'd liked Styles' no-nonsense efficiency and selfless courage at once, but the way Beth Katz's eyes flashed sometimes told her there was more to her than met the eye. She'd talk to Kane and maybe Jo later, but for now, she needed an extra person to keep Tauri safe and would give her the benefit of the doubt. She looked at Beth. "So it would seem."

FIFTEEN

STANTON FOREST

Hearing voices, Serena froze. A man and woman were heading her way. Relief flooded her for a few seconds before she caught a better look of the woman. She'd seen her calling out to Grandpa before he'd sent her out to collect eggs. There must have been something about the people that concerned him. He'd never told her to wait to make sure they'd left before she returned. On occasion, lost hunters dropped by for directions and she'd thought nothing of it until she'd heard the shot.

She recalled seeing blood on the woman's face, but now she'd cleaned herself and wore one of Grandpa's jackets. The woman didn't look happy. Black bruises covered one cheek and she walked with a limp. As they came closer, panic gripped her and she urged Thunderbolt deeper into the forest. Tree branches caught in her hair and smacked painfully against her cheeks as they moved along a narrow pathway. Thunderbolt seemed to understand her anxiety and had been as quiet as a mouse, his ears twisting this way and that as if listening for danger. She stroked his silken neck and, keeping her voice to a whisper, talked softly to him, urging him on. Hidden in the dense forest, she turned to watch the couple walk by. No one else followed. The men had split up, and now she didn't know which way to go. They wouldn't return to the cabin, not now they'd killed Grandpa. She wanted to go back to the cabin and use the CB radio but had gotten turned around so many times she'd never find her way home. Hungry and tired, tears wet her cheeks. *Which way do I go?*

Heartsore for her grandpa, she lay on the horse's neck and sobbed. She couldn't believe those horrible men had killed him for nothing. The sight of him being dragged to the pigpen had stuck in her brain and she couldn't stop seeing it. The way they'd laughed as if he meant nothing. Someone must be in the forest she could go to for help, but she hadn't heard gunshots from hunters close by. The forest was unusually quiet, as if the birds knew something was terribly wrong.

In her mind's eye, she could see Grandpa's smiling face and hear his gentle voice. He was a good man. He didn't deserve to die. Remembering the days she'd spent in the forest with him collecting fallen trees and dragging them back to the cabin brought back happy memories. Some of the wood was used to warm the small home, but other pieces, her grandpa would carve into animals and birds to sell or trade at the markets. He'd been the best grandpa a girl could have and she valued the times she'd spent with him. The vision of him using the harness on Thunderbolt to drag the tree along the trail came into her mind. It was as if her grandpa was there right beside her. He'd used the same words every time. Would Thunderbolt take orders from her? Serena, straightened. "Home, boy. Take us home."

The horse's head raised and he moved off at a swift trot, taking her by surprise. Hanging on and gripping tight with her knees, Serena urged him into a canter. Soon they came to a wide trail. Thunderbolt snorted and then whinnied. As they turned the bend ahead, four men on horseback came toward them with a dog running alongside. She stared in disbelief. One of the men was wearing a sheriff's department uniform. Another man had FBI written across the front of his jacket, and two others followed some ways behind. Urging Thunderbolt on, she waved as they got closer. Tears spilled down her cheeks. "Help me."

SIXTEEN

Urging his horse forward, Carter met the crying girl and grabbed her horse's bridle. "Hey there. I'm an FBI agent. My name is Ty Carter. That man coming along is Chief Deputy Zac Rio out of Black Rock Falls. What's your name?"

"Serena Lee." Tears streamed down her eyes and she pointed behind her. "Men came to Grandpa's cabin. One of them is back that way in the forest, but he's heading away from here. He has a woman with him. She called out to speak to my grandpa."

"Then what happened?" Rio came closer.

"I don't know. Grandpa said to go and collect the eggs and stay out of sight until the strangers left. He didn't trust strangers." She covered her face and sobbed. Dark hair spilled over her face and her body trembled.

Not being good with kids, Carter looked at Rio and tipped his head toward the girl. When Rio shrugged, Chaska, one of Blackhawk's cousins, came forward and spoke to the girl in his native tongue. She raised her head and replied, her words fluent but punctuated by sobs. Carter looked at Chaska. "Do you know this girl?"

"I know her mother, and she visited the res some years ago." Chaska indicated with his chin back the way they'd come. "The cabin back there belongs to her grandfather Troy Lee. Her mother is Kaya. She moved to Black Rock Falls with her husband. Her grandfather teaches her about the forest. He was a good man."

Wanting to push and discover what had happened, but curbing his enthusiasm, Carter nodded. "Okay, so does she know what happened?"

"She heard a gunshot, not her grandfather's shotgun, and hid. Two men came by, dragging him to the pigpen. She could see he was dead. He had blood on his shirt. The men and the woman all went inside, and she snuck away on the horse and has been avoiding them ever since. She was heading back to the cabin to call for help."

Carter looked at the girl, who had calmed since speaking to Chaska. "Did you see where the other men went? We followed them to the cabin and they look like they're headed back to the river."

"No, they were all at the river and I headed in another direction. I got lost and then heard one man and the woman, and told Thunderbolt to go home. We cantered all the way here. The man was heading the other way." Serena hiccupped and scrubbed at her eyes. "I saw something else, a drone, flying along above the river toward them. It was carrying something. Next time it went over, it was flying high and the box was gone."

Concern gripped Carter. Something wasn't right. Sure a group of prisoners could arrange a bus wreck, but organizing men capable of shooting the bus driver from a chopper and now drones dropping supplies? This manhunt had just gone to the next level. He turned to Rio. From his expression, he didn't need a rundown. "We'll take her to the cabin to collect her things." He turned to Chaska. "Can you get her safely away from here and onto the res?"

"Yeah, we have trails no one has discovered." Chaska moved his horse close to Thunderbolt and looked at Serena. "Would you like to stay with your grandmother until we catch these bad men? I will contact your mom when it's safe to do so." He glanced at Carter. "Is that okay?"

Nodding, Carter turned his horse around. "Yeah, we'll head back to the cabin and inform the others. We'll get her something to eat and then you must get her out of here. She's a witness and these men won't hesitate to kill her the moment they find out."

"You have my word." Chaska met his gaze. "She is family. I'll keep her safe."

"Thanks. Will you contact me when you arrive?" Rio handed him one of his cards. "We'll need to know you're safe."

"Yes, I'll call." Chaska headed back to the cabin with Serena at his side.

Standing guard as Serena packed her belongings, his gaze scanning the forest alongside Rio and Blackhawk's other cousin, Takoda, Carter hit his com hoping that it would carry the distance to Kane. "Kane, do you copy?"

"*Copy.*"

Carter brought Kane up to date. "This is bigger than we imagined."

"*Yeah, seems to me there's something going down that we haven't anticipated.*" Kane heaved a sigh. "*We're coming up inland toward you, so we will no doubt run into one of the groups. From what you are saying, it will probably be the man and the woman. That has to be the prison guard. If she is hurt, she was either injured in the wreck or the prisoners have been abusing her.*"

Carter shook his head slowly. "She might have been in on it. It's strange she isn't dead, considering the company she's keeping."

"Maybe. I guess we won't know whose side she's on until we get there." Kane sighed. *"She's the least of my problems. If someone is dropping packages to them in the forest, it's likely to be weapons. I figure this escape is twofold. They needed to get Eduardo Souza out of prison, and he likely put a very high price on my head. The men he's chosen to hunt me down have nothing to lose. His wealth is a bottomless pit and he could give them a new life just about anywhere. Souza has had so many identities that finding him again is going to be difficult."*

Seeing so many potentially bad scenarios, Carter ran a hand down his face. "Right now, we need to concentrate on the serial killers. Souza is an escaped felon and the entire FBI has him in their sights. Investigations didn't stop when he was imprisoned. We needed to close down all the branches of his empire. This hasn't yet been accomplished, but I can assure you that some of the best are hunting down and clearing out rats' nests as we speak." He blew out a breath. "None of this is logical. Three serial killers, armed or not, wouldn't have a snowflake's chance in a brushfire to take us down. They kill innocent people and we're all military trained. I'm starting to believe this is a ruse to get us away from Black Rock Falls."

"Well, Souza is no fool." Kane's boots crunched through the underbrush as he walked. *"He would be aware of the involvement of you and Styles by now. As you said, he has fingers in every pie. He would have someone to infiltrate the FBI's files, just like Kalo, and discover who was involved in taking down him and his men. Getting us out here and splitting us up is a way to take us down. We don't have intel on what weapons they're carrying or their communication devices. With an eye in the sky, they'll know our location. If we can locate them, we have the numbers to take them down. I'm just hoping Jenna made it safely back to the ranch. A chopper can't land there. The ranch is secure and she has three FBI agents to watch her back. I'm waiting on her call."*

Carter shook his head. "Call her now. You have drones at your ranch, right? Get her to pack one up and use the other to bring one to our coordinates. Then we'll be on an even playing field."

"I don't want her going outside. You know darn well she's a target. So is my son."

"Styles here. Do you copy?" The familiar voice came through Carter's com.

Rolling his eyes, Carter stared at Rio. "Yeah, I'm here. Can we dispense with the 'copy' and 'over and out' shit?"

"Sure." Styles sounded amused. *"Beth will send the drone. She'll get the job done. You can rely on her."*

Straightening and sweeping his gaze over the forest again, Carter cleared his throat. "You okay with that, Dave?"

"Copy. There's a cabin one mile south from your position. We'll meet you there. If we run into the prisoners, you'll hear us coming. Over."

Carter rubbed Zorro's ears. "I'll never get the military out of that man."

SEVENTEEN

Kane led the group into a thicker part of the forest and quickly gave everyone a rundown of their theories. He looked at Raven. "Have you seen combat? I know you were flying a chopper and in the medical corps."

"Unfortunately, yes, I have." Raven touched his sidearm and shrugged. "Killing is against my Hippocratic oath, but I'm sure that it doesn't cover psychopathic serial killers trying to kill me." He shot a glance at Wolfe. "I'm sure you've been in similar situations since moving to Black Rock Falls."

"Yeah, it's the difference between right and wrong." Wolfe gave him a long steady stare. "No normal person wants to kill, but no one is expected to come under attack and not defend themselves. They have laws in this state for just that, which I'm sure you're aware."

Desperately wanting to contact Jenna but needing to get his team all on the same page, Kane looked from one to the other. "I figure we're coming up against a very well-planned ambush. We don't know for sure what resources they have up their sleeves. The drones these days could easily pass as birds flying over-head. Some of the sophisticated ones don't make a sound. We have no idea how long we've been under observation, so we'll need to make things difficult for them. Now we know what's going on, we can easily turn the tables. My main concern is for the women. They must have guessed we left them to guard Jenna. When you think about it, it was the most logical thing to do. It would be difficult for her to join us in the forest in her condition, and stubborn as she is, they'd know she'd use common sense." He pulled out his satellite phone. "I need to call Jenna." He made the call and gave her a rundown.

"Yeah, I can send a drone at first light. It will take a time to get to you. Send me the coordinates." Jenna's footsteps sounded on the polished floor. *"Okay, I'm in our bedroom. What's really going on?"*

Kane waved the others forward and urged Warrior into the shadows. "It doesn't feel right. For serial killers, these guys are acting like they're on a mission. I'm not sure if it's to get to me or if it's to split us up. They must know we have reinforcements on the way. These men are usually loners. Knowing they're working together is freaky." A chopper flew overhead and began to do sweeping circles. "I figure the Two Bear Air Rescue has just arrived, but they won't be here long. It's getting dark."

"I've heard from the DOC. They've pulled in teams from all over the state to assist in the search. They'll be setting up a command station at the forest warden's office at Bear Peak. It has the biggest parking lot, so once people arrive they'll be used to relieve others out searching. I gather the general consensus is that they believe the prisoners will die of starvation or be eaten by a grizzly. I did explain that they've already killed someone and ransacked their home, but they're not listening to me."

Rubbing the back of his neck, Kane peered through the trees. The night mist was already rising and rolling through the lengthening shadows. "They're not taking in the big picture. They figure this is all about Souza escaping from jail and the other guys just came along for the ride. In fact, it was well planned and there are things going on we don't know about. You will need to keep on your guard at all times."

"After seeing the chopper flying over the house, it was pretty obvious. It's fortunate we had Beth here with us. She was able to hack the helicopter's computer and send it all the wrong messages. I don't figure they'll be trying to get in that way again. I had some idea that Beth Katz was high up in her field, but she makes Kalo look like a novice."

Kane reached for a bottle of water from his saddlebag and took a sip. "Yeah, from what Styles said, she's completely fearless and a little bit eccentric. I've heard a lot about her from Wolfe. No personal information, but that she has a different way of looking at things than most people. She has the unique ability of being able to imagine what a serial killer is going to do next. He puts it down to her father being the notorious serial killer Cutthroat Jack. She lived with him for many years not knowing he was out murdering people until he murdered her mother. Apparently, she didn't witness her death and insists she has no memory of that night. Likely, she's blocked out the horror of what happened. Maybe that's why she's one step ahead of a serial killer. She might have the same mindset."

"If she's carrying the gene." Jenna cleared her throat. *"If she does, it doesn't mean she'll become a serial killer. She's worked many murder cases and nothing's happened yet, so I think I'm safe."*

"She hasn't tried to kill Styles yet either. I'm sure he would have told us by now." Kane grinned into the darkness. "We're heading to a cabin now to meet the others. We'll sleep over and wait until the other teams arrive and then decide what to do. As these prisoners are in our county, we should really have representatives chasing them down."

"We'll be taking turns keeping watch overnight. Please don't worry about us. If anything happens, I'll lock everyone into the

safe room and call you right away." Jenna's footsteps came again. *"Tauri would like to talk to you."*

Warmth crawled around Kane's heart as his son's voice came through the earpiece. "Hey, have you been helping Nanny Raya make cookies today?"

"No, we made pasta and I got to turn the handle on the machine." Tauri giggled. *"Now Auntie Jo is making sauce out of tomatoes and she touched that pot of basil you have growing on the window ledge. She said you wouldn't mind."*

Smiling into the darkness, Kane sighed. The basil had been a pet project of theirs, along with other herbs they'd grown from seed. Every leaf on every plant was precious to Tauri. "That's okay. We grew that to make really good sauce for our pasta. You be a good boy now and help Mommy. I'll speak to you again soon."

"Okay." The phone was dropped onto a table before Jenna's voice came back. *"He's enjoying having Jo here. He likes to cook, just the same as you. I'd better go. It must be dark there. I'll see you soon. Love you."*

Missing her swamped him. "Love you more." He disconnected and urged Warrior back along the trail, moving swiftly to catch up to the others. As he reined in beside Wolfe, his friend turned to greet him."

"It will be dark soon. What's the plan?" Wolfe scanned the forest. "There's no sign of anyone in the vicinity, no smell of a fire. They must have moved in another direction. If we hole up in a cabin overnight, the teams from Helena should arrive by morning. I know the DOC has a plan to catch these guys. Do we go or do we stay and take down these men?"

Kane removed his Stetson and ran a hand through his hair, thinking. He'd never walked away from a fight or left a criminal running loose. Yet Jenna was unprotected. Sure, she had Beth and Jo with Nanny Raya as backup, but they hadn't faced the evil Souza was capable of delivering. "I figure we should discuss our options when Carter and Rio arrive. I'm torn between staying and capturing three violent criminals and protecting my family. Maybe my judgment isn't as sound as it should be right now."

"It's sound." Wolfe urged his horse down the trail. "You've made the right decisions all along. If it had been as simple as just finding the felons, it would be straightforward. We've been thrown an unexpected curveball."

"If you want my opinion"—Raven followed close behind— "with you and Souza, it's personal. I find it difficult to believe he doesn't want to be in on your murder. Using Jenna and Tauri as bait would be sensible, but by now, he'd know that just isn't going to happen so long as she is on the ranch. I figure his plan is about to change."

EIGHTEEN

Stumbling over tree roots as darkness fell all around them, fear gripped Amy Clark. The last thing she wanted to do was spend a night alone with Margos. As the smell of woodsmoke drifted through the forest toward them, he poked her in the back. Terrified he would murder her at any moment, she glanced over one shoulder to see him smiling.

"There's a cabin ahead." Margos pointed through the trees. "I want you to go right up to the front door and knock. Tell them you got turned around in the forest and lost your friends. Just get the front door open, get invited inside, and I'll do the rest."

Heart thundering in her chest, Amy gaped at him and then looked away quickly. "What are you going to do to them?"

"I haven't rightly made up my mind." Margos slid a knife out from his belt and ran his thumb along the blade. "I'm not planning on shooting anyone. I don't want to make a noise and alert the cops. They'll be somewhere close by, but my friends are watching them. They'll be coming soon to meet up with us. Once I have dealt with the owner, I'll give them a call." His lips spread into a wide grin. "I bet you're looking forward to another night with us. Isn't that right, Amy?" He gave her a little push. "Off you go now and do what you do best."

Staggering along the dark trail, Amy searched her mind for something to say to the homeowner to alert him that Margos was intending to kill him, but Margos was keeping very close behind her and would hear every word. Could she stand by and see another person murdered? She stumbled out of the forest and into a clearing before a log cabin. Just knocking on the door of a cabin in the middle of the forest at night was dangerous. It was a given that people were armed in this vicinity. The wildlife was dangerous, and it surprised her that they hadn't run into anything that considered them as a potential meal. Trembling, Amy lifted her hand and knocked on the door. "Hello, is anyone home?" The sound of footsteps came from behind the door and the curtain across the window beside the front door moved slightly.

Stepping back to be seen in the shaft of light streaming from the window, Beth held up both her hands, so that the person peering at her from inside could see she wasn't armed. When the door cracked open an inch and a man's face appeared, she formed a gun with her fingers and indicated behind her with the other hand. Hoping the man would understand her, she lifted both eyebrows and mouthed, "Help me."

The man appeared to be oblivious to her gestures and just stared at her as if she had gone completely mad. The door opened a little wider, and the next second, a knife flew through the air and with a sickening *thunk* stuck in his throat. The man grasped at his neck, eyes bulging, and made frantic attempts to remove the knife, and then he fell back, crashing to the floor and sending a statue of a horse on a side table toppling. Terror-stricken, Amy stepped to one side too shocked to speak or scream. From behind her, Margos appeared out of the gloom. He pushed past her and walked straight into the house, bending only to pull the knife from the man's throat before checking each room. Paralyzed, Amy stared at the man as bright red blood gushed out and spilled across the floor. His eyes locked on hers and, horrified, she watched his life slip away.

"Get in here." Margos stood at the door to a kitchen. "Make supper."

Fear had turned the blood in her veins to ice. She couldn't move. A sticky crimson slick had pooled around her feet. The smell of it and the dead man's voided bowels made her want to puke. She covered her face with both hands, unable to believe what was happening. She jumped when Margos' voice came from close behind her.

"Turn this way and walk around the blood." Margos shook his head and grabbed her by the arm. "You can't possibly be that stupid." He sighed. "Ah, well, I guess maybe you can." He gave her a shove toward the kitchen.

Desperate to survive, Amy pushed her thoughts in another direction. So far, she'd practically ignored them and not complained. Although she had endured mental and physical abuse, they hadn't killed her. Every minute she remained alive was a chance to escape. Perhaps when they were asleep, she might be able to sneak away. Margos mentioned there were cops in the area. Likely when the others arrived, they'd speak about them. If she discovered where to locate the cops, she'd be able to get to them. It seemed that playing dumb was her only chance of survival. Hunting through the kitchen to discover ingredients to make supper, she found a large container of chili in the fridge. She lifted the lid and sniffed. The container was full and from the smell had been made only recently. She recalled how her mother had made slow-cooked chili over six to eight hours and then left it to sit overnight in the fridge before serving it the following day. She had always said that the next day's chili was the best. Maybe this man had the same idea?

The poor man who owned the cabin kept a well-stocked pantry and she found the fixings for making cornbread. Trying to keep her mind on her task helped a little to keep away the horrors of what had happened. Her hands trembled as she prepared the cornbread. Margos announced he'd found alcohol and she could hear the clink of glasses as he dropped them on the coffee table in front of the fireplace. As she slid the cornbread into the oven, voices came from the front of the cabin. The other men had arrived and they went about dragging the body from the front door down the steps and into the forest. Risking a peek around the kitchen door, Amy watched as they dragged a rug from another room and placed it over the smeared blood trail inside the door. They closed and locked the door behind them and went into the bathroom to wash up, all chatting as if on a great adventure. She caught enough of the conversation to know they had a plan to deal with the cops, but they didn't discuss anything in front of her. The sight of their grinning leers made her sick to her stomach. The depravity they would make her endure overnight terrified her. As they filed into the kitchen one by one and sat at the table, she avoided their gaze and kept herself busy. Perhaps with the drink and full bellies they'd fall asleep. It would be her only chance to escape.

NINETEEN

Wolfe followed Kane as they did a recon around the cabin they'd discovered. It was a reasonably sized hunting cabin. One large room, divided up into a small cooking area with an old wooden table and mismatched chairs. A Dutch oven hung on a tripod over the grate in a large fireplace, in front was a ratty old sofa. Two sets of bunkbeds along one wall had rolled up mattresses tied with twine. It was dusty but reasonably clean and had a few emergency provisions inside, but the air smelled old and musty with an undertone of critter pee. Whoever owned the cabin hadn't been by for a long time. The boarded-up windows and back door would suggest they wouldn't be coming by again soon. The front door, with wide metal strips across it, reminded Wolfe of one on an ancient castle. Each side of the thick door, strong metal brackets held a thick piece of wood that slotted in. At one end, a large padlock held it in place. It would keep most folks out, but Kane had taken less than a minute to unlock it.

As he followed Kane around the back of the cabin, they took a small path through the trees to a clearing some twenty yards away. A corral had been erected and on one side was a small shed that held bales of hay. A water trough in the corral was fed by an artesian well, which piped fresh water to the house as well. Impressed, he turned to Kane. "Nice setup. We won't need to worry about the horses tonight, will we? We can store our saddles in the shed. This area is completely hidden from the trail. I figure they'll be safe enough here."

"Yeah, I haven't heard anyone or seen any signs that people have passed this way. There's no smell of woodsmoke in the air. Raven mentioned there was another cabin approximately half a mile away on this trail. With the wind blowing from behind us, if there was a fire, we wouldn't smell it. I figure we'll need to stay on our guard even though this place looks safe." He turned and led the way back to the others. "We'll collect our horses and get them settled first. We have plenty of supplies, and the kitchen looks clean. I figure I'll be able to rustle us up a decent meal."

Smiling, Wolfe slapped him on the back. "Right now, I'd eat the stewed leather off the soles of my boots."

They met the others and collected the horses. Wolfe grinned. "Dave has volunteered to make supper."

"I'll help." Raven rode to his side and handed him the reins of his horse. "Living alone for so long, I've been able to make a meal out of practically nothing."

The sound of horse hooves came from the opposite direction and they all turned, hands on weapons, as Carter, Rio, and Takoda headed toward them. Wolfe lifted his arm to wave, and as they stopped beside them, he looked from one to the other. "Any sign of the prisoners?"

"Nope, we lost their trail once they got into the forest. The pine needles are so thick they cover footprints." Carter shrugged. "We know they split up. The girl was able to give us very good descriptions of the men. Margos is traveling with the prison guard. Callahan and Romero followed the river for a time and then went inland. They didn't follow any of the trails but weaved in and out of the trees. After a time, we lost any hope of following them. How they are getting around without getting lost or eaten by wildlife, I have no idea, unless the package dropped by the drone contained satellite phones with GPS." He looked from Wolfe to Kane. "This situation is getting crazier by the second. We apparently have three men who've been incarcerated for years and yet they're able to vanish in the forest like smoke in a place they've never been before and with no supplies whatsoever. If you don't figure that's unusual, I've slipped into a different dimension."

"I'm convinced something's going on." Kane took hold of Warrior's reins and led him around the back of the cabin. "Right now, we need to get out of sight. We might not be able to see them, but they could be watching us with binoculars. We have no idea what was dropped to them from the drone."

With the horses settled and Kane and Raven working in the kitchen preparing a meal from the supplies they'd brought with them, Wolfe removed the old Dutch oven from the grate and lit the fire. Once the wood glowed red, he filled and then placed a large kettle in the embers. Whatever Kane made for supper, they'd all need coffee. Once that was done, he got the others together to organize which order they'd stand watch. "Two hours max. I'll take the second watch because y'all know I work until midnight most times. I figure Kane, Carter, Raven, and Styles need to sleep. They're able to rack out anywhere and it would be an advantage to have them fresh."

"We'll take the first watch." Blackhawk indicated to his cousin. "We'll head into the forest after supper and take up a position where we can watch the trails. If we hear or smell anything, we'll let you know."

"I'll take the third with Rowley." Rio removed his hat and

dropped it onto the table before the fire. He looked at Carter and Styles. "Can you go from two?"

"Yeah, sure." Carter moved a toothpick across his mouth and dropped onto the sofa in a cloud of dust. He waved one hand coughing. "If I survive this sofa." Beside him Zorro sneezed.

"One thing." Kane pushed food wrapped in aluminum foil into the hot coals and straightened. "Keep your kit and weapons beside you. We don't know what surprises these guys have up their sleeves." He turned and took a large pot from Raven and suspended it over the fire. "I figure they're trying to turn the tables on us. If I'm right, we're the hunted."

Later that night, only the sound of breathing surrounded Wolfe as he sat by the window observing the forest. He'd moved around peering through the boards covering the windows, but nothing but the wind stirred the trees. The fire had long fallen to ashes and darkness filled the cabin with only a few streaks of moonlight filled with dancing dust motes penetrating the gloom. He kept his movements silent and changed up his routine, going to different windows each time. Aware his blond hair might be noticed in the shafts of moonlight, he'd pulled on a black knitted cap. He moved again, checking each window. One mistake and they could all die trapped inside the cabin. A scraping sound came from the front porch, and immediately on alert, he stepped carefully around the men sleeping on their bedrolls and crossed the living room floor. Another very slight creak came from outside, but it was difficult to tell if it was the wind blowing through the forest or someone stepping on a creaky floorboard. He slid with his back against the wall to peer through the cracks in the wooden panels nailed across the window.

Nothing moved outside and he continued his vigilant

rounds of each window. Loud thumps on the roof woke everyone with a start. In seconds, Kane was beside him, peering out of the window. The smell of burning filled the air and curls of smoke drifted down between the logs making up the ceiling. Zorro, Bear, and Duke barked a warning and ran around in circles. Bear jumped on Raven and then on everyone else on the floor until they were on their feet.

"Grab your gear and get out." Kane pushed Blackhawk and his cousin toward the front door. "Fan out and keep low. This might be a trap."

"The door's locked." Blackhawk had one foot on the wall and both hands on the door handle and was pulling. "It won't move."

Wolfe pulled on his backpack and looked at Kane's unreadable expression. The smoke was getting thick and burning his throat and nose. "I heard a sound earlier but didn't see anything. Maybe they dropped the wood into the crossbar lock?"

"Seems that way." Kane glanced around. "It's almost as if they prepared this cabin for us, to burn us to death. The back door is the same and the windows have been fortified with iron bars." He turned to the others. "We'll need to blast our way out of here. With luck whoever is out there will hightail it into the forest." He looked at Styles. "Jenna mentioned you carry a Magnum. Maybe you need to put that bad boy through its paces."

"Help me drag those bunkbeds away from the wall." Carter coughed and then headed toward the beds. "That's the weakest area."

"Spread your fire from left to right. We only need a hole big enough to crawl through." Kane aimed his assault rifle at the wall. He turned to Carter. "You go first. I'll cover you. Take Duke and Bear with you and get clear. Get the dogs out first."

"No worries." Carter picked up his rifle.

Flames licked through the logs above them and the smell of

gasoline permeated the smoke. Wolfe picked up his rifle and joined the others in a line. They all aimed their weapons. He looked at Kane as blackened wood rained down on them. His throat and chest burned. "On your command."

"Fire."

TWENTY

The prisoners' mood had become jovial after Romero returned from some type of mission in the forest. They'd spoken in hushed tones and Amy hadn't heard anything. Later, Margos discovered forty bottles of moonshine neatly stacked in the root cellar, along with a still. They drank from glasses but after a short time decided to drink straight from the bottle. Amy kept out of their way, remaining in the kitchen to wash dishes and appear to be busy. As she moved around, it was as if they'd completely forgotten she existed, and she liked that just fine. Discovering an old backpack hanging in the broom closet, she moved back and forth very carefully to stock it with bottled water and small food items she could carry easily. She found a flashlight and a Zippo. In the passageway, she'd noticed a few old jackets hanging on pegs along with a cowboy hat. Staying as quiet as a mouse, she waited.

"Woman." A slurred voice came from the sitting room. "Food. Bring us food."

Frantically searching the pantry, she discovered a few packets of potato chips and hurried into the living room and dropped them on the coffee table in front of the fire. "Do you want me to keep looking to see if there's anything else?"

"Yeah." Margos' red-rimmed eyes flicked over her and then he waved her away before returning to the others. "Do you know what the worst thing about using an ice pick is? It gets stuck in bone. Sometimes it really messes up your rhythm." He chuckled, raised the bottle in a toast, took a long drink, and thumped his chest. "Drinking sure seems like a better way to die."

As laughter rang out, Amy escaped back into the kitchen. She found bars of chocolate in a plastic container in the pantry and added them to her backpack. After helping herself to home-made cookies in a jar, she brewed a pot of coffee. The last thing she needed to do was fall asleep at the kitchen table. The conversation in the other room was starting to fade. She could only hope they would fall asleep in front of the fire.

A cool breeze brought the heavy smell of smoke through the open kitchen window. Knowing the devastation a wildfire could inflict on a forest, panic gripped her as she looked outside, horrified to see an orange glow in the night sky. The forest was on fire, and from the direction of the wind, it was heading her way. It was now or never. She must escape. Heart thundering in her chest, she snuck quietly into the passageway, grabbed a jacket and pulled it on. Inside the pockets she discovered a knitted cap and a pair of leather gloves. Snores came from the other room, but too afraid to look around the door, she tiptoed back into the kitchen. After pulling on the backpack, she grabbed a long carving knife from a block on the kitchen counter, pushed it into her backpack, and headed for the back door.

Freezing midstride when a cough came from the other room, she grasped the doorknob and listened for any sounds of movement. Only snuffling and snoring came along the passageway. Knees shaking, she turned the handle and pulled open the door. The grinding squeak as the hinges complained terrified her. She wanted to bolt out of the door and run wildly into the forest, but her attention rested on a key hanging beside the door. Without hesitation, she grabbed the key, eased out through the door, and pushed it shut. As it screamed in protest, she thrust the key into the lock with trembling fingers and turned it. Outside, smoke filled the air and she pulled her T-shirt up over her nose and mouth. It was clear which direction the fire was heading. The cabin sat on a fire road, and it would be easy enough to head in the opposite direction to the blaze. With luck she may encounter a local volunteer fire department, and she could explain who she was and where the prisoners were hiding.

Using the flashlight, she moved as fast as possible, terrified to look behind her in case Margos was creeping up behind her, ice pick in hand. She'd heard so many terrifying stories, told with relish, it had made her sick to her stomach. From the articles she'd read about serial killers, they didn't hang out together, but these three seemed to really enjoy each other's company. They all wanted to know exactly how they'd murdered their victims, and each of them gave blow-by-blow descriptions. Then they would look at her as if deciding what her fate would be and which one of them would get the pleasure of murdering her. How she had survived so long she had no idea.

As she ran along the fire road, ahead she made out the headlights of a truck as it turned full circle to head back along the way it had come. As she got closer, she made out a large horse trailer. A woman jumped out, ran to the back of the horse trailer, and opened the doors, pinning them back. She waved her flashlight. "Hey."

The woman turned and stared at her, and Amy lifted her flashlight. "I need help."

"I'll give it to you if you take that darn flashlight out of my eyes." The woman walked to meet her. "What are you doing out here in the middle of the night alone?"

Gasping, Amy grabbed at her arm. "I'm Amy Clark, the prison guard who was kidnapped by the prisoners from the state pen when they escaped in the car wreck. I was able to get away. They murdered the man in the cabin back there." She indicated behind her. "They found his stash of moonshine and are asleep right now, so I was able to escape."

"I'll help you but I need to get my horses before they burn to death in the fire. It's heading this way." She indicated frantically toward a cabin set way back into the forest. "Can you help me and then we'll drive into town and contact the sheriff?"

Staring behind her, Amy wanted to say no because this woman didn't understand how dangerous the men were who could be following her. Instead, she nodded and ran beside the woman to a corral where two horses were moving around restlessly. "What's your name?"

"Colleen Troiani." She swung open the gate. "Grab the Appaloosa. She's gentle. Just talk nice to her and we'll load them in the trailer."

Exhausted and running on pure adrenaline, Amy followed instructions, and in minutes they loaded the horses, but as they closed the doors a shot rang out and thumped into a tree beside Amy's head. She didn't look around and just climbed into the truck. "They're coming."

"They won't catch us." Colleen pushed the truck into drive and they took off along the fire road.

The next moment they were on the highway and going fast. Heart thundering in her chest, Amy burst into tears. Swiping at her face, she looked at Colleen. "Do you have a phone? We need to call the cops?"

"Yeah." Colleen pressed a button on her steering wheel and the dash lit up. "Call 911."

As the call went through Amy leaned back in the seat. In

the side mirror the glow in the forest was spreading fast. As they headed closer to town, firetrucks flashed past them sirens blaring and lights flashing. It seemed that everyone in the county was heading toward the fire. As they approached the town, she turned to Colleen. "I can't thank you enough for saving my life. If those men had caught us, they would have murdered us and stolen your truck."

"You don't have to worry about them now." Colleen smiled at her. "I'm taking you to the sheriff's office. Maggie, the receptionist, will meet us there as all the deputies have been out hunting down the escaped prisoners."

As the truck slowed outside the sheriff's office, an African American woman with a broad smile wearing PJs with a jacket over the top waved at them. Exhausted, Amy practically fell out of the truck and staggered toward her. "Are you Maggie?"

"I am indeed." Maggie smiled at her. "Jump into my truck. I'm going to take you straight to the ER. From what Colleen said on the phone, you're in bad shape. Did those monsters hurt you?"

Nodding, Amy dissolved into tears again. "Will I be safe at the hospital?"

"Yes." Maggie started the engine and they drove away. "We have a special ward there for prisoners and people needing protection. You'll be very safe there and I will stay with you until one of your family arrives. Your mom and dad are both staying in town. They've been here since you went missing from the bus wreck. Once I get you to the hospital, I'll call them and you can speak to them." She patted her on the arm. "The doctors will need to do a few tests. It's important so these horrible men can be charged for what they did to you. The deputies will be coming to speak to you as well. Not right away. They're heading back to town now."

Turning in her seat to look at her, all Amy could see was deep compassion in Maggie's eyes. "I understand what is going to happen next but it won't make any difference to them because they were never to be released anyway." She looked down at her clenched fists. "Two were asleep after drinking moonshine when I left. The other one was shooting at us. I know I shouldn't say this, but I hope the wildfire gets to them before they can escape. They deserve to burn in hell."

TWENTY-ONE

The noise inside the cabin was deafening. Wood chips flew in all directions, spinning away in cartwheels. The fire was creeping down the cabin walls. Flaming debris and roof shingles fell and ignited the furniture. Intolerable heat burned exposed flesh, and although Kane had covered his face, breathing was difficult. The fire had sucked all the oxygen from the room. They kept firing as a hole appeared in the wall. The sudden rush of air fed the flames and all around them an inferno roared. The team didn't stop firing until the hole was big enough to step through. Kane reloaded. "Carter, you first. Stay low and run toward the corral. I'll put down cover fire over your heads. Stay low. Go, go, go." Beside him Blackhawk pushed Duke and then Bear through the hole.

"Zorro, with me." Carter dived through the shattered wood and took off with the three dogs close behind.

Flames crept across the floor, heating Kane's boots as he sprayed the forest. The last man to leave was Raven. With the loud buzzing in his ears from the gunshot, he turned when he touched his arm and only just made out what he was saying.

"I'll be your wingman." Raven gave him a nod. "I'll go right and cover your back." He ducked out of the hole and began to lay down fire for Kane to escape.

This wasn't the first time Raven had been beside him when they faced great danger. He'd saved Kane's life during a deployment. That time didn't exist for him any longer. That person died in a car bombing in DC almost seven years ago. Dave Kane had emerged from the ashes with a new identity and face. If Raven recognized him, both of their lives could be in danger. With his fingerprints removed, the only way Raven could identify Kane would be by a retina scan. Hopefully, Raven's old friend would just be a memory. He pushed the past away and ducked through the hole. His backpack stuck tight and he turned to tug it free and then jumped down. To his right, Raven kept firing in wide arcs, his bullets tearing through the pines splintering branches. Fire licked the broken boards around the hole. Coughing with eyes streaming, he turned to Raven. "Get out of here."

Backing away from the inferno with Raven at his side, Kane sent bursts of gunfire into the trees and then they ran for their lives as the forest exploded into flames. As he reached the others at the corral, everyone was frantically throwing saddles onto their horses. He turned to see the cabin light up the clearing. The roof had caved in and the intense fire would soon spread. Nothing they could do would save it now. Duke ran to his side barking, but he could hardly hear him with the buzzing in his ears. Wolfe, his face blackened and eyes red and running, came over with Warrior's tack, and Kane stood, his burning-hot rifle against the corral fence, and saddled Warrior. The horse held his head high, nostrils flaring and stamping his feet eager to leave. He'd been through forest wildfires with Warrior before and he was as solid as a rock. He lifted Duke onto the saddle. The dog trembled and tried to arrange his fat body, almost slipping before Kane climbed on behind him. He rubbed Duke's ears and held him tight. "It's okay, boy. You're safe."

He looked around at the soot-streaked faces, lit up with the light from the fire, and pointed into the wind. They took off in single file following a track heading north. As the track came out onto a fire road, Kane got his bearings. They'd ridden to Bear Peak. Ahead of him, Wolfe was on the phone. He rode alongside him and waited for him to disconnect. "Fire department?"

"Yeah." Wolfe coughed and spat. "They'll need someone out here before the forest burns to the ground." Wolfe turned to Kane. "Paramedics are on their way. We're heading to the forest warden's station and they'll meet us there. We need oxygen and treatment for our eyes." He coughed again and turned red-rimmed eyes to Kane. "They must have used drones to drop incendiary devices onto the roof." He waved a hand toward the forest. "This entire escape has been a ruse to take down Jenna's team and the FBI agents you use. Souza has masterminded all of this and he's using notorious serial killers like puppets."

The same conclusion had crossed Kane's mind. Everything that had happened was slick and well thought out. Souza had been one step ahead of them all the time. The next steps to take could be fatal. This man spearheaded the import of illegal arms and drugs, specifically fentanyl, which was killing hundreds of thousands a year. In prison he still maintained his cartel no matter how many of his soldiers were apprehended. The vicious hold Souza had on his cartel meant no one in his organization dared to disobey him. He made examples of them by brutally murdering their families.

Determined, Kane stopped, pulled out a bottle of water, washed his eyes, and then drank and spat. A vision of Jenna holding a newborn and sitting beside Tauri slid into his mind. Would he ever get to see his child? Would he be there when Jenna needed him the most? The odds wouldn't be in his favor. In front of him, Duke trembled as if he understood the impossible position this incident had put him in. He looked at Wolfe and couldn't believe he'd made the decision. It was the only one to keep his family, friends, and America safe. One phone call to POTUS and he'd become the sniper again, the secret government asset needed to remove Souza from existence once and for all. "The team here can deal with the escaped prisoners. We'll have reinforcements by daylight. The escape was just a distraction. Call it in. It's time I took down Eduardo Souza."

TWENTY-TWO

BLACK ROCK FALLS

Wednesday

Jenna gripped the phone so tight her fingers ached. The man at the end of the phone, her loving husband, had turned into the combat-ready sniper. Fear gripped her as she waited to hear the words she dreaded. "What do you mean you're not coming home?"

"All that's happened over these last couple of days has been masterminded by Eduardo Souza." Kane kept on clearing his throat and turned his face away to cough. *"They used drones earlier this morning in an attempt to burn us to death in a cabin. We kept vigilant all night and didn't see it coming. We figured they dropped incendiary devices on the roof. I believe they've been following us from the moment we entered the forest. This was a deliberate act to take out your team and the FBI. Most likely Wolfe as well. They wouldn't know about Raven. I've asked him to stay at the ranch for a few days. I suggest you put the men in the cottage and keep the women in the house. Duke will be coming home with Carter. They'll be working the escaped prisoner case alongside our team, but Raven will be there to*

protect you along with the women." He sighed. *"This is nonnegotiable, Jenna."*

The fire department sirens screamed in the background. "Okay, sure. I hear sirens. Where exactly are you, Dave?"

"I'm at the office. Firefighters are coming from all surrounding counties. Everything is under control. The DOC is handling the hunt for the escaped prisoners. They have a ton of men coming from everywhere. Once our team has rested and recovered from smoke inhalation, you can send them to assist, but it might be in our best interest for you to keep them in town. We don't know what the prisoners are doing or what intel they have. They could be heading for town."

Trembling, Jenna kept her voice steady. "Okay, but the young girl Carter found, did she make it to the res?"

"Yeah, Chaska called the moment she arrived. She's with her grandma. You should leave her there until this is over. It's not safe for her in town just now." He blew out a long sigh and wheezed. *"I'm real sorry about this, Jenna. Don't you figure I want to come home to you?"*

Pressing a hand to her belly, Jenna nodded as if he were in the room with her. "Yes, I know you do. Please don't tell me you're going after Souza alone?"

"Yes and no." Kane paused as if not wanting to continue the conversation. *"Wolfe made the call, so I'll have a support team. I'll rely on their intelligence and follow their plan. I'm aware of the risk, but it's our only chance for a normal life."*

Jenna's grip lessened on the phone. "I figured having him in prison would stop him. I was wrong."

"We all were. The powers that be believed once they had him in prison, a new leader would emerge, but running the cartel without contacts or finances would be doomed to fail. They didn't realize Souza had the power to control his empire from prison, and as his people live in fear of him, it was business as usual. Once he's gone, there are plans in place to break up his

cartel. *It will be a start because there are many cartels out there, but I won't be involved in taking down the others."*

Swallowing a sob, Jenna recalled Wolfe's warning about being Kane's Achilles' heel. She tried very hard to control her voice. "That's good. I won't ask when you're leaving. I'm guessing you'll be holed up somewhere getting prepared." Knowing her calls were safe from being intercepted, she needed to know one last detail. "Wolfe will be where he normally is, won't he?"

"Oh, yeah." Kane chuckled. *"I couldn't go hunting without him. I'll see you soon. Love you and give Tauri a hug for me."* He disconnected.

Rocking back and forth on the bed, the phone clutched in her hand, Jenna allowed the tears to fall. Kane was going to take down Souza. He was under orders from POTUS, as his own secret weapon to rid the world of a threat to America. An asset they called him, but to Jenna, Dave Kane was flesh and blood, a wonderful husband and a great father. She wanted to scream, wail, and punch the walls. There was no guarantee she'd ever see him again.

Getting slowly to her feet, she placed her phone on the nightstand and went into the bathroom. No one could know about Kane's mission and she had a house filled with FBI agents. As she showered, she ran excuses for why Kane and Wolfe had gone missing. She finished, dried her hair, and dressed. Head high, she walked into Tauri's room to find his bed empty. Panic gripped her and she turned and ran along the passageway. Relief flooded over her as she found him at the kitchen table making hotcakes with Beth. "Oh, there you are. Daddy called and he sent you a hug." She bent to hug him. "He's helping the firefighters along with Uncle Shane."

"Duke doesn't like fires." Tauri frowned.

"Uncle Ty just called. He'll be along soon with him and Warrior." Jo walked into the kitchen. "He'll be driving the

Beast." Her gaze narrowed and she raised one eyebrow at Jenna. "You sure Kane is okay?"

Nodding, Jenna forced a smile. "Yeah, he's with Wolfe. He didn't want to risk leaving his truck in the forest to get burned up and Carter needed to get here somehow. I gather he'll be bringing Styles as well?"

"Nope." Beth looked at her. "Styles is coming with Raven. Apparently, they and the dogs needed treatment for smoke inhalation. They were all on oxygen for a time. Someone locked the cabin and set fire to it. They needed to blast their way out." She shrugged. "Styles is bringing a mess of rib eye, enough to feed an army. He said Kane made a call and they need to go and collect it on the way here." She looked at Jo. "Kane told him to use the steaks in the freezer first and the new ones can be stored in the freezer in the garage." She looked at Jenna. "I didn't know Kane and Wolfe had joined the volunteer fire department. Styles said they might be out there for a week trying to contain the fire." She raised both eyebrows. "Maybe the prisoners will run out of the forest or, better still, be burned up."

"I guess that would solve a few problems." Jo served breakfast and passed the plates around.

"Who is getting burned up, Mommy?" Tauri's eyes were as big as saucers.

"Beth was joking." Jo chuckled. "No one is getting burned up."

"Tauri, why don't you come with me?" Nanny Raya smiled at him. "We'll take our breakfast into my place and watch cartoons. What do you say?"

"Can I go, Mommy?" Tauri tugged at her arm.

Dizzy with stress, Jenna sat down. "Yes, of course you can, sweetheart." She waited for him to leave and the connecting door to the nanny's quarters to close behind them before she looked at Jo. "We still need to catch those prisoners. I'll contact the DOC command center and try and figure out what's happening."

"Do it after breakfast." Jo gave her a long look. "If you want my opinion, you need to take it easy for a couple of days. You don't look so good."

Running both hands down her face, Jenna wanted to scream about the injustice in her life. Loneliness surrounded her. An empty void had opened where Kane should be. She needed him, even with the wonderful caring people around her. How long before she discovered if he'd completed his mission or died trying? *No one must know.* Gathering her inner strength, she looked at Beth and smiled. "Don't worry. I'm not planning on going anywhere until the team arrives and I've eaten breakfast. Plus the guys will need a few hours' shut-eye. They've been awake all night." She leaned back in her chair and shuddered. "And I couldn't miss my delicious cup of decaffeinated coffee." She pulled a disgusted face. "I miss Dave's special blend."

"You can have a cup of regular coffee, Jenna." Beth's gaze moved over her. "Sure, drinking a ton of strong coffee isn't advised, but one cup in the morning wouldn't hurt. You can drink it in moderation when you're breastfeeding as well." She sucked in her lips. "I'm sorry. I shouldn't have presumed you'd be nursing your baby. It's not for me to comment on something so personal."

Seeing Beth in a different light, Jenna squeezed Beth's arm, feeling the instant tightening of her muscles. The woman was like a curled snake. She removed her hand. "I appreciate your interest. Not having a mom to talk to about pregnancy, I need to rely on friends' advice." She looked at Jo. "Did you drink coffee when you were expecting Jaime?"

"A little. Like you, I stuck to milk most times." Jo chuckled. "Jaime was a small baby, so my OB was constantly telling me to eat more meat and cheese as well."

Relaxing, Jenna glanced at Beth. As far as she knew, Beth had no kids. "Thanks for the advice. Styles mentioned you have a very wide knowledge base."

"It comes with the territory." Beth smiled. "Working on computers constantly and delving into all areas of existence, I tend to absorb knowledge along the way. I don't have any personal advice to give you, but I'm sure Jo will be able to assist you with more in-depth information." She leaned forward conspiratorially, but Jenna could see vulnerability in her eyes. "What else did Styles say about me? I'm still trying to work him out."

"I can probably answer that question." Jo pushed a cup of real coffee across the table to Jenna and then sat down to eat. "We worked together recently, and he spoke about you all the time. He was very concerned about you being with Carter. He regards Carter as a loose cannon and was concerned about putting the pair of you together. I believe Styles is a little over-protective with you, when it's blatantly obvious it's not required. We all know you can take care of yourself."

"Really?" Beth laughed and lifted her fork. "I found Carter to be very professional, kind, and considerate. He has a great mind for crime solving. Who wouldn't enjoy working with him? He's the ultimate sexy cowboy. I'm not surprised he's still single. It would take a very special woman to tame him." She burst out laughing.

Looking from one to the other, Jenna moved her attention back to Beth. "I know that Styles respects and admires you. Why are you worried about his opinion of you? Has he said or done something to upset you?" She lifted a forkful of eggs to her mouth and chewed.

"No. I do find him hard to read sometimes, but we get along just fine." Holding a slice of toast between finger and thumb and waving it around as she spoke, Beth sighed. "I figure I'm like a puzzle to him, and right now he can't find all the pieces."

TWENTY-THREE

Scanning the horizon, Johnny Raven assessed the threat. He figured his cabins alongside the river were far enough away from the blaze to cause concern. He'd left no dogs at home. The personal protection dogs he'd trained had already been delivered to their new owners. The next batch would come from a litter of pups especially bred by Blackhawk. Both having an interest in dog training, they'd decided Blackhawk would stay in a cabin close by to assist him. It had become a good and lucrative partnership. In between times, Raven would train suitable rescue dogs. If they didn't make the grade, he'd still ensure they found loving homes with new owners. He formed a great relationship with the local dog rescue.

He'd driven Styles back to his cabin to shower and change. As Ben and Bear lounged in front of the cold fire, both exhausted from their horrific night, he put on a pot of coffee and made toast and eggs. They couldn't just descend on Jenna's ranch this early in the morning and expect her to feed them. He had no idea why Kane had insisted he stay with her when she was surrounded by FBI agents. Maybe Kane had felt the same familiarity he had with him and trusted him to guard his wife. It was very strange how they had clicked immediately, as if they'd been longtime friends. When the cabin exploded into flames, it had seemed natural for him to stay and watch Kane's back. Maybe it was because he reminded him of a sniper he'd met during a deployment in the desert.

Disobeying orders, he'd flown into enemy territory after the sniper's ride had been shot down. His chopper didn't make it either, but the sniper had dragged him from the wreck, and the pair of them spent some time together before they made it out of the country to safety. He had discovered later the man who called himself Junior was the son of a three-star general. He'd been saddened to discover Junior had died along with his wife in a car bombing in DC some years later. Although their paths had never crossed again before his death, he'd never forgotten the skill and courage of the man who'd gotten them through enemy lines to safety. Dave Kane, apart from being younger, and without the broken nose, scars, and tattoos, could be his double. The build was the same and the way he moved, in that fluid confident way, reminded him so much of Junior. It had impressed him how Kane had laid down cover so they could all escape. There was no doubt that Dave Kane was a natural leader. Dragging his mind back to the present as Styles came into the kitchen, he waved him to a chair. "Breakfast?"

"Man, it's five-star here." Styles grinned. "You have hot water and solar power. This is a great setup."

Raven filled a plate and handed it to him. "Thanks. It took some time but it's home now. If it doesn't burn to the ground while I'm away."

"Nah." Styles picked up his fork. "I spoke to the local volunteer fire chief and he said it's already under control. They have it surrounded already. Everyone came from all over to fight it."

Nodding, Raven sipped his coffee. "I've had this strange feeling I've met Dave before. It's like we have a past connection. I could have known his brother maybe. He must have been an older brother, and his name was Junior. What do you know about him?"

"He has no living relatives, served in the military, then became a cop in Chicago, I believe. He was shot in the head on the job and came here to semi-retire. Ended up marrying the sheriff." He chewed and swallowed. "He's never mentioned a brother or anyone by the name of Junior. There're no photographs in his home of anyone but him, Jenna, and Tauri. I noticed a few of all of us at cookouts, but then I haven't worked alongside him. I've worked with Jenna, but funnily enough, I was interested in his background too. I guess it's the cop in me." He chuckled. "He screams military to me, takes the lead like it's natural. He's a good man. I'd follow him into battle. I like him."

Nodding, Raven smiled. "Yeah. I never figured I'd say this, but I believe we'll be close friends. He asked me to watch over his wife. He intends on assisting with the fire cleanup and then joining the hunt for the prisoners. He just doesn't give up."

"He's trusting you with Jenna?" Styles' eyebrows narrowed. "You be careful. Kane is the jealous kind. His family means everything to him."

Laughing, Raven shook his head. "You don't need to worry about me. I already have someone I'd like to know better, but I need to get on the good side of her dad before I risk asking her out, even though I believe she's twenty-two."

"Oh, Lord." Styles ran a hand down his face and then looked up as if seeking divine intervention. "Emily Wolfe?" He snorted with laughter. "Good luck with that."

TWENTY-FOUR

Carter, filthy and stinking of smoke, finally arrived in the Beast, and Jenna bombarded him with questions as Duke ran around her legs demanding attention. Of course, with Kane sending him away, the old dog couldn't understand why he'd ended up in the Beast with Carter. She rested a hand on the dog's head. He still wore his harness, and her hand came away dirty when she rubbed his ears. The fire must have terrified him. She bent to meet the dog's eyes. "It's okay, Dave's gone for a ride. He'll be back soon."

Duke didn't like the noise of the motorcycle and stopped fussing and leaned against Jenna's leg, but a tremble went through him. She kept one hand on Duke's head as she turned her attention back to Carter. "Was anyone hurt? I couldn't get any details from Dave. He was anxious to get going."

"We're all fine." Carter's white teeth shone brilliant white in his soot-blackened face. "A bit singed around the edges. I was the lucky one. I went out first with the dogs. Dave was last with Raven, but they're okay. The paramedics put us on oxygen for a time and then we were able to go." He frowned. "Wolfe was on lookout and saw nothing. He heard a noise but no more than a creak when someone locked us inside. The place was all boarded up with metal railings on the windows. We figure they used a drone to drop an incendiary device on the roof. Luckily, we had our rifles and blasted our way out."

Relieved, Jenna nodded. "That's good to know. Jo brought your bags from the office. You'll be staying with the guys in the cottage. Why don't you wash up and come by for something to eat and then you'll need to get some rest."

"I'll take a shower and eat, but I'm good. We slept from dark until the fire. Wolfe will be exhausted and yet he insisted on remaining behind with Dave."

Thinking on her feet had become normal. "Yeah, well if they're chasing down serial killers and putting out fires, they're going to need an extra doctor. Wolfe would never turn his back on the people of Black Rock Falls."

"Obviously not, but he didn't ask Raven to remain behind." Carter gave her a long considering stare before indicating to the dogs. "The dogs need a bath. I'm happy to wash both of them."

Duke took off so fast his claws scratched the polished floor as he skidded down the passageway and ran into Jenna's bedroom. Raising both eyebrows she stared after him. "Darn, you only have to mention the word *bath* and Duke hides under the bed. We'll have a terrible time getting him out of there. He turns into a solid statue, with hooks on his feet to stop anyone moving him. Dave usually has to lift him out. There's a tub around the back of the house with running water. Dave had it specially installed so that Duke could have a hot bath."

"Do you figure if he sees Zorro having a bath, it will help?" Carter rubbed his chin with his filthy hand, leaving streaks of soot behind. "I'll wash Zorro first, or I'll get my clean clothes wet."

"I don't believe it's safe for you to go outside." Jo stood in the middle of the family room with her hands balled on her hips.

"There could be snipers out there just waiting to take you down."

"They'd need to be mighty fine shots to get me around the back of the house. It's enclosed by trees and they'd need to shoot through the fence." Carter shrugged. "I'll get Duke. You open the back door."

Amazed as Carter maneuvered Duke out from under her bed and then carried him outside, Jenna went to the door to watch. After getting a nice warm flow of water going in the tub, Carter bent to rub Duke's ears. The poor dog trembled, and Jenna leaned out of the door to hand Carter the dog shampoo. "It's going to be okay, Duke."

Attached to the fence, Duke wasn't going anywhere.

"Wanna take a bath, Zorro?" Carter grinned as Zorro did a happy dance, his backside wiggling and stumpy tail making circles. Then the dog took off and bolted around the house. He came back, mouth stretched in a doggy grin, and put his front legs on the edge of the tub. "Good boy." Carter shampooed Zorro and the dog stood still, his head held high as Carter rubbed the soap through his coat and then rinsed him.

Handing Carter a towel, Jenna looked at Duke. "See, it's okay. Nothing bad is going to happen to you."

She held her breath when Carter slipped off the harness and lifted Duke into the tub. Usually Duke gave a good impression of a bucking bronco at this stage, but he set his big sorrowful eyes on Jenna and whined. "Good boy."

"Me or him?" Carter chuckled. "I don't figure he wants to be shamed in front of his friend. You know they think just like us. People don't believe they understand but they do."

Watching in astonishment as Carter finished the chore and lifted Duke out of the tub, she passed him another towel. "Just be careful. I'll get him inside or he'll find something nasty to roll in. He only does that when he's wet."

Her phone rang and Jenna stared at the ID. "It's Maggie. I hope everything is okay."

"I've just taken the missing prison officer to the hospital. Her name is Amy Clark. She ran into a woman leaving the mountain with her horses and she brought her to the office."

As Carter pushed Duke through the back door and into the mudroom, she waved him inside to listen to the call. "Has that poor woman been with the serial killers all this time or has she been lost in the forest?"

"They held her prisoner and used her to convince cabin owners to open their doors to her. From her account, they killed at least two of them, and she believes there is a girl alone in the forest. She found clothes belonging to a possible twelve-year-old at one of the cabins where an elderly man was murdered." Maggie let out a long sigh. *"She is not in good shape. From what I can see, she's been beaten. I gave the hospital as much information as I'm able and asked the doctor to do a rape kit. They will be keeping her in the security wing until further notice. I'm just about to contact her parents. They're in town waiting for news about her. Will they be allowed to see her or do you want to interview her first?"*

Wishing she had Kane and Wolfe close by, Jenna chewed on her bottom lip. Conflicted by Kane's insistence that she remain on the ranch and the overwhelming need to be there for this poor woman, she stared at Carter. "Hang on a minute, Maggie. Carter, will you be able to drive me to the hospital to interview this woman? We'll take Jo and Beth with us as well. Tauri will be fine here with Nanny Raya."

"Yeah, sure, as soon as I get cleaned up. Zorro, stay." Carter took off at a run toward the cottage, zigzagging as he went to avoid a sniper's bullet.

Jenna stared at Zorro, who stood for a few seconds before sitting down and turning into a statue, his eyes locked on the disappearing figure of his master. "Maggie, how long has it been since the doctors arrived to examine her?"

"They just went in now. I'm standing outside in the hallway of the secure area." Maggie sounded as strong and dependable as always. *"I figure you have some time before they're through examining her. They're familiar with the rape protocol and mentioned taking pictures, blood tests, swabs, and CT scans. From previous experience, I would say they'll take one or two hours. I'll wait here for as long as it takes. I promised I'd stay with her until her folks arrived."*

Heading back toward the kitchen, Jenna scanned the expectant faces of the women. "Okay, we'll be right along. Don't allow the parents into the secured area until I've spoken to her. Thanks for helping out, Maggie, I really appreciate you."

"Thanks, but I'm just doing my job." She disconnected.

"Tell me you're not planning on leaving the ranch, are you?" Jo glared at her. "Dave asked you not to leave the ranch because it isn't safe, and the second his back is turned you want to go into town. Have you lost your mind?"

Leaning her hands on the table, Jenna looked from one to the other. "I'm the sheriff. The team is burned up and we're the last men standing. Whoever is doing this couldn't possibly know we're heading for the hospital. We'll use the underground parking lot and take the elevator to the secured floor. That means we'll be going from the Beast into a secure area. We'll do the same on the way back. Carter will be driving and I'll sit in the back with Jo. No one could possibly see us behind the blacked-out windows. If anyone is watching us, they'll see two blond-haired people leaving in a black truck." She looked from one to the other. "Jo, can you get Carter something to eat? I'll feed the dogs and then get ready." She looked at Beth. "There are liquid Kevlar vests in the hall closet. Can you grab one for Carter?"

"Sure." Beth headed along the passageway.

Pumpkin, Jenna's black cat, jumped onto the chair, and Jenna ran her hand down the cat's silken black coat. She smiled at her. "I'm sure you can care for yourself while I'm gone." She turned as Tauri came running through the door to Nanny Raya's separate quarters. "There you are."

"I saw Uncle Ty running toward the cottage. Is Daddy home?" Tauri peered behind her.

Swinging her son into her arms was out of the question now. He'd grown so fast and weighed a ton. She bent to hug him. "He's out fighting fires and hunting down bad men with Uncle Shane. I'm not sure when he'll be back but he sent you a hug."

"Okay." He held up paint-stained fingers. "I'm very busy painting." He frowned when Beth dropped Kevlar vests over the back of a chair. "Are you going to work?"

Nodding, Jenna straightened. "For a little while. A lady was hurt and I need to go and see her at the hospital." She clicked her fingers and Duke came running. "Duke would like to stay with you today."

"Okay. I'll go and finish my painting." Tauri hugged her around the legs. "See you later." He scampered off through the connecting door. "Come on, Duke."

"He's a beautiful boy." Beth leaned her back against the sofa. "Was he in foster care for a long time before you adopted him?"

The question came from left field as Jenna had pushed the fact that they'd adopted Tauri from her mind. He was her son in every sense of the word. She assumed Beth's time in the system had influenced the question. "From birth until four and then Blackhawk became his guardian. He lived with him and his mother until he came to us. It was a remarkable day, the moment we arrived, we had a connection to him and he told us he'd been waiting for us. He believes we're his parents, even though he knows his father was a Native American. I figure his father is dead. We know his mother died soon after giving birth. Blackhawk has this crazy idea their spirits sent us to find him."

"That's truly remarkable." Beth folded her arms across her chest. "Not just for the fact you found each other, but that he came through the system unscathed. He's one of the lucky ones."

Jenna searched Beth's face but the woman hid her emotions as well as Kane. "I've run across many serial killers who came out of the system or from abusive parents. There's no doubt in my mind, the majority of psychopaths are triggered by abuse in one form or another. As long as I draw breath, I'll fight to keep the children safe." She met Beth's cynical gaze. "Abuse of women, men, and kids, and the use of cohesive control, is just another word for *prolonged torture*. The worst thing is when kids, especially, try and speak out, most times no one believes them, or they blame the child. Women are told their husbands have a right to bash them and tell them what to do. Domestic abuse is out of hand. There's no place a woman or kid can go for help. The shelters are filled to overflowing, and you don't want to know my opinion of the foster care system. Here in my county, we introduced stringent rules and frequent visits. This is why we founded the Her Broken Wings Foundation. It started small and now it's growing by the year. It's funded by donations both in money, time, and expertise. It's no good just talking about helping or pretending terrible things don't happen behind closed doors. People need to face the facts and actually do something."

"Trust me," Beth nodded slowly and her lips curled into a small smile, "you're preaching to the choir."

TWENTY-FIVE

STANTON FOREST

Disorientated, Mason Margos, the Ice Pick, blinked eyes filled with dust and tried to straighten. Somehow, he'd fallen sideways on the sofa and the top of his head was resting on the floor. Pain shot through his temples and his stomach rolled with even the slightest movement. Pushing himself into a sitting position, he moved a dry tongue around a dryer mouth, tasting spew, and yet he couldn't recall vomiting at any time during the evening. In fact, he couldn't remember the evening. He wrinkled his nose at the smell of smoke, and slowly the events over last night dropped into place. Holding his head to prevent it from rolling off his shoulders, he turned slowly to look at Callahan and Romero, stretched out on the filthy rug in front of the hearth with bottles of moonshine clutched in their hands.

Muted sunlight pushed through the smoke-filled air and cut into his corneas like knives. He quickly looked away as a rush of nausea gripped him. Where was the woman? "Kitty kitty, get your ass in here."

Shouting split his head in two and he groaned in agony, but no sound came from the bedroom or the kitchen. Staggering to his feet, Margos kicked Romero and Callahan to wake them.

"Wake up. The woman has gone. She'll be able to bring the sheriff's men right here. We need to leave now."

Moans and complaints greeted him, and it took two more kicks to get them fully awake. He found a water dispenser in the kitchen, poured a cup, and drank greedily. The cool water slid down his parched throat like honey. He splashed his face in the kitchen sink and hunted for provisions. As he threw a few things into a box, a bunch of keys hanging on a peg by the door caught his attention. He grinned at seeing a key fob with the name Ford written on it. "Move it! We gotta leave now. From the smoke, the fire could be heading this way." He grabbed the keys, the supplies, a rifle and ammo he'd found earlier and then headed for the back door.

"I ain't going anywhere until I've had a drink." Callahan grabbed him by the arm. "You sent me out to lock the cops inside the cabin last night. No one is going to be chasing us. That place was secure and no one would have gotten out alive."

Turning slowly and eyeballing him, Margos waved a hand around the room. "I don't care about them. The woman escaped and she'll be on her way to town to tell them exactly where we are. They could be waiting out front for us right now ready to take us down."

"Listen to him, Callahan." Romero went to the sink and stuck his head under the tap. He shook his head like a dog before turning, grabbing a cup, and taking his fill of water. With fluid running down his chin, his dark eyes settled on Callahan. "Drink some water and let's get the heck out of here."

Holding up the keys triumphantly, Margos smiled. "It looks like we have a ride into town." He looked at Romero. "Souza made provisions for us to get to a pickup point. Call the big man and tell him we're ready to leave this place." He pushed open the back door and headed down the steps.

The only building standing in the small yard was a barn. Margos pushed open the doors and inside discovered an older-model Ford pickup. He climbed behind the wheel, inserted the key, and the engine roared into life. He smiled as the others piled into the truck. "The gas tank is full. Now we just have to find our way out of this darn forest."

"I guess you just head in the opposite direction of the smoke." Callahan leaned casually against the door, his fingers running the length of a carving knife he'd taken from a block in the kitchen. He turned his head toward Romero as he disconnected from his call. "What did he say?"

"I never got to speak to Souza." Romero's expression changed from excitement to anger. "He said we needed to split up and hang around town and he'd contact us as soon as possible."

"Our photos will be spread all over the news by now." Callahan's eyes bore into Margos. "We'll need to split the cash and go our separate ways. They'll be looking for three guys."

They'd found money at both properties. The first old man had a roll of bills in a coffee can on a shelf, the other kept his stash in his nightstand. They had over six hundred dollars. Margos flicked him a glance. "Sure, but I figure we'll be fine. We planned for this and we've changed our appearance since the mug shots. Most men in these parts have beards and we have shades and ball caps or cowboy hats. We'll fit in just fine. They don't know we took clothes from the cabins, and they'll be looking out for men in prison garb."

Margos turned the truck onto the narrow two-track dirt road and headed downhill. Thick smoke curled its way through the trees and masked anyone there. Convinced no one would know they'd taken the truck, he decided to take the backroads. By avoiding the highways and possible roadblocks, once they arrived in town they could melt into the local population. He had some knowledge of Black Rock Falls. It was a tourist destination, with people coming for the whitewater rapids, fishing, and hiking. Then there was the rodeo circuit and other festivals throughout the year. Strangers, it seemed, were welcome in town. "We have our phones. I'm sure we can survive for a few days. The money we discovered will keep us going for a time. Just keep a low profile until we can get away cleanly."

"I figure we should drive to the next town, where no one will be looking for us." Callahan sneered at him. "We could be walking into a trap."

Margos wondered how these men had managed to outwit the cops for so long before being captured. All their suggestions would make it easier for the cops to find them. His idea to burn the FBI agents and deputies alive had been pure genius. He shook his head, unable to understand how come these idiots didn't see the problem of hitting the highway. "What's the first thing the cops would do when they knew we'd escaped?"

"I ain't playing twenty questions with you." Callahan blew out a long sigh.

Shrugging, Margos kept his attention on the road ahead. "The first thing they'd do is set up roadblocks. If we try and leave the county, they'll catch us. It's what they would be expecting us to do, so we have to do the opposite. This is why Souza wasn't caught for over fifteen years. He made one stupid mistake and that was to go to a meet personally. In his business, all he needs to do is to sit tight and direct traffic. If the guys he sends walk into a trap, he has another hundred waiting in line to take their places. The last place they'll look for us is in Black Rock Falls. If they find kitty, she'll tell them what we wanted her to know. She'll tell them we're heading for Louan." He chuckled. "Them cops are gonna be running all over the place."

"How are you planning to get past any roadblocks into town?" Romero looked at him through the rearview mirror. "You mentioned you've never been here before."

He realized in that moment that these men had been imprisoned for twenty years or more and didn't understand technology. "You recall I showed you how to use the GPS on the phone? Well, we'll use the same map, to find our way via the backroads to Black Rock Falls. Why don't you give it a try now? Turn on your phone and ask it to show you a scenic route to the town of Black Rock Falls."

After a few tries, Romero's phone displayed the map. He laughed hysterically when the GPS gave directions. Margos flicked a glance at him. "There you go. It will connect you with both of us as well if you ask it. You can use the contacts if you like, same as you did when you called Souza, but these days all you have to do is speak."

"What do you mean?" Romero's eyes flashed. "Are you messing with me?"

"Ask your phone to call me." Callahan turned in his seat to look at him. "Try it. Phones do everything now."

"Okay, but if you're messing with me, this ain't gonna be a good day for you." Romero spoke into his phone and seconds later Callahan's phone rang.

"Hello." Callahan grinned at him. "Cool, huh?"

The idea of being out in public again concerned Margos as well. He gripped the steering wheel. "Many things will be different. They have a different code of conduct, more rigid, especially toward women. You can't tell them they look nice or hold open a door for them."

"What?" Romero raised both eyebrows. "I had an interview with that psychologist woman for her book. She asked me some weird questions, man. She wanted to know the reason I murdered, and how it made me feel." He sniggered. "I told her it made me feel good."

"What reason did you give her for killing?" Callahan picked the dirt out of his nails with the tip of his knife. "She asked me the same questions and I told her I don't need a reason. She came up with a few medical explanations why I'm like the way I am."

"She was surprised when I told her I didn't believe I was

any different from anyone else." Romero shrugged. "It's obvious that hundreds of thousands of people go missing never to be found, so there are people out there just like me clearing out the rotten fruit. I'm no different to a trashman." He met Margos' eyes in the rearview mirror. "Is that the same as what you feel? It's not something I've discussed with any of the inmates."

It had been some years ago since behavioral analyst Jo Wells had arrived at the prison to speak to various people. Margos looked from one to the other. "I didn't think we needed to explain anything. We did the crime and we're doing the time. We all have our own reasons. I figure the general consensus would be that we only kill people who deserve to die. For me, there's always someone out there who looks at me the wrong way, as if they're better than I am."

"For me, it's those women who look at you as if they're all that and when you ask them out for a drink, they look at you as if you've got two heads." Callahan twirled the knife in his fingers. "I got my name by wringing their scrawny necks, but I figure I might change now I'm out." He waved the knife across his throat. "Maybe I'll leave them with a smile?" He chuckled. "From ear to ear."

Laughing, Margos slapped the steering wheel. "Nice, and what about you, Romero? What's this rotten fruit you talk about? Come on man, you can't leave a person hanging."

"They make out like I killed every woman I met." Romero wiped the back of his hand across his mouth. "I used to be a handyman in a number of apartment buildings. You would be surprised how many of the women would give me the come-on." He lifted his hands in the air and dropped them in frustration. "It was always the married women. They were lounging at home eating candies and watching soap operas while their husbands were out working to make ends meet. It happened to me, so I figured it shouldn't happen to anyone else." He shrugged. "I took out the rotten fruit, is all."

"The thing is, they bring it upon themselves and someone has to teach them a lesson, right?" Callahan's mouth twitched into a wide smile. "When Ms. Wells asked me how it made me feel, I wanted to tell her it made me feel mighty fine, but I told her it made me sick to my stomach and I'm ashamed of what I did because that's what she wanted to hear. That's what they all want to hear. They figure, by locking us up, it will make us stop killing. Well, they're right, aren't they? I can tell you I looked everywhere but I couldn't find a woman cheating on her husband inside them prison walls."

Nodding, Margos turned onto a narrow blacktop, and after traveling for ten minutes, they came to a sign at a crossroads that indicated they'd arrived in Black Rock Falls. He turned onto the highway. "Ah, that must be the town just ahead. While I'm waiting for Souza to contact me, I might just find me some rotten fruit."

TWENTY-SIX

Wearing Kane's liquid Kevlar vest because it fit over her baby bulge and surrounded by Carter, Jo, and Beth, Jenna made it into the hospital by the back door without any problems. They took the staff elevator to the security ward and met Maggie, sitting outside one of the rooms. Jenna smiled at her. "Thank you so much for coming to the hospital. Did you happen to see Dave before you left?"

"I did see him climb into the medical examiner's truck, but I left Agent Styles and Deputy Raven in charge of the office." Maggie stood and gathered her things. "I couldn't ask either of them to accompany her to the hospital. She doesn't need the company of men at this time." She shook her head, and her eyes filled with compassion. "Amy is in a bad way. I doubt she will ever return to the prison service." She lifted her chin. "Agent Styles did have a message for you. He said that Dr. Wolfe had instructed him to have any victims taken to the morgue and put on ice until he returns. The Department of Corrections personnel will take photographs of any crime scenes they encounter in the forest. If he is delayed, Norrell is quite capable of conducting autopsies with Emily to assist."

Stomach flip-flopping at the thought of Kane being away for a long time, Jenna stared at her. It hadn't entered her mind until that moment. Hunting down Eduardo Souza might take weeks. How could she possibly explain the reason he and Wolf were missing for so long? *I guess I'll have to worry about that when the time comes.* She nodded. "Thanks, Maggie, I really appreciate it. You must be starving. Why don't you head off now and get something to eat before you go back to the office? Put it on our tab."

"Thanks, I'd like that." Maggie squeezed her arm. "Amy Clark's parents are outside in the waiting room. I told them that I would be staying with her until you arrived and then they would be able to see her. I didn't give them any details. I just told them that she would be okay."

Walking her to the door, Jenna wondered how she could ever make it as sheriff in Black Rock Falls without Maggie running the office. She was the constant who kept everything moving along. In rain or shine, Maggie was always behind the counter as solid as a rock. "I'll go and see them the moment I've spoken to Amy."

When she turned around, two female doctors stepped out of the room. Jenna walked up to them and introduced herself, along with agents Carter, Wells, and Katz. "We're all involved with this case. Is there a room where we can speak to you in private?"

The doctors led them a short way along the passageway and into an examination room. Jenna looked at them expectantly, waiting for them to give her information about Amy Clark.

"In normal circumstances"—a doctor who introduced herself as Dr. Ann Bradley clutched a file in front of her chest and looked from one to the other—"I wouldn't be able to give you any information on my patient. Amy, however, has instructed me to give you all the necessary details to bring the men who assaulted her to justice."

"Did she suffer any injuries in the wreck?" Carter had his notebook in one hand and pen raised.

"Yes. Superficial injuries from broken glass, we assume from the windshield. We removed quite a few shards from her face and head. We found bruising as well, but it is difficult to determine if that came from the bus wreck or when she was beaten by her assailants."

Jenna shot Carter a look to silence him. "I assume you did a rape kit? Was there any sign of sexual assault?"

"I'm sorry to say, there was." Dr. Bradley's eyes flashed with anger. "She was subjected to multiple rapes over the time she was with them. They didn't use protection and we've taken swabs to test for DNA and multiple diseases, but she will need to be tested regularly over a long period of time before we know she is clear." She sighed. "Then there's also the chance of pregnancy. We've offered her a number of options and she has yet to make a decision." She cleared her throat. "She's not in shock, but you'll need to tread very carefully when you interview her. I haven't administered medication, but I will be placing her under sedation for a few days at least. I hope you will allow her to remain here under our care."

"Sheriff Alton really doesn't have any choice in the matter." Beth stared at the doctor, eyebrows raised. "Amy Clark is a victim and it's her choice if she remains in the hospital or not. We can only advise her to remain here at least until we have apprehended the men who did this to her."

Beside Jenna, Beth was like a coiled snake and had been getting worse with every step closer to the victim. She had some understanding of Beth's upbringing from the fact that she was the daughter of a serial killer named Cutthroat Jack, who was still alive and living in the state pen. She found it difficult to believe that Beth, with her unstable background, had passed all the tests the FBI had thrown at her. According to Styles, apart from being slightly eccentric in her way of doing things, she'd proved her worth as a very capable crime solver.

During her stint as an undercover DEA agent and having to endure physical abuse from her faux husband, Jenna understood firsthand how facing similar cases could evoke flashbacks. She wondered if Beth was reliving bad memories, as before they'd even spoken to the victim, she was standing up for Amy's rights. This was very noble but it didn't help the situation. They couldn't go in and rush Amy like bulls at the gate. They needed to treat her with kid gloves.

Taking a step closer to the doctor, Jenna needed to exert her authority. She looked at Beth. "I'll be interviewing Amy, along with Jo. We'll need to treat her very gently. Have you had experience in cases of this nature before?"

"I've lived through cases like this before." Beth's gaze hardened and changed to predatory. "It's in my file that I was abused as a child in foster care. I don't suffer from PTSD, but I do have some idea of what she's been through, and yes, I can be considerate. My anger is for the perpetrators and the need to catch them before they do this again."

Jenna nodded. "Okay." She waved Beth toward the door and caught Jo's inquisitive gaze on her.

In that moment she wished she had time to sit down and talk to Jo about her concerns. Although Beth must have passed all the necessary tests to be working in the FBI, she hadn't convinced Jenna. Taking in the entire picture, it surprised her that Jo hadn't come to the same conclusion. Beth Katz fit the profile of a serial killer. She had a psychopathic parent and she'd been living in the house when her father was on his killing spree. Likely, she'd witnessed her mother's death by his hand and then suffered long periods of abuse in foster care. She completely understood that not every child inherited the psychopath gene from their parent, but the look Beth had just given her had chilled her to the bone. She had seen that same cold evil expression in many serial killers she'd arrested.

TWENTY-SEVEN

As Jenna entered the hospital room, the sight of Amy Clark's battered face pushed all thoughts of Beth's psychopathy to the back of her mind. Maybe she'd chat with Jo later or leave it until Kane returned. Up to this moment Beth had been nice and extremely helpful. Being angry about abuse was something she'd experienced many times, so maybe she was being a little harsh toward Beth. She couldn't blame the poor woman for the sins of her father. She approached Amy and introduced everyone before sitting beside the bed. Jo and Beth sat opposite. Jo had a notebook ready to take notes, but Jenna pulled out her phone, laid it on the side table, and activated the record button. "Amy, so we don't miss a single detail, I'm going to record this interview. Are you okay with that and is there anything I can do to make you feel more comfortable?"

"No. I don't mind, and Maggie told me you help many women who've been through the same experience. I'm feeling very safe here in this secure ward." Amy glanced at Jo and Beth. "I appreciate you sending women doctors and FBI agents to speak to me. I'm not very good around men right now."

Nodding, Jenna wanted to hold her hand to comfort her in

some small way, but being direct and professional would be best. "Can you tell me what you remember from the time you left the prison? Was everything normal during the bus ride?"

"Yes, it was very quiet. The prisoners didn't speak to each other at all. They just stared out of the windows. They seemed to enjoy the view." Amy pushed a strand of hair behind one ear and stared into space. "Then I heard the sound of a chopper overhead. It seemed to follow us for some miles until we got onto an open stretch of highway. There were no vehicles for miles ahead of us. It just dropped out of the sky and hovered in front of the bus."

"Can you describe it?" Jo glanced up from her notebook. "Did you see anyone inside?"

"Yes." Amy turned her head slowly toward Jo. "It looked like a military helicopter but it was black. It had open doors with men sitting along the edge aiming assault rifles at us. The men were dressed in black, like the SWAT teams you see on TV."

She went on to describe the incident as it occurred with surprising clarity. Jenna noticed how Amy became distressed when she described approaching the cabin. "How far would you estimate the cabin was from where you'd left the bus wreck?"

"Maybe a mile. It was difficult to gauge. It could have been two miles. We were moving very fast." Amy blinked a few times. "I could hear water running, so I figure it was near a river." A large tear rolled down her cheek.

Having to ask this poor woman questions was tearing Jenna apart. "I know this is difficult for you, but can you tell me exactly what happened when you arrived at the cabin?"

"I didn't know they were going to shoot the old man." Amy picked at her fingernails. "They told me they just wanted to get inside the house and find some clothes. It wasn't necessary to kill him. There was washing on the line. They could have taken it without anyone knowing."

"The prisoners are lifers and violent criminals. Did one of them take charge?" Jo looked at her. "I understand you must have been facing the old man, but do you know who shot him?"

"Margos gave the orders. He was in charge the entire time." Amy scrubbed at her forehead as if trying to remember. "I'm not sure who shot the old man. It could have been Margos or Romero. They were the two carrying weapons."

Jenna cleared her throat. Asking about sexual abuse was difficult but the questions needed to be answered. "Do you remember which one of the men assaulted you?"

"They all did frequently." Amy lifted up her knees and, with her elbows resting on them, placed her head in her hands. "I fought back at first, but how many times can you be punched in the face before you give up? Margos was the first and he wanted to tie me to the bed to stop me fighting, but at that time they hadn't found the rope." Trembling and allowing the tears to fall, she went on to describe the horrific time with the men.

"There are hundreds of people out searching for them. They won't get away with hurting you." Beth's fists were clenched. "You have my word."

"Did you find the girl?" Amy looked from one to the other. "I know she fled the cabin. I saw her hair ribbon caught in a tree."

Nodding, Jenna gave her a small smile. "Yes, Serena is safe. The prisoners didn't find her. She ran into part of my team hunting down the prisoners in the forest." She sucked in a breath and pushed on. "During your time with these men, were there any discussions on where they were heading or what they planned to do?"

"No, they did mention the town Louan a number of times, as if they wanted me to remember it." Amy gave Jenna a bleak look.

"You must remember I was either in the kitchen cooking for them or in the bedroom. They only discussed things when I was out of earshot. When we left that cabin, we split up for a time, I went with Margos and the others headed for the river. They acted excited and later came back with a package, which one of them let slip came from a drone. It contained weapons, ammunition, and satellite phones, along with some instructions that I didn't get to see."

"Going on to the second cabin, can you recall anything specific about it? Was it by any unusual rock formations or can you think of a way we can find it again?" Beth's gaze moved over Amy as if assessing her injuries. "I know we have Serena to show us how to get to the first cabin, but I'm wondering if, in light of what you said about them receiving instructions, it was specifically chosen for a reason?"

"No, I can't remember anything specific about the second cabin." Amy shook her head slowly. "It was just a cabin in the woods alongside a fire road."

Jenna shot Beth a look to prevent her butting in and turned back to Amy. "Forget the second cabin for now. Anything else you recall of significance from the first cabin?"

"It smelled of pigs, and Margos told the others to feed the old man to the pigs." Amy shuddered. "I was pushed inside and didn't see what happened to him."

Leaning back in her chair to relieve the pain in her lower back, Jenna swallowed the sick feeling crawling up from her belly. Pigs would eat anything, including the man who fed them from the time they were piglets. "Can you tell me what happened when you left? Did you see anyone else in the forest?"

"No, I didn't see anyone at all, but as I told you before, I did see a yellow ribbon snagged on a pine tree. How Margos didn't spot it I'll never know. I kept looking around the whole time, but I didn't see hide nor hair of her."

Amy described how they moved to the next cabin and the

same deception was played out again. Margos had stabbed the owner of the cabin and dragged him into the forest. Later, as she prepared supper, she heard Margos call out that he'd found moonshine in the root cellar. They'd all dashed down to get some and commenced drinking before they'd eaten a meal. It didn't take too long for them to fall asleep. She turned her attention to Jenna. "When this happened, I gathered a few things and ran away. I noticed the smell of fire when I got outside. I headed back to the fire road and ran downhill. Along the way I met a woman who was trying to get her horses off the mountain and away from the wildfire. She gave me a ride into the sheriff's office and Maggie brought me here."

"I know they beat you pretty bad." Beth leaned forward in her chair. "Did any of them actually try to kill you? The men are very dangerous psychopathic murderers. I'd like to know how you managed not to trigger them into killing you?"

"I recalled that trying to make yourself useful to them sometimes prevents triggering them. I avoided eye contact, kept my head down, and did everything they asked me to do. Yeah, they beat me, but it wasn't to kill me. I was part of their twisted sexual behavior." Amy took a long shuddering breath. "Those men are animals."

Nodding, Jenna couldn't resist patting Amy's hand. "Is there anything you believe might be important for us to know?"

"No, I figure I've told you everything." Amy leaned back in her pillows looking exhausted.

"Do you have any questions about what happens next?" Jo's expression was filled with compassion. "Has the doctor explained about the morning-after pill? Unless, of course, you have a religious reason not to take it. There will be a number of tests to ensure you haven't contracted any diseases from the men. I'm afraid some of these must be repeated over a period of time."

"Yes, they did explain everything to me. I just want to speak to my parents before I make any decisions." Amy stared at her hands. "It's not a decision I can make immediately. An hour either way is not going to make any difference."

Pushing slowly to her feet, Jenna stopped the recording. "I'll contact the men searching the forest and see if they can pinpoint where both of the cabins are located. Although with the wildlife hunting through the forest at this time of year, it will be difficult to find any remains." She sighed. "I'll send your parents in now, but I would like you to follow the doctor's advice and stay here in the secure ward until she believes you are fit to leave. I can't order you to do this, but we don't know where the prisoners are at this moment. It might be safer for you to remain here."

"I'll stay here for a couple more days until I get some of the test results back and I don't look so bad." Amy tried to smile but her split lip prevented her. "Then I guess I will return to Helena with my parents, although I don't believe I will be working in the prison service again. From now on I want a quiet life."

Backing away, Jenna cleared her throat. "Someone will be by with a statement for you to sign. It's likely to be Maggie." She headed out the door and met Carter and Zorro in the waiting room chatting with Amy's parents. She introduced herself. "You can go in and see her now." She gave a wave to the guard on the door.

"You must find the men who did this to her." Amy's mother gripped her arm like a python.

Jenna nodded. "Oh, I know who did it. We have the forest crawling with law enforcement to bring them in. They won't get away with what they've done. I promise."

TWENTY-EIGHT

As Jenna stepped out into the bright sunlight, her heart missed a beat at the sight of a tall muscular man dressed in black leaning against the Beast. For one wonderful second she believed Kane had returned, but this man had a dog sitting beside him and it wasn't Duke. Two steps closer and she recognized Johnny Raven. His handsome face creased into a broad white smile that would melt most woman at the knees. She couldn't force herself to smile after speaking to Amy Clark. "Raven, what are you doing here? I thought you'd be taking a few hours rest."

"I'm rested well enough, thank you, ma'am, and Kane's instructions were to watch over you as if you were my little sister." Raven nodded to Carter and held out a set of keys. "You can take my ride. I'll be driving Jenna. My bags are in the back. I'll be bunking with you guys in the cottage on the ranch until we catch these guys."

"Can I have a word with you please, Jenna?" Carter took the keys but walked with her a few paces away. "Are you good with this arrangement? You hardly know this man? Why do you think Dave would choose him over me to watch over you?"

Not really understanding the reason herself, Jenna met his

gaze. "First, I don't need anyone to watch over me, and second, as someone is obviously trying to kill my team, I figure as Raven is new, it's likely whoever is doing this doesn't know about him. He's dressed like Dave, so perhaps it was Dave's idea to have Raven impersonate him while he's away. It's no secret Dave wanted to be in the field, hunting down those responsible for the fire. Shane is his best friend and would never let him go off alone. I figure he asked Raven to stand in for him, for that reason only and not to slight you in any way."

"I guess." Carter moved a toothpick across his lips and stared toward the mountains. Smoke rose from the forest curling up in gray wisps. "It appears that the fire is already out. We could go and assist in the search for the missing prisoners."

Shaking her head, Jenna took in the dark circles under Carter's eyes and hadn't missed his raspy voice from inhaling smoke. "No, I need you all in town. From the interview I had with Amy Clark, there have been two murders in the forest. Right now, these are our priority. The Department of Corrections has teams of prison guards and deputies from various counties' sheriff's departments combing the forest. Once they are sure the fire is out, they will have choppers up as well. We've played our part in this search for now. I'm not giving them another chance at killing you."

"Where do we go from here?" Jo had walked up behind her. "What about the girl? Who is interviewing her?"

Jenna indicated toward Beth and Styles, who were chatting to Raven beside the Beast. "You and Jo come with me and Raven. Styles and Beth can take the other truck. I figured the best thing we can do is to head out to the DOC's command center. They've set up at the forest warden's station out at Bear Peak. We'll find out what's happening with the search and have them go and investigate the cabins where the murders took place. They will have plenty of capable deputies available to secure the scene. In emergencies like this, I give them blanket jurisdiction to act on my behalf. It will be necessary for them to bring out any remains and take them to the morgue. Norrell will perform the preliminary autopsies." She walked slowly toward the others. "Once we're done there, we'll head out to the res. I'll call Blackhawk. I have no idea if he's contacted the girl's parents. Everything seems to be happening at once."

"Then what?" Carter walked beside her.

As her mind made plans and then dismissed them, Jenna turned to him. "Hopefully, by that time Rowley and Rio will be rested enough to take over the office. There's not much we can do until we get a sighting of the prisoners. I figure we head back to the ranch and get Kalo and Beth onto the CCTV footage in real time, just in case they make it into town. They can run the facial recognition programs continuously. Kalo has done it before and I'll release another media report to have all the townsfolk aware they could be heading this way." She reached the others and brought them up to date. "Then I want everyone well fed and rested. We need to be ready to take down three serial killers."

Climbing into the Beast was getting more difficult by the day. She glanced at Raven as he slid behind the wheel. First Carter and now Raven, Kane had never allowed anyone to drive his truck. Did he believe he wouldn't be coming back this time? The thought of him out there somewhere risking his life made her heart ache and she clutched her chest.

"Are you feeling okay?" Raven turned to look at her. "I'm a doctor. I know you're a strong and determined woman, but you're also in your third trimester. Delivery at any time could be imminent. If you're experiencing any pain, you need to tell me."

Shaking her head, Jenna stared straight ahead. "Don't worry, I'm not having this baby without Dave." She flicked him a glance. "Think you can handle the Beast?"

"I figure we'll find out soon enough." He started the engine.

"Is it true that you or Dave don't need a key to start the vehicle?"

Waving her tracker ring at him. "Yeah, it's the same as carrying the smart key I guess. We have the technology on us at all times. If someone gets into the vehicle, it locks and then the alarm sounds. The engine immobilizes. Trust me, without the key you'd need a crane to move it without either of us."

"Don't stamp your foot on the gas." Carter chuckled from behind him. "It takes off like a rocket."

To her surprise, Raven handled the Beast as if he'd been driving it all his life. They headed out of town and after passing through a roadblock on the highway, they drove along Stanton. As they headed alongside the forest, Jenna made out groups of people wearing jackets with wide bands of yellow. She indicated to the forest. "That must be the DOC search parties."

"They're just starting off, by the look of it." Raven pulled the truck to a halt outside the forest warden's station. "I'll leave the dogs in the back." He looked at Carter. "You okay with that?"

"Yeah, sure." Carter closed his hand around Jenna's arm as she climbed down. "Take the assistance. I'm concerned you'll fall flat on your face."

Carter had taken some time to regain his filter once he decided to join civilization again, but this sudden show of concern for her well-being surprised Jenna. "Thank you. Carrying all this extra weight makes it difficult to move around sometimes." She headed to the door of the forest warden's station and pushed inside.

A heavy scent of sweat filled the humid room, with people moving around, collecting backpacks, maps, and radios before moving away in groups. Raven, being able to see over the heads of most of the men in the room, took her by the elbow and guided her to the command center. Which turned out to be four men surrounding a map pinned to a whiteboard. "Who is in charge here?"

"That would be me." A man in his mid-sixties, rotund and wearing glasses, turned to look at her. He held out a hand. "You must be Sheriff Alton. I'm Peter Angle, head of the taskforce."

Shaking his hand, Jenna peered at the map. "Any signs of the prisoners?"

"Not yet, but we haven't given up looking." Angle indicated to two red pins on the map. "Those are the cabins they ransacked. Deputies from Louan and Blackwater are there processing the scenes. There are no remains at the first cabin. All they discovered were a pair of boots in the pigpen. At the second cabin there were remains of a male, but they had been disturbed by wildlife. They are bringing out the remains as we speak. I've notified the medical examiner's office and they will be sending a van to collect them." He searched her face. "I'm aware that your team has been on the job since the escape. We can handle it from here, but I do need to know there's a team in town on alert in case they slip through the net."

Jenna nodded. "Okay, thanks." She turned to the others. "I need to go and speak to Serena." She turned to Styles and Beth. "Can you head back to the office? Rio and Rowley will be back later and I need a team there. If the prisoners found a vehicle, they could be in town now." She turned to Carter. "I'd like you to go as well. There's a couch in the conference room. Try and get a couple of hours shut-eye. We're going to need to be alert overnight." She thought for a beat. "Maggie will order meals from Aunt Betty's Café or pizza for you. Just tell her what you need and they'll deliver."

"I'm not sure if that's a good idea." Carter shook his head. "I'm an extra gun and Raven will be driving."

"Hello!" Jo glared at him. "I'm standing right here. Are you suggesting I can't shoot straight?"

"Nope." Carter held up both hands in surrender. "Okay, I'll

go." He spat out his toothpick and strode to the Beast and opened the door for Zorro to jump down and they headed for the other truck.

Jenna stared after him. "Is he always this temperamental?" She walked toward the Beast with Jo at her side.

"Not always, no." Jo stared after him. "If you really want my honest opinion, all the men are concerned about you. With Kane away, they all believe it's their responsibility to keep you safe." She waved a hand absently toward Raven, who was watching the byplay with a smile. "Dave was thinking on his feet when he chose Raven. Apart from being mistaken for him, he made sure you had a doctor with you."

Wishing Kane were with her, her stomach gave a jolt. What would he be doing right now? Was he risking his life? She forced a smile. "Yes, he thinks of everything. Come on, let's head to the res before anything else happens." She turned to look at Raven, who was staring into the forest. "You coming?"

"Sure." Raven hurried after them. "I didn't figure the bears came this close to the highway, with the eighteen-wheelers thundering by so often."

Jenna stopped and turned to look at him. "They can be anywhere, especially here at Bear Peak." She shook her head. "You live in the forest and you're not bear aware? How did you survive so long?"

"I often ask myself the same question." Raven shrugged. "Just lucky, I guess."

TWENTY-NINE

Jenna called ahead to tell Blackhawk they were on their way. The security on the res would be on high alert because of the escaped prisoners. The tribal police were evident as they drove across the bridge and entered the res. They knew Jenna and the Beast by sight and waved her through. She buzzed down her window to speak to the officer on duty. "Any sign of any strangers?"

"Nope, all quiet here." The man narrowed his gaze. "Everyone is on alert. We'll know if they wander onto our land."

Nodding, Jenna noticed the schoolhouse had closed shutters. "I see you've kept all the children at home."

"Indeed." The man nodded. "Everyone is at home with the doors locked until these men are caught."

She waved as Raven headed into the res. Jenna gave him directions to Blackhawk's cabin. "Have you been here before?"

"Nope, but I was due to come by soon." Raven headed past cabins and up a road surrounded by forest. "Atohi has a litter of pups we are planning to train as K9s. Once they are old enough to be trained, we'll both be working with them. It's a joint business."

Glad to hear that Raven had a partner, Jenna smiled. "That's great. Atohi is an amazing dog trainer. His tracking and hunting dogs are known all over for reliability, as are his horses. I'm very fond of him. He is part of our family." She pointed. "There he is."

"You should be at home." Blackhawk shook his head, an expression of disapproval crossed his face. "Dave told me you'd be at home. It's not safe for you in the forest."

Giving him a hug, Jenna frowned. "Apparently, it's not safe for me anywhere while Souza is free. I have Raven and an FBI agent with me. I'll be fine." She indicated toward his cabin. "Is Serena here?"

"Yeah, but she's been staying with her grandma. Her mom is here too." Blackhawk trudged up the front steps to the porch. "They came here when I called them and told them you'd be coming."

Jenna loved the coziness of Blackhawk's home. He lived with his mom, who had a cabin of her own, currently occupied by Atohi's two cousins, but she liked the company of living with her son. The home was open plan and filled with comfortable furnishings and a handcrafted wooden coffee table before a local stone fireplace. Many craftsmen on the res produced beautiful wooden furniture and it was evident inside the cabin. They also produced exquisite silver turquoise jewelry and leather goods to sell at the res tourist store or in a store in town. She'd commissioned one of the artisans to design Kane's belt buckle. She smiled at the young girl sitting on the sofa, her head bowed over a tablet.

"There you are." Blackhawk's mom waved them to the long wooden kitchen table. "This is Kaya, Serena's mom."

Jenna noticed her red-rimmed eyes. "I'm so sorry for your loss."

"Thank you." Kaya sniffed. "Serena came so close to being killed by those terrible men."

"Don't worry, we'll find them and make them pay for killing your father." Raven dropped into a chair, his face grim.

"I have coffee and fresh baked cookies. Rest awhile. You all look exhausted." Atohi's mom raised her voice. "Serena, the sheriff would like to speak to you." She went about pouring coffee.

After Jenna had introduced Jo and Raven to the young girl, she explained why they were there and set up her phone to record the interview. This girl was a witness to a murder, and Jenna needed as much information from her as possible. "How many men did you see at the cabin?"

"Two, but I could hear more voices." The girl's eyes carried fear. "There was a woman there as well. I didn't see her or hear her at first. When I was riding into the forest, I heard her screaming. I figure they might have killed her too."

Shaking her head, Jenna kept her voice low and conversational. "No, she is fine. Her name is Amy Clark. She is one of the prison guards who were with the men in the bus wreck." She took an array of photographs out of her folder and splayed them across the table in front of Serena. "Do you recognize any of the men who were at the cabin in these pictures?"

"Yes." Serena pointed to Callahan and Romero. "Those men dragged my grandpa to the pigpen. I could see he was dead. His eyes were just staring at nothing. It was terrible. I could hear the pigs rushing toward him when the men tossed him over the fence. I had to get away but I was too scared to move."

"We understand how terrible it was for you, Serena." Jo leaned forward in her chair. "Did you hear someone shooting your grandfather?"

"Yes, I did." Serena gripped her hands together on the kitchen table, her eyes stricken. "I know the sound of my grandpa's shotgun. It is very loud. The other noise was softer but loud enough to make the birds fly out of the trees. Grandpa had told me to go and hide in the henhouse because he didn't recognize the people coming out of the forest. He told me to run to the next cabin and get help if anything bad happened." A big tear ran down Serena's cheek. "Something bad happened and I couldn't find the next cabin in the dark. I couldn't go past the front of the house on the horse—the men would have seen me—so I went into the forest and tried to go around in a big circle to get back to the fire road but I got lost."

Glancing down her list of notes, Jenna met the girl's eyes. "So you remained in the forest overnight alone?"

"I was with Thunderbolt. He would let me know if anyone was coming or if any wildlife came close." Serena dashed a hand across her cheeks as if annoyed to be crying. "As soon as it was light we kept moving, but the men had left the cabin, and no matter which way I went, I could hear them. I rode around for a long, long time and then I saw a man wearing a jacket that had FBI on the front. He was with another man who was dressed as a deputy. I rode up to them and told them what had happened. Atohi's cousin Chaska sneaked me along secret paths to the res. I was glad to see my grandma."

"Are you having nightmares?" Jo looked at Serena.

"No, but I think about what happened to Grandpa all the time." Serena pointed to her head. "It feels like it is stuck in here and won't go away."

"It will go away." Jo patted the girl's clenched hands. "When you start having those thoughts about what happened, try and think of something nice. Do you like flowers or seeing horses running through the paddocks? Think about them. It might help."

Appreciating Jo's kind words, Jenna nodded, but in her opinion, Serena needed professional help, and she would make sure she received that through the Her Broken Wings Foundation. Assistance was available to everyone who needed it.

"Thank you, Serena. We'll talk to your mom now. You've been very helpful. Don't worry, we'll catch these men very soon."

When Serena returned to her game on her tablet, she turned to Kaya. "You've both been through a terrible experience and we have people available who can help you in Black Rock Falls." She handed her a card. "It doesn't cost anything to speak to one of our counselors and any treatment either of you require will be free." She paused for a beat as Kaya read the card. "I would ask you to remain here on the res if possible. Serena is a witness and those men are still at large. As far as we are aware, they don't know she exists, and we would like it to remain that way for as long as possible. The media will know that your father was shot by them, and if they happened to mention Serena was at the cabin at the time, she could be in danger of her life."

"Don't worry, my husband is taking his vacation and will be arriving here this afternoon." Kaya's lips quivered into a small smile. "My family will keep us safe. Thank you for offering to help Serena get over her bad thoughts. Once this is all over, if she is still troubled, I will take her to Her Broken Wings Foundation and ask for their advice." She nodded slowly, not taking her eyes off Jenna. "It is a nice thing that you and your husband do. I only hear praise about your foundation, and you never turn anyone away. You must have a good heart to want to save so many damaged people. I hope the sun always shines brightly upon you both."

Moved by her lovely words, Jenna blinked back unshed tears. "Thank you." She inhaled the smell of cookies and smiled. "I'm going to need the recipe for these cookies. They smell mighty fine."

"They taste good too." Raven wiped crumbs from his beard and his cheeks colored as everyone looked at him. "I did leave some for you."

Jenna raised both eyebrows, glad the tension in the room had eased. "Just as well." She reached for a cookie and nibbled on the crumbly delight. "These are so good. I'll be fighting you over the last one."

THIRTY

Elaine Harper locked the door to the library and headed down the steps. She took the quiet, dimly lit alleyway between the buildings and pulled her coat tighter against the cool evening air. The sun had set, and the last traces of twilight faded into long shadows cast by the buildings. Her rhythmic footsteps from the heels of her sensible shoes echoed through the alleyway. Shivering as the wind from the mountains whisked up discarded papers and other bits of garbage littering the ground, she pushed on in the darkness. As she moved past the dumpsters, the light along the road at the end of the alleyway glowed like a beacon. She hurried along as a prickle of unease crawled over her. She turned a corner and stared both ways along the unusually deserted street. With each step the streetlights flickered ominously, creating distorted images of the way ahead.

Heart thumping in her chest, she glanced over her shoulder. A shadow moved behind her, or had it? She couldn't be sure, but the feeling of being watched was undeniable. Senses on high alert, Elaine picked up her pace. The once familiar route had suddenly become a labyrinth of potential threats, with every sound amplified—the ticking from a vehicle engine cooling, the distant howl of a dog, the wind whispering through the trees. She kept moving. A crunch of gravel followed by slow deliberate footfalls came from close behind her. Should she stop to look behind her again or keep going? Trying hard to swallow her fear, she reached in her purse for her phone and her hand came up empty. Frantically, she searched her pockets—nothing.

Panic had her by the throat. Had the escaped prisoners made it to town? Was one of them stalking her? She stared ahead to the small clutch of houses in the distance. If someone was following her, would she make it there in time to ask for help? The footsteps behind her grew louder, more deliberate, whoever lurked in the shadows was getting closer. Maybe the person behind her wasn't a threat, but could she dare risk it? Mind racing, she scanned the dim light ahead looking for a place to hide. She'd walked along this sidewalk a thousand times before, but panic was fogging her brain. She moved faster, and ahead, the shadowed maw of an alleyway yawned. Hidden by a cloak of darkness, she could slip inside, hide behind a dumpster, and wait for him to go by.

With each beat of a heart pounding in her ears, she chanced a glance over one shoulder. No one followed her, but as she backed into the alleyway the *crunch, crunch* of boots on gravel split the silence, and the silhouette of her pursuer detached from the darkness. Unable to take her eyes from the approaching man, she walked backward into the alleyway. Her feet tangled in a bunch of loose packing material and she stumbled, falling heavily to the ground. Pain shot up her arm and something sharp stuck into her hip. The footsteps were getting closer. Terrified, she dragged herself to her feet, and gritting her teeth, pushed herself to keep moving despite the pain. The stink of garbage seared her nostrils as she shuffled a few steps, slipping on the spilled grease making the ground like ice. It seemed to take forever to get between two dumpsters and press herself against the wall. Panting with terror, she trembled, but not from the cold. Sweat dripped down her back, tickling a path between her shoulder blades.

The footsteps paused at the mouth of the alleyway and then moved slowly toward her. Trying to calm her breathing, with every muscle tense, she fought back a scream as he started to hum. There was no escape and she held up her hands as a large shadow filled the gap between the dumpsters. A low rumbling chuckle made the hairs on her neck raise and she choked out a strangled scream. As a cloud moved away from the moon, she caught the metallic sheen of a knife as he raised it in the air.

THIRTY-ONE

Shivering against the cold wind, Fatima Hagerstrom strolled along Main. Streetlights cast puddles of gold across the sidewalk, but between the buildings, long shadows cloaked the entrances of the alleyways. Glad to have her dog, Max, trotting happily beside her, with his leash slack in her hand, she scanned the darkness. Tonight this part of Main was empty and only two vehicles parked outside the café in the distance. Aunt Betty's Café was open until eleven most nights, and as the wind was getting colder by the minute, she'd have time to stop by and grab a to-go cup of coffee for the walk home. Being out alone at night always spooked her, but having a dog carried responsibilities, and walking Max even after a long day's work was necessary. They'd taken this route countless times, but tonight the air was thick with an uneasy stillness. The usually vibrant, noisy, tourist-filled town was silent.

Suddenly Max's ears pricked, and before Fatima could react, the leash slipped from her hand and he bolted toward a dark alleyway. She stared after him. "Max, no!"

In seconds the dog disappeared into the shadows. He never chased cats. Why had he run away from her? Pulling her phone from her pocket, she accessed the flashlight and flooded the darkness. Heart pounding, she hurried after him, moving the flashlight back and forth. Alleyways transversed this end of town and he could be down any one of them. She aimed the phone at the first one, and her white dog was nowhere to be seen. Unease gripped her as she moved to the end of the next store. "Where are you? Max, come here, boy."

Moments later, Max emerged from alongside the Chinese restaurant, his white fur matted with something dark and wet. As she shone the flashlight beam over him, the black patch turned to crimson. Horrified, Fatima squeezed her eyes shut at the sight. Max bumped into her leg and whined in distress. She opened her eyes and stared at her blood-soaked dog. Someone might be hurt, and she needed to make sure. She scanned Main in every direction for someone to help her, but the sidewalk was empty. She gripped her phone and in hesitant steps moved forward, her knees trembling. "Is anyone there?"

Nothing.

Holding her phone out like a shield, she stepped into the dimly lit alleyway. Heart thundering in her chest, she stepped over tangles of packing material. Ahead and behind her, darkness closed in around her in a sinister embrace. In an exhalation of breeze, the metallic scent of blood washed over her and every fiber of her body told her to turn and run, but morbid fascination drew her forward. One step, two steps along the side of the filthy dumpster and she caught sight of a shoe. Taking a steadying breath, she forced herself to peer around the side of the bin and stared into the sightless eyes of a woman sprawled on the ground in a pool of blood. Fatima gagged in horror, her throat tightened, and unable to scream, she backed away. Suddenly a shadow shifted in the far corner of the alleyway. Someone was watching her. Terrified, the phone slipped from her grasp as she turned to run.

Sprinting along Main with Max bounding along beside her,

his leash trailing behind him, she ran toward Aunt Betty's Café. The eatery's lights spread across the sidewalk, offering comfort and safety. Chest tight, she ran for her life past the dark storefronts and gaping alleyways. In the distance, the café seemed a mile away. Fear pushed her on and she sobbed with relief when she finally made it. Gasping for breath, she burst through the door, startling an elderly couple waiting at the counter. From the back, Wendy, the assistant manager, came out carrying a take-out bag and handed it to the elderly couple.

"Your dog is covered with blood." Wendy came from behind the counter, her eyes filled with concern. "Fatima, what's happened?"

Panting, Fatima stared over one shoulder, terrified the killer might be right behind her. "Call 911." She waved a hand behind her. "There's a dead woman in the alleyway alongside the Chinese restaurant. She's been murdered and I saw someone in the shadows."

"You better stay here." Wendy turned to the elderly couple and then ran to the door and bolted it. "I'll grab my Glock. Trust me, no one is coming through that door until the sheriff arrives."

THIRTY-TWO

The insistent chime of her phone woke Jenna, and believing it was Kane, she sat up in bed and grabbed it from the bedside table. Seeing on the caller ID it was Rio, uneasiness crawled over her as she accepted the call. "I'm assuming this is something really bad if you're calling me at one in the morning?"

"Afraid so." Rio didn't sound the least bit apologetic. "We have a homicide in an alleyway beside the Chinese restaurant on Main. A female approximately twenty-five years old. Evidence of knife wounds to the chest, face, and neck. There are no footprints in the blood apart from a dog's and no obvious evidence. The victim was discovered by Fatima Hagerstrom walking her dog. She is currently with Wendy at Aunt Betty's Café. She ran there after she discovered the body, and Wendy locked the door and kept everyone inside as Ms. Hagerstrom believed she saw someone lurking in the shadows."

Placing her phone on speaker, Jenna stifled a moan. Her back had been aching all night. She slipped from the bed and dressed. "Have you secured the scene? Did you call Rowley?"

"Yes and yes. Rowley has just arrived." Rio's footsteps echoed on the sidewalk. "I'm currently clearing the alleyways between the Chinese restaurant and the beauty parlor, but we haven't seen anyone else on the street at all since we arrived. A few eighteen-wheelers rumbled along Main and one truck. We've waved down the truck and spoke to the driver. They were leaving home for night shift. I have his details and verified his movements with the security company that employs him."

Jenna pushed her feet into her boots and hurried into the kitchen. "I'll call in the team. You and Rowley stay on scene until we get there. Is there anything else you need?"

"Nope. Wendy from Aunt Betty's Café has been supplying us with Thermoses of coffee. There was an old couple in the café taking shelter and I sent them home, but I asked Ms. Hagerstrom to wait in the diner until you can speak to her. She did see someone near the body. Just a second." Muffled voices came in the distance before Rio returned. "You don't need to call in Norrell. She just showed with Colt Webber and Emily. I've already taken photographs of the scene without getting too close to the victim. Do you want Norrell to go ahead and process the scene?"

Sighing with relief, Jenna turned on the coffee pot. "Yeah, sure, I'll wake Raven and ask him to drive me into town, and maybe one of the FBI agents will want to come along and take a look. I'll call them at the cottage now."

"Okay. Don't worry, Jenna, I'm on it." Rio disconnected.

Being chief deputy now, Rio was more than capable of handling any situation. He'd processed many murder scenes in his time with the team and as a gold shield detective in LA, but Jenna wanted to be involved for as long as possible. However, this murder would give her a good idea of just how well the team worked without her. Once the baby arrived, she'd be on leave for six months along with Kane and needed to be sure the office would run without her. She called Carter first, mainly because he had his nose out of joint when Kane asked Raven to look out for her. When he answered his phone, she gave him the details of what had happened. "I'm not calling you to come with me. I do understand you all need your rest after what happened in the forest, but I can't drive there alone. Do you mind very much waking Raven and explaining?"

"Yeah, sure I'll wake Raven for you, but I'm coming too." Carter cleared his throat. "Dave was concerned Souza might come after you to get back at him. I know you're not mentioning where Kane and Wolfe vanished to and I don't expect you to, but I'm not stupid. If Dave has decided to go after Souza, he should have taken me with him. I don't figure a medical examiner is going to watch his back like I would." He sighed. "Right this moment, we don't know if this murder is a setup to get you out of the house—do we? I mean, Souza did escape with three serial killers and he doesn't do anything without a good reason. We know someone is in contact with the prisoners, which means Souza could be directing traffic. Are you sure you don't want to stay home and leave this one to us? I mean, being pregnant and all?"

Jenna lifted her chin and stared out of the kitchen window into the darkness. She'd faced many dangers in her lifetime and never shown weakness. Pregnant or not, she could do her job well and bring down serial killers. "Don't worry about me, Ty. I can assure you, I might not be able to take a perp down in a fist-fight right this moment, but I can darn well shoot straight."

"That's good to know." Carter sighed. "But I'm here if you need me. Don't hesitate to call if you need assistance when the baby arrives."

Getting Thermoses out of the cabinet, Jenna cleared her throat. "My job as sheriff is very important to me and I can assure you I will still give a hundred percent to any case that I'm on. I have already made provisions for my children that allow me to do this without interrupting their care. If I can't do my job to the fullest extent, that is the day I walk away from this town forever."

"*I understand.*" Carter blew out a breath. "*Can you tell Jo and Beth what's happening? I don't want to be accused of not including them in the case. I'll go and wake Raven now.*" He disconnected.

Suddenly missing Kane, Jenna stared at the phone. Had she been too harsh with Carter?

THIRTY-THREE

It didn't matter that summer was fast approaching in the alpine town. The nights were still cool, and as Jenna stepped from the truck, an icy chill bit through her clothes. As she walked toward the alleyway, crime scene tape fluttered in a breeze carrying the scent of blood and death. Voices came from deep within and floodlights lit up the filthy alleyway so brightly Jenna needed to shield her eyes after being in the dark street. With Carter on one side and Raven on the other, she made her way along the alleyway to the crime scene. Norrell was bending over the victim. She lifted the young woman's shirt and took the temperature of the victim's liver to determine the approximate time of death. Beside Norrell, Colt Webber was videoing the scene and recording her dictation.

Scanning the scene, Jenna turned a full circle, she couldn't imagine why anyone would take this particular alleyway as a shortcut to Maple when there was a laneway with a streetlight right next door. She glanced at Carter. "Do you think that she was dragged in here and murdered?"

"It's hard to say until we have a look at the other end of the alleyway." Carter moved a toothpick across his lips, staring unblinking at the scene. He motioned to Rio, who came forward to speak to them. "Any sign of a struggle?"

"I figured the attack happened beside the dumpster." Rio indicated behind him with his thumb. "There's a lot of garbage at the other end of the alleyway and it doesn't look like anyone's been dragged through it. Maybe she ran there to hide, which would indicate this guy was either stalking or chasing her."

The moment Norrell stopped speaking, Jenna moved forward. "What have you got for me, Norrell?"

"I haven't confirmed the identity of the victim yet, but we did find a purse and inside was a driver's license for Elaine Harper. She resembles the image, but her face has been so badly damaged I'll need fingerprints or a DNA match to verify her identity." Norrell bent and gently lifted up one of the victim's arms. "As you can see, she tried to defend herself against her attacker, but confined within this small area, she didn't have a chance. Her clothes appear to be intact, so I don't anticipate any sexual abuse." She turned to wave a hand toward the entrance of the alleyway. "There are no bloody footprints, apart from the dog's. The witness who was walking her dog and found the body mentioned that she believed there was someone lurking in the shadows, but I have searched every corner of this alleyway and have found nothing unusual. In other words, it doesn't mean that they weren't here; it does mean that they left no trace DNA behind."

Peering at the poor woman spread out on the ground, sliced up, and left to bleed to death, with her eyes pleading for Jenna to discover a murderer, saddened her. Seeing someone cut down in the prime of their life sickened and horrified her. She moved closer and a jolt of familiarity hit her. "I know her. She's a librarian. I spoke to her when I took Tauri there to show him the books. She was very helpful and directed us to a bookcase filled with interesting reading for his age. Why would anyone want to murder her?"

"Likely a random thrill kill." Raven crouched down beside the body, keeping outside the pool of blood. "This couldn't have happened too long ago. Rigor is just setting in now. Taking the coolness of tonight into consideration, I would say she'd been dead for approximately two to three hours."

Jenna's gaze shifted over the body, searching for evidence. The crime scene itself usually gave away many secrets. Garbage littered the ground and would disguise and likely eliminate any trace evidence. "Did you find a phone? Was there one inside her purse?"

"No, there wasn't one inside her purse and we haven't found one anywhere near the body but there was one in the alleyway. It was the one the witness, Fatima Hagerstrom, dropped after she found the body. She has already identified it as hers." Rio met Jenna's gaze. "I walked with Rowley around the immediate area, including a short way along Main and Maple, searching for the victim's phone and found nothing."

"Personal effects?" Carter came to Jenna's side. "What was inside her purse?"

"House keys, a small pack of tissues, a pen, makeup, and some feminine products. I don't figure she had a vehicle." Rio held up an evidence bag containing a woman's purse. "She lives in that group of houses about half a mile from here on Maple. It would have been an easy walk from the library. It's probably one she does every day. Perhaps the killer waited for her to pass and then chased her down here."

As Norrell and Emily went about placing the victim into a body bag, Jenna took out her flashlight to search underneath the dumpsters but found nothing interesting. She groaned as she straightened and Raven leaned in close to her.

"If you need to look under dumpsters or anything else, why don't you ask me?" He lowered his voice to just above a whisper. "How long has the backache been worrying you?"

Jenna narrowed her gaze at him. "For months. I'm getting

used to it now, but I sure as heck won't miss it once the baby is born."

"Is it a constant ache?" Raven frowned and his gaze moved over her face filled with concern. "If it is, please ask your obstetrician to check you out in case it's the first stages of labor."

Trying to keep her mind on the case, but not wanting to snap at Raven like she did with Carter, she smiled at him. "If it becomes a problem, I'll be sure to call her but right now we have a dead woman lying brutally murdered in an alleyway and a serial killer or maybe three of them loose in town. I figure we need to keep our minds on the priorities."

After Emily and Webber loaded the body into the back of Wolfe's van, Jenna went to Norrell's side. "Will you be conducting the autopsy or are we waiting for Wolfe to return?"

"The deputies from Blackwater delivered the remains of Robert Moore late yesterday afternoon. He was the man the prisoners murdered at the second cabin." Norrell peeled off her examination gloves, rolled them into a ball, and tossed them into a dumpster. "He has sharp force trauma to his neck, but I will need to conduct an autopsy to determine cause of death. With multiple murders, I have no choice but to take them in order. I'll try and get to her on Friday." She sighed and removed her mask and then led Jenna deeper into the alleyway. "Wolfe didn't give me any details of where he was going or when he would be back. He explained to me when we decided to marry that there was a side of him I couldn't ask about and it concerned his time in the military. He said, when he needs to go away for a time, he prefers having Dave with him." She gave Jenna a long searching look. "Do you know what's behind it? Should I be worried?"

Jenna looked over one shoulder glad to see Carter and Rio discussing something just outside the alleyway. They wouldn't be overheard. It wasn't her decision to explain anything to Norrell and obviously Wolfe wasn't going to risk it either. There was too much at stake to tell anyone about Kane's secret past. "I don't know but I do know it's something we shouldn't discuss. I'm sure if there was anything they could tell us about, they would. They don't go away very often, so it's not something you should be worrying about." She searched her face. "They both served in the military under fire. Maybe it's something they need to do to keep their heads straight? I know for sure Emily and the girls know nothing either."

"So we never ask?" Norrell folded her arms across her chest. "Doesn't it worry you that your husband keeps secrets from you?"

Barking a laugh, she met her annoyed expression. "Everyone has secrets. Wolfe has explained that he can't discuss his with you. I'm sure you will find him open and honest about everything else in his life. It's the same with Dave. He tells me everything apart from what he does with Wolfe when they're away. I believe everyone deserves to keep one special secret, so I never ask." She smiled at Norrell. "One thing's for darn sure, it doesn't involve women."

THIRTY-FOUR

Yawning, Jenna climbed from the Beast outside Aunt Betty's Café. They left Ben the K9 asleep on the back seat. Rowley opened the eatery door for them and then locked it behind them. Inside, she found a woman resting her head on her arms seated at a table and Wendy making sandwiches and coffee. Jenna waved Rio and Rowley to a nearby table and sat down with Raven and Carter beside the woman. A blood-soaked white dog growled at them but sat immediately when Raven gave the command. "Ms. Hagerstrom, I'm Sheriff Alton. Thank you for waiting for us. This must have been such a shock for you. Are you up to explaining what happened?"

"Before you start, I have fresh coffee and sandwiches for everyone." Wendy pushed plates of sandwiches on the table and then went back for pots of coffee. "It's been a long night." She went back to the kitchen and then carried plates of sandwiches and coffee to Rio and Rowley.

After pouring the coffee and adding the fixings to her own cup, she looked at Fatima Hagerstrom. "When you're ready and in your own time."

Fatima Hagerstrom went about telling her story from the

moment she left home. The route she took every night at the same time walking Max. She mentioned that it had been very quiet in town and only one or two vehicles went past her during the entire time. She hadn't seen anyone on the streets and there were only two vehicles outside Aunt Betty's Café when she looked along the road.

As Carter was taking notes, Jenna kept the questions flowing. "Did you hear anything? A scream or a scuffle? We believe this woman was murdered around the time you left home. As it was so quiet, are you sure you didn't hear anything at all?"

"No, I did notice it was too quiet." Fatima dabbed at tear-soaked eyes. "When I'm walking Max, I usually hear a dog barking or the screech of an owl, but I didn't hear anything. I wouldn't have known she was there if Max hadn't run away and come back soaked in blood. In hindsight, I should have called you immediately rather than going to look myself, but I was concerned that someone was in trouble. Maybe they had slipped in the alleyway and injured themselves." She took in a long shuddering breath. "I had no idea I would find a poor murdered woman. I could see she was dead, but when I saw a shadow move, I didn't wait around to check. I just ran away as fast as I could. This was the only place open. I couldn't call for help. I dropped my phone between the alleyway and here."

"The person you saw in the shadows, can you describe him?" Carter lifted his gaze to Fatima. "Did you believe it was a man? If so, how tall would you say he was? Fat or thin?"

Jenna rested a hand on the woman's arm. "Close your eyes and think about being in the alleyway and looking at the shadows. What do you see?"

"It's hard to tell but I think he was wearing a cowboy hat. He was broad but not as tall as you." She indicated to Carter. "He was surrounded by shadows, so it's difficult to be sure of what I saw. I do know that someone was in the alleyway. I had to get away. Do you figure they will come after me now?"

Shaking her head, Jenna pushed the sandwiches toward Fatima. "It was very dark. I doubt very much he would have seen your face. I figure he escaped from the other end of the alleyway and will be long gone from here by now. Eat something and drink the coffee. It will make you feel better. When we are done here, I'll have one of my deputies take you home." She looked into the woman's eyes. "If at any time you have concerns, call me and I'll make sure someone is there immediately. We will keep your name out of this, so no one will know who you are."

"Thank you. I appreciate it, but my husband will be coming by for me once we've finished here. I thought it would be better if he waited at home." Fatima lifted a sandwich with shaking fingers and looked at her dog. "I just hope the man who murdered that poor woman doesn't recognize Max. I think for the next few days, I'll keep him hidden in the backyard."

"Do you want me to write a statement?" Carter indicated to the statement pad Jenna had placed on the table. "It might be better if Ms. Hagerstrom remains at home until we catch this guy."

Bone-weary from lack of sleep, Jenna nodded. "That would be a great help, thanks." She smiled at him. "Please, eat something first. You look exhausted."

"I will." Carter took a sandwich and ate it in two bites, sipped coffee, and then went to work using his notes for a reference.

"I'm a doctor." Raven peered at Fatima with concern in his eyes. "If you have any concerns, trouble sleeping, flashbacks, or night terrors, call me." He handed her his card. "I don't have a practice in town. I only do house calls."

When Jenna's phone chimed her blood ran cold. She stared at the private number ID and stood to walk away from the others. "Sheriff Alton."

"I'm sorry to disturb you, Sheriff, this is Bob Cutter. I'm with the DOC search party. The coordinator instructed me to call you with an update on the prisoners."

Pushing a hand through her hair, Jenna sighed. "It's fortunate that I am out on a case at the moment. Usually, I'm asleep at this time of the morning. Go ahead, what have you got for me?"

"As you are aware, we discovered the cabin and the remains of Robert Moore in the forest. There is a garage attached to his property, including a gas tank. So we surmised he owned a vehicle and checked him out with the DMV. Further to this we scouted the area for tire tracks and discovered fresh marks heading toward town. Going on the time these men were at this cabin, if they took the backroads, they could have avoided the roadblocks and be in town by now. We are moving our search to the area of Stanton Forest on the perimeter of town."

Shaking her head in disbelief, Jenna took a deep breath to steady herself. "How long ago did you know about this?"

"I've just come on shift and received my orders. I believe the information was available at the time they discovered the body." Cutter cleared his throat. "I apologize for not getting the information to you sooner. We've all been so busy it must've slipped through the net."

Fuming, Jenna turned as Carter and Raven came to her side. "This lack of communication, Mr. Cutter, has cost a woman her life. We would have informed the townsfolk if there had been any inkling that these men had arrived in town. Now a poor woman walking home has been brutally murdered. This is why I'm out in the middle of the night investigating a homicide. I suggest you move your team right away. You need to be checking the outlying ranches and cabins. They'll be using one of them as a hideout. These are seasoned criminals, vicious killers, they will know exactly how to avoid law enforcement and they won't care how many lives they take in the process. I suggest you get your act together and do your job."

"Yes, ma'am." Cutter disconnected.

Jenna scrolled through the contacts on her phone for her media acquaintances. She made the same call to each of them. "I'm sorry to call you so late, but this is an emergency. Three serial killers who were involved in the bus crash on the highway have arrived in Black Rock Falls. It is imperative that we get the information and photographs of these men across all channels. I need people to stay at home when possible. Anyone moving around should do so in groups. Do not attempt to walk the streets alone at night. We have already had three homicides that we believe are connected to the escaped prisoners. More information will be forthcoming once the next of kin of the victims have been notified. The Department of Corrections and deputies and sheriffs of other counties are currently searching the outlying properties of Black Rock Falls. They will be wearing easily identifiable uniforms. Please inform the townsfolk not to open the door to anyone not clearly wearing a law or DOC uniform." She disconnected and looked at Carter and Raven. "The reign of terror has begun."

THIRTY-FIVE

Friday

Crisp cool air lifted Maya Brooks' hair as she ran along the trail. A gentle breeze rustled the trees, bringing the fresh scent of pine and snow from the ice-capped mountains. As the first light of dawn filtered through the dense canopy of pines, it cast golden spears of light across the forest floor, sparking her imagination with dancing fairies. At this time of the morning, the forest was magical and gave her a sense of peace. After a run, she could face the day and any stress that came along with it. As she moved along the familiar pathway, a break in the canopy drew her attention, and engaged by the view, she stopped. The sky changed from deep blue to various shades of pink and orange and moments later the sun illuminated the peaks of the surrounding mountains. The forest came alive all at once. Squirrels scampered up trees, and birdsong filled the air. She moved on, taking in the fresh green ferns and wildflowers along each side of the trail. As usual she would run to the first bridge, cross over to the other side of the ravine, and then take the trail back to the parking lot.

As she crossed the bridge, the smell of fire came on the wind. Aware of a brushfire in the forest the previous day, she turned to look in the direction of Bear Peak. No smoke was visible and she turned to scan the forest below the bridge. If there was any danger of fire on the other side of the ravine, she would turn back and go the way she came. Seeing nothing, she proceeded across the bridge and headed down the track on the other side. People used this trail for hiking and running. This area of Stanton Forest was never a designated area for hunting, so everyone could move around without fear of being shot. Two hundred yards along the trail, she noticed a makeshift camp. Three discarded sleeping bags sat beside a small fire. As they were some distance from the river, and hunting wasn't allowed, she wondered why these people camped in the forest. She wrinkled her nose at the smell of the smoke. What had made them leave an unattended fire? She scanned the forest, turning around and looking in all directions. A wildfire this close to town could cause massive destruction as all the outlying homes were made of wood.

With no one in sight, Maya headed toward the fire. Whoever had lit it had dug a small hole first, and she used the soil to kick over the embers until it stopped smoldering. She spun around at a sound behind her and stared into the faces of three smiling men. She lifted her chin. "You can't go off and leave a fire unattended in the forest."

"Is that right?" One of the men allowed his jacket to fall open, displaying a gun in his belt. "And you're the law in this forest, are you? Or are you just a busybody?"

Suddenly afraid of the men leering at her, Maya turned and ran. The men were blocking her way back to the trail, so she zigzagged through the forest. A gunshot rang out and a thump hit her leg. Searing agony shot through her thigh, and staggering a few steps, she fell flat on her face. Unimaginable pain streaked through her in red-hot waves. Pine needles filled her mouth and she spat them out, panting through the agony. *They shot me.*

Terrified and trembling, she scanned the forest searching for the men, but no one followed her. Lying as still as possible, she waited and listened. The forest had fallen silent after the shot as if everything was holding its breath. She looked all around again and breathed a sigh of relief. She'd lost them. Struggling to sit up, she gaped at the groove cut through one side of her thigh. Shrugging out of her backpack, she found the first aid kit she always carried with her and bandaged her leg. Unsure if she could walk, she pulled out her phone. She needed help and dialed 911. She gave her details and approximate coordinates to the woman who answered the phone. She needed to get back on the trail where she could be easily found by the deputies and paramedics who would be on their way. Using the trunk of a pine to pull herself to her feet, she moved slowly from tree to tree in an arc to avoid the men's camp. Maybe they didn't know that they'd hit her and only shot to scare her away. Surely if they meant her harm, they would have come after her? A rustling came from the left, and gripped by panic, she hobbled faster, trying to make out the trail through the trees. If she made it there, the deputies would find her.

Pine needles crunched, and a soft laugh came so close behind her terror shattered through her. She didn't have time to run before a hand clamped on her forearm and closed like steel, crushing her bone. She screamed and lashed out, punching the man in the throat. When he gasped and let go of her arm, she tried to run, but a second man stepped out from behind a tree and scooped her up as if she weighed nothing. "Let go of me."

"That's never gonna happen." The man carried her to the trail and body-slammed her to the ground.

Air rushed from Maya's lungs and it hurt to breathe. The man stood over her laughing. Trembling, she stared at him and held up her hands. "Please let me go. I won't tell anyone you shot me."

The man ignored her and looked into the forest as the man with the gun came crunching through the underbrush.

"See, I told you if you wait long enough, they'll come to you. You don't need to risk going into town." He pulled a knife from his belt and handed it to the other man. "You can have this one. If I start killing now, I'll never stop and there are plenty more where she came from, but don't shoot her. It's too quick."

"I've waited twenty years to smell a woman like that, all hot and sweaty after running." A third man crunched out of the forest, bent over her, and inhaled. "The kitty kittys at the prison smell like antiseptic but they scream the same—if you can catch one." He snorted with laughter. "Even her blood smells sweet." He grinned at the man holding the knife. "Show me what you've got."

Maya gaped at the men, discussing her as if she weren't human. Tears ran over her cheeks in hot streams. "Please don't hurt me. I won't tell anyone."

"They always say that, sweetheart." The man with the gun stared at her with cold dark eyes. "It turns on guys like us and makes us want to hear you plead and moan for a long time. It takes skill to slice and dice."

"I can never make it last long enough." The man with the knife chuckled and looked from one man to the other. "You sure had it right when you said once you kill again, it's hard to stop. I sure like being free. You guys can do what you like, but I'm gonna head back into town and have me some fun." He stood over her smiling. "Run."

Terrified but not beaten, Maya rolled onto her knees determined to run away. She crawled, dragging her injured leg behind her. *I must get away.* She had escaped these men before and could do it again. Deep laughter filled the suddenly silent forest, and the next second, someone grabbed her hair, wrenching her head back. Cold steel crossed her throat, stinging her flesh. She opened her mouth to scream but no sound came out. She fell forward into the well-worn dirt path and then the beautiful magical forest spiraled into darkness.

THIRTY-SIX

"What?"

Jenna hurried from the kitchen and went into her bedroom, pressing her phone to her ear. "Are you saying that this woman called in her own murder?"

"I guess she did." Rowley's footsteps echoed on tile as he walked into the morgue. *"She called to say she'd been shot in the thigh by one of the three men she found camping in the forest during her usual morning run. At the time, no one was pursuing her. She had bandaged her leg and was trying to make it back to the trail. She gave her name and her approximate coordinates. I contacted the paramedics and Rio right away, and we headed for the forest. It took us forty minutes from the time the call was logged until we found her on the trail with her throat cut. We secured the scene, called out the forensics team, and searched the forest. We found the firepit but there was nothing there. We did locate the woman's backpack. It was empty. So her phone and any other items she had with her are missing. In the phone call to Maggie, she mentioned she had driven to the parking lot, so the prisoners will likely be in a silver GMC. I'll text you the plate number. Rio has notified everyone in the search and put out a*

BOLO. *Like I said, I'm at the morgue to fill out the paperwork. Norrell and Emily have already processed the scene and collected evidence. I've uploaded a video onto the server."*

Shaking her head, Jenna stared at her reflection in the mirror. Dark circles ringed both eyes and she appeared pale and drawn. "Why didn't you notify me the moment the call came in?"

"At the time we didn't know it was a homicide." Rowley cleared his throat. *"If we'd known, we would have called you right away. It wasn't until we found the body that we knew it was a homicide. We figured we were investigating a stray bullet. Rio did everything by the book. He figured, after you'd been out all night handling the other case, he'd take the lead in this one."*

The indignation of not being told about a murder dissipated as Rowley explained. Being so close to her confinement, the thought of leaving her team without a leader had concerned her, but now she had confidence her team could handle any situation in her absence. "It seems you have everything under control. I'll be coming into the office. Styles, Raven, and Beth will be coming with me. Carter and Jo are staying at the ranch to ensure that Tauri is safe. Catch you later." She heaved in a deep sigh and rubbed her belly. "I hope your daddy will be home soon."

"Is something wrong?" Beth appeared in the doorway and looked at her with raised eyebrows.

Chewing on her bottom lip, Jenna nodded. "Yeah, we have another murder. This one is very strange. From what Rowley just told me, the victim called it in. We know she was attacked by three men." She went on to explain the murder in detail.

"The prisoners?" Beth took a step inside Jenna's bedroom. "So they must be camping in the forest just on the outskirts of town. It sounds like an opportunistic thrill kill. They haven't been out long enough to have planned her murder."

Tapping her bottom lip as she ran the scenario through her

mind, Jenna nodded. "Yeah, I agree. It does point in that direction, the same as the alleyway murder. The problem is, what if there is a fourth serial killer in town totally unrelated to the prisoners? As both these women did these activities regularly at the same time, they'd make perfect targets." Jenna pushed her hair behind one ear and leaned against the foot of the bed. "One thing about serial killers is that they come in every variety, and the escaped prisoners are a mixture. Only one of them is a stalker, Callahan, but he strangled and raped his victims. He would have taken his time to plan each murder and pick his target when he knows they are totally alone. It's a safe and very deadly way of murdering someone."

"Whereas an opportunistic thrill kill is dangerous because they run a greater risk of being caught." Beth leaned casually against the nightstand. "Which leaves us Margos and Romero. Neither of them cut throats."

"Who is cutting throats?" Jo walked into the room and looked from one to the other.

Beth brought her up to date. "We are hoping there isn't a fourth serial killer in town. It's possible. After all, this is Serial Killer Central."

"These men have been locked up in prison for a very long time." Jo folded her arms across her chest. "They have been exposed to other serial killers and every one of them loves to relive their kills by telling stories to each other. After so long, it wouldn't be inconceivable to believe that they had changed their MO. They might not be able to change their fantasy because that seems to be part of them, the small thing that drives them to kill, but listening to others' stories could create new fantasies." She lifted one shoulder in a half shrug. "It's not something I've studied in detail as there's no data to study. We don't release serial killers. The only one of note who escaped was Ted Bundy and his murders became more heinous and depraved as he escalated."

Incredulous, Jenna stared at her. "Are you saying that after a long time in prison their triggers could change?"

"With these three, I would say most definitely because they all have fantasies about murdering women and they didn't kill the prison guard right away. She must have been of some value to them, so raping her was fine but killing her was forbidden." Jo met Jenna's gaze. "Up to now, they've killed out of necessity."

"I agree." Beth shrugged. "Killing the men meant nothing to them. It didn't give them a thrill. For them, taking those men's lives was no more than swatting a fly. The three of them have problems with women, so perhaps they shared the recent kills. The biggest problem I can see is they've been blooded again and are now escalating."

Needing to address every angle, Jenna paused a beat to consider the evidence. "I'm keeping an open mind on a fourth serial killer for now. We'll need to contact the victims' next of kin to find out if Elaine and Maya followed the same routine each day, but I agree with you, it sounds more like both women were just in the wrong place at the wrong time."

Jenna gathered her things and took her shoulder holster from a hook behind the door. Her M18 pistol was in a locked drawer beside her bed, and she collected it before waving them out of the room. She looked at Jo. "We'll need to get into the office. I was going to ask you and Carter to stay here today to protect Tauri, but I need boots on the ground in town. If the prisoners are keeping to the forest, they'll still need to eat and gather supplies. We have facial recognition programs available and believe they're driving a silver GMC."

"I'll stay." Beth paused in the passageway. "I can liaise with Kalo and we can keep the town under surveillance. I can work from your office and be on hand if anyone decides to drop by."

Nodding, Jenna smiled at her. "I'll contact the DOC command center and bring them up to speed. They'll need to concentrate their search closer to town."

"Don't forget"—Beth walked backward into the kitchen—"serial killers are very good at slipping into society without being noticed. You could have one right beside you and not know. They'll have changed their appearance, so be aware of their eyes. It's one part of the body that's the most difficult to disguise and these men wouldn't have access to contact lenses or wigs." She looked from one to the other. "After this long, they won't look the same as their mug shots anyway. This was a well-planned escape, so assume they have beards and badly fitting clothes, and are dirty and smelling bad from living in the forest."

The door to Nanny Raya's apartment opened and Tauri bolted through. Jenna opened her arms to hug him. "There you are. Mommy's going to work now. Do you want Duke with you again today?"

"Yes." He looked shyly at Beth. "Is Aunty Beth staying today? She said she would teach me how to play games on the computer."

Jenna raised both eyebrows. "Really?"

"The games require math skills and recognition." Beth lifted her chin. "They switch on the parts of the brain that understand technology. The younger the better, but if you disapprove, I'll understand."

As Beth was an IT genius, Jenna wouldn't miss the chance to have her tutor her son. She nodded in agreement. "I think that would be a great idea." She looked at Tauri. "Beth has to work as well, so don't be a pest."

"I'll be good." Tauri grinned broadly.

"Don't worry, we have a few things to do as well today." Nanny Raya walked into the kitchen. "I'll check in during the day, so you can be sure everything's okay."

Jenna's phone chimed. She looked at the caller ID and smiled. "The guys are waiting outside for us." She bent and kissed Tauri on the cheek and ruffled his hair. "I'll see you later.

Be a good boy." She turned as Duke came toward her and rested his head against her leg. He obviously missed Kane. "Stay and look after Tauri for me." Duke gave her his doggy smile and wagged his tail.

As Tauri disappeared through the connecting door with Duke on his heels, Jenna shrugged into her jacket, picked up her things, and headed for the door. She peered into the sky, searching for a helicopter. Apart from the murders, everything had been quiet on the home front. Perhaps Kane was keeping Souza busy. She sent up a silent prayer to keep him safe and climbed into the Beast. *Let this be over. I need you here with me.*

THIRTY-SEVEN

HELENA

Stuck inside a cabin on the outskirts of Helena, Kane stood from the table and paced up and down. With each step, the old cabin creaked under the weight of years, its wooden beams darkened by time and the elements. He inhaled air thick with the scent of pine and the faint, lingering aroma of woodsmoke. A small fire crackled in the stone hearth, casting flickering shadows on the rough-hewn walls. He stared into the flames. His retentive memory for faces and names had proved useful. Since arriving he'd scanned so many files his eyes hurt. Along with Wolfe, he'd discussed different plans of action, and Wolfe had quizzed him repeatedly on faces and names he might come in contact with during the mission. Knowing the difference between a potentially brutal killer and a gofer was vital information. In a shootout, he didn't intend to take down innocents. Souza was his main target, but he'd been given the green light on other key members of his new team. When told they'd be expecting collateral damage, it was a nice way to say "kill them all" without giving a specific order. He took only specific orders.

He'd been deployed into some of the harshest places on earth and there'd always been one or two friendlies. This time they were throwing him into a nest of mercenaries—men paid by Souza to do his bidding. Many of these men were trained military who'd placed wealth over their country. This was the problem with allowing a cartel kingpin to escape prison. They always had a supply of money hidden somewhere, or more likely, supplies of money. Enough to rebuild an empire of death and destruction. Even though the FBI and DEA had literally destroyed Souza's organization, he had enough gullible people to start up again in seconds. Mercenaries were plentiful as the riches were great, and in this mission were an unknown quantity he'd need to deal with face-to-face. This regurgitating of an empire happened almost overnight. So many people were willing to sell their souls to distribute drugs or sell woman and children into slavery. Money had a dreadful allure. In the right hands it could do great things, and in the wrong hands it could ruin lives. The choice was a frightening one, and poor people trying to feed their families would take the risk. These were the people Souza recruited, expendable and replaceable couriers and distributors to move his product. The only way to stop Souza was to remove him permanently. However, getting to him would be another matter.

At the sound of an engine approaching and wheels on gravel, Kane pulled his weapon and pressed his back to the wall to peer out of the window. It was the height of the tourist season in Helena and their arrival hadn't caused as much as a ripple, but *caution* had become his middle name. He peered through the net curtain without moving as Wolfe climbed from the truck, carrying pizza boxes, a six-pack of beer, and a bottle of red wine under one arm. Kane opened the door and stood to one side. His stomach growled as the pizza's cheesy aroma mingled with the earthy scent of the cabin, creating a comforting, homey atmosphere. Food was a comfort he indulged in and as he grasped the bottle of red wine he grinned at Wolfe. "Pinot noir, you sure know the way to a man's heart."

"Well, we don't know what kind of food we'll be getting when we hit the next town. From the intel coming in, most of the places Souza has visited are dives." Wolfe dropped the boxes on the table alongside the beer and went to the sink to wash his hands. "The eggs and bread we brought with us will do for breakfast. They'll send me the meeting place coordinates first thing in the morning. I figure it's going to be a cloak-and-dagger mission. I'm to leave my chopper here. One will be supplied for me to fly to the meeting. What happens next, we'll find out on the day. Do you figure you're ready?"

Kane washed his hands and then went to the table, lifted a slice of pizza, folded it, and took a bite. He hummed in delight and then fixed his gaze on Wolfe. "I'm always ready."

The office hummed with activity. Jenna gathered everyone into the conference room and her first priority was contacting the next of kin of the two victims. She sent Rio and Rowley with the bad news and asked them to inquire if both women followed a pattern. Did Maya run at the same time each morning and did Elaine close the library and walk the same way home every night of the week? This information was imperative if they discovered that there was a fourth serial killer in town. Once Rio and Rowley had set out, she placed her phone on speaker and called the DOC command post to notify them about the current murder. "I don't have the manpower to send out our drones, so I'll need your teams moving closer to town and checking all the outlying cabins in the immediate area. We know what vehicle they have available to them and we have BOLOs out on them. We have had no sightings of either the prisoners or the vehicle in the vicinity of Stanton Forest."

"We've found various camps with hikers and guys fishing. All of these left their vehicles in the parking lot on the edge of Stanton by the hiking trail and walked to their destinations." The coordinator let out a long sigh. *"Although we haven't seen*

*any drones in the area, and the forest is vast. It seems real strange
that we haven't encountered any sign of the prisoners since they
left the last cabin. I figure that someone is giving them the heads-
up about where we are, and they are taking evasive action. We
have fresh boots on the ground this morning and they are moving
slowly toward town along the eastern side of the river. If one of
the prisoners did commit the murder this morning, then we have
no reason to believe they're moving in a westerly direction. I will
notify you immediately if we come across any evidence."*

Twirling her pen in her fingers, Jenna looked at her team.
None of them had any questions and she gave them a small nod.
"We'll be searching empty buildings around the perimeter of
town. I've released another immediate report this morning, and
I expect the townsfolk to call in on the hotline if they see
anyone suspicious hanging around. Thank you for your
assistance. I hope to hear from you soon." She disconnected.

The moment she placed her phone on the table it chimed.
The caller ID told her it was Norrell calling from the medical
examiner's office. "Good morning. Do you have an update?"

*"I recall Wolfe mentioning that you preferred to have the
preliminary findings on murder victims ASAP. I went ahead and
examined the two female victims. I believe my findings are
conclusive, but I will be completing both autopsies today. Just as
a side note, I worked late last night to complete the autopsy on
Robert Moore, the second forest victim. Time of death concurs
with the timeline in Amy Clark's statement. Death was from
sharp force trauma to the neck. I'll send you a detailed report
later today."*

"Do you believe that Moore's and both of the female
murders were committed by the same person?" Jo leaned
forward in her chair. "As we have three serial killers on the
loose, it would be interesting to know if they are all killing."

*"The sharp force trauma in three of the murders appears to
be inflicted by the same knife but I'll need to wait until the DNA*

evidence is processed. We'll have the murder weapon, but who wielded it in the women's murders is inconclusive at this stage. I have taken swabs, but if these men were wearing gloves, it will be difficult to find any trace evidence." Norrell tapped away on her keyboard. *"The first female victim, who we are assuming is Elaine Harper, sustained twenty-five sharp force trauma injuries. Most of them were used to inflict pain. It was a vicious attack by someone who knew what they were doing, so I surmised this was the work of one of the serial killers as it fits the MO of Carl Romero. When he was done, the final blow was an upward thrust under the sternum to slice the heart in two. This was the kill shot."*

Jenna placed her pen on the desk, reached for a cup of coffee, and took a few long sips. The details of the murder were horrific. Even after all the times she'd stood in an autopsy room during an examination, the horror of what one person could do to another still made her sick to her stomach. Kane had always insisted that empathy was a good thing, and once she lost that, she needed to quit her job. "Okay and what about Maya Brooks?"

"She suffered a flesh wound caused by a gunshot to her upper thigh. This had been treated and I concur that this happened as recorded in the 911 call. Her cause of death is from massive blood loss from a severed carotid artery, resulting in cardiac arrest. There are no signs of sexual assault in either victim. Once I have completed all my tests, I will send you a full report."

Twirling her cup in her fingertips, Jenna frowned. "Defensive wounds?"

"Not in Maya Brooks. She has scratches consistent to running through the forest, but from the angle of the wound to her throat, she was attacked from behind and above. I'd say she was on the ground, maybe on her hands and knees, when attacked."

Picturing the scene in her mind, Jenna nodded. "Thanks.

Rio and Rowley are notifying next of kin. They are local, and Rio and Rowley will collect DNA swabs of the victims' mothers' for identification."

"That's good. I already have positive IDs on both male victims. They are, as you suggested, Troy Lee, from the first murder, and Robert Moore, from the second. If that's all, I'll get back to work."

Jenna searched the faces of her team. No one had questions. "Okay, thanks, Norrell." She disconnected and leaned back in her chair. "Suggestions?"

"I figure we need to spread out across town and hang out anywhere they might drop by for food." Carter waved a toothpick held between finger and thumb. "They wouldn't be foraging for food. All of them are city folk. We know they have cash. The cabins were ransacked and they have clothes as well."

"They'll park some ways from their target store and walk. Two vehicles and three men. One might remain with a vehicle." Styles stood and refilled his cup from the coffeemaker. "We're not dressed like FBI and won't be noticed." He carried his cup to the table and sat down. "Taking them in will be a problem. They have nothing to lose and might take hostages if cornered."

Shrugging, Jenna blew out a long breath. She would be noticed. Her face was all over the front pages of the newspapers this morning alongside the pictures of the prisoners, and moving through town would make her a target. Leaving the ranch had put her in danger. She needed to be sensible. "I'm sure you are all competent in taking down these men. If you spot one, call for backup. Rio and Rowley will be back soon, and Raven is available as well. Use your coms and keep me updated. If Beth or Kalo gets a sighting, I'll call you."

Everyone stood, apart from Raven, and headed out talking among themselves. She turned to Raven. "I can't sit here doing nothing." She opened a drawer and pulled out a tourist map. "I figure we check out these old buildings." She circled them with her pen and pushed them toward him. "If we see signs of habitation, the DOC teams are close enough to call in for backup."

"You're not concerned about being shot at?" Raven raised both eyebrows.

Shaking her head, Jenna looked at him. "I'm not planning on getting out of the truck. All these places, we can drive around."

"Dave said his truck was bombproof but guys exaggerate." Raven shrugged. "I'm not sure if risking your life is what he had planned for me."

Standing, Jenna holstered her weapon. "Dave never exaggerates, and trust me, the escaped prisoners don't have the weapons to take out the Beast. Let's go."

THIRTY-NINE

Hours later, exhausted, Jenna climbed from the Beast, and grabbing her cup of to-go hot chocolate, headed inside to her office. For once in her life, she regretted having her office at the top of a flight of stairs. Her back had been getting worse over the last couple of days, and with Wolfe being away and Norrell being so busy conducting the autopsies, she didn't have anyone to ask if this was a normal part of pregnancy. She went into her office and sat down in her chair, putting her feet up on the footrest Kane had given her. Keeping her feet elevated prevented swollen ankles he had insisted. She smiled as she recalled his concerned expression as he slipped it under her desk and lifted her feet onto it. She checked her watch. It was a little after five and she wondered what he was doing right at this moment. Not knowing was driving her crazy. She had dated many men in the military during her time with the DEA while living in DC and realized that being the wife of anyone in the military would be extremely stressful. Forcing her mind back to work as Raven came into the office carrying bags of takeout, she glanced up at him. "All the sightings of the escaped prisoners that came in on the hotline didn't pan out. Rio and Rowley have been running around town all day. I just sent them home. We might need them later."

"It's been a washout." Raven went to the coffee machine and refilled it before sitting down in one of the chairs before her desk. "They can't have been noticed by the prisoners. They visited anywhere that sells food and swapped venues back and forth all day. Oh, and Styles went to collect Beth and drop Jo at the ranch. Beth did the same group of eateries and didn't see any of the escapees. I've no idea what they're eating unless they took supplies from the last cabin they ransacked."

Ravenous, Jenna pulled a pack of sandwiches from one of the bags. She'd missed lunch, but Raven had insisted she drink the milkshake he grabbed for her from the convenience store at the end of town. "That's likely, but after being away for so long, a burger would be tempting. The eateries are open late, so maybe they'll come into town again tonight."

"I figure what's tempting them is more likely to be someone to murder." Raven helped himself to a burger and fries. "Beth and Styles are grabbing a meal at Aunt Betty's. Carter is on his way in, so I ordered enough food for everyone."

The egg salad sandwich tasted like ambrosia, and Jenna let out a long contented sigh. "That's good. I hope you ordered a ton of it because I'm starving." Recalling that Raven was a registered GP, she eyed him over the top of her to-go cup. "I know you're not an obstetrician, but do you know if a really bad backache is a problem in pregnancy?"

"Many women suffer backaches during the third trimester. Mainly due to the weight of the baby and the position. I can see that your baby has dropped dramatically in the last forty-eight hours or so. This is quite normal as they are getting ready to be born. When are you due?"

Rubbing her belly, Jenna smiled. "About three weeks, but my obstetrician believes the baby is a little more mature than the dates would indicate. She believes it will be early."

"Well, sometimes backache can be early labor pains, so if you get any contractions, you'd better let me know." Raven gave her a long look. "I'll take you to the hospital and notify your obstetrician you're on your way. Don't panic, babies take their own time, but if your water breaks, we'll need to leave right away."

Nodding, Jenna smiled. "No contractions and my back feels better now I'm sitting down, but thanks. It's good to know I have you looking out for me."

"My pleasure." Raven nibbled on a fry. "I'm enjoying being involved in this case. I've learned a great deal being with you this week." He turned to toss his dog, Ben, a fry. "Do you have any dog food here? I'll be happy to replace it. It's time to feed Ben."

Jenna pointed to the closet behind her. "In there, the stuff in the blue bag belongs to Carter. Zorro is picky. We have bags of it at the ranch as well because Duke will eat anything. The red bags are high protein and they make Duke drool just looking at the bag, so I think in dog food, they must be like steak. Use what you like, no need to replace it. He's one of the team and it goes on the office tab."

"Thanks." Raven went to the closet, took out a clean bowl and filled it. He placed it beside the water bowl and indicated toward it. "There you go, Ben. Enjoy." He sat down and lifted his burger. "Best burger in town, like everything else from Aunt Betty's."

"You got that right." Carter walked in the door. "I hope there's one of those burgers in the bag for me."

"Yeah, I ordered enough for everyone." Raven pushed the bag toward him. "Hot food in this bag and there's peach and apple pies in the refrigerator."

"There's always pies in the refrigerator." Carter removed his toothpick and tossed it into the garbage. "Dave usually has a constant supply. When they're cooking cherry pies at Aunt

Betty's Café, he doesn't need to order. They just bring them right along." He grinned and pulled out a burger and a packet of fries. As he sat down, he looked at Jenna. "I figure the prisoners are going to move into town at dusk. They won't be together. I believe they will drop one of them on the outskirts of town, and the other two will split up."

Chewing slowly, Jenna swallowed her bite of sandwich. "I was just discussing that with Raven before you arrived. We are all trained to handle missions and move around unnoticed when necessary. The storeroom here is filled with tactical gear and everything we'll need to move around town like shadows. The problem is this is a big town, and we'd need to have sightings before we move out. We can't just hang around town on the off chance that one of them walks by." She sipped from her to-go cup and then placed it on the desk. "It has been very quiet in town. People are staying off the streets, and if Kalo had noticed them, he'd have called right away. We need to be alert, so we rest up for the next couple of hours." She looked from one man to the other. "If you're not aware, there are showers and plenty of fresh towels in the men's locker room." She took a key from the drawer in her desk and pushed it across the table toward them. "Here's the key for the storeroom. The small key opens the gun locker. Take what you need, including ammo. When you've finished eating, we'll meet back here in my office at seven and hope that these escapees make the mistake of walking into my town tonight."

FORTY

JEZABEL

A little after six, Kane sat at the bar in a little backwoods town by the name of Jezabel, his feet resting on the brass footrail polished by a century of boots. He'd taken a position away from the growing gaggle of loudmouthed men at the opposite end. It was like stepping back in time. His room wasn't much better. It smelled old and musty, and he figured, by the surprised expression of the barkeep when he'd requested a room, not many people stayed above the saloon. He'd noticed a decent motel as he'd driven the battered old truck into town. No doubt Wolfe would be staying there. The saloon was what he might describe as quaint. Brown paint peeled from the outside of the saloon, and the worn floorboards creaked when he headed for the entrance. Out front, a hitching rail bleached from the sun over the last hundred years or more sat waiting for the last group of cowboys to ride into town looking for a drink.

He imagined a stagecoach pulling up, its horses wet with sweat and filled with passengers looking for a better life. The sign out front, hung at a jaunty angle from rusty chains, had greeted hundreds of people over decades. It had seen better days. The faded green letters with red surrounds were barely readable and a stark contrast to the neon sign on the corner. From inside whiskey-tainted air mixed with a smell of leather, and beer spilled onto the sidewalk. Balls on a pool table clinked, and from an old jukebox, the sweet voice of Patsy Cline came over the mumble of voices. From the number of men sitting on stools hugging glasses of beer or whiskey along the long polished bar, this place was the hub of the town. From the smell, Kane figured they all worked with cattle.

After Wolfe had attended an extensive briefing conducted by a small group of trusted agents, Kane decided the best way forward would be for him to step into an ongoing DEA under-cover investigation into fentanyl distribution. From the intel, while in prison Souza had continued his illegal importation of fentanyl from China and been organizing dealers with wide-reach setups to purchase the drug from him. Fentanyl was a perfect drug for trafficking, mainly because such a small amount was needed to be smuggled. Disguised as a packet of salt, it often slipped into Mexico and then was carried into the US using drug mules. From there it was added to various substances to make pills, which were easier to sell on the streets.

It disturbed Kane how fast this drug was spreading into the US. As little as two milligrams could be lethal, which meant one single kilo of fentanyl could potentially kill half a million people. The plan in place, the major concern was that Kane was known to the organization, although they last saw him wearing a partial disguise. This time he'd used a professional movie FX artist to add fake tattoos. He now displayed full sleeves on both arms and a rattlesnake crawling up his neck. They'd added a long jagged scar down one cheek. He'd kept everything apart from the scar well-covered as he hurried back to the chopper supplied to Wolfe.

It had taken two chopper rides for him and Wolfe to arrive outside of Jezabel, where they'd parted company. He glanced at his reflection in the mirror behind the bar and a stranger looked back at him. Wolfe had picked up untraceable weapons, the rest of his disguise, and a suitcase filled with old clothes. After being dropped at a gas station ten miles from town, he'd changed in a filthy toilet. He wore a shoulder holster carrying an M18 pistol, same as his own, under a blue and gray plaid shirt, hanging open over a faded black T-shirt, threadbare jeans, and his own scuffed work boots. He'd found an old truck waiting for him and headed into town. The disguise had given him over-the-collar light brown hair, brown contact lenses, and tattoos that looked so real Wolfe had walked past him on the sidewalk outside the saloon. It was fortunate that when two or three big guys sat at the bar alongside him, for once in his life he didn't stick out like a sore thumb.

Uncomfortable at having his back to the door, Kane sipped a bottle of beer and kept his attention fixed on the reflection in the mirror. He'd balked at wearing the brown Stetson the powers that be had supplied him with and picked up a trucker's cap from the gas station. Communication would be difficult. Souza's crew would know every trick in the book and be checking him out. They wouldn't know about the GPS subdermal implant, something he'd vowed never to agree to again, but after his last encounter with Souza's men, he wasn't taking the chance of not being found. He also had a tiny communication device set inside a stud earring with an unde-tectable speaker the thickness of a hair curled inside his ear. The clarity of the sound was remarkable. Being able to access experimental military inventions made his life easier. Although, how he'd explain having a pierced ear to Jenna when he arrived home would be difficult. That's one thing he liked about Wolfe. If new inventions became available, he'd get them.

The conversation inside grew louder as more cattlemen flowed through the doors. Most were dressed much the same as him, with the exception of dusty cowboy hats. The influx of ranch hands was much the same as in Black Rock Falls. Work was plentiful at this time of year, and on Friday nights many of the men left the confines of the bunkhouses to spend time in town. Along with the men arrived a number of what he would describe as barflies. These women squeezed in among the men crowded around the bar, filling the room with the scent of cheap perfume. He dropped his gaze to his beer as a woman with bright red lipstick and long dyed black hair hanging down to her waist sidled up toward him. He figured her jeans had been sprayed on and a bare midriff showed underneath the shirt tied above her waist. He regarded her from under his lashes as she managed to climb onto the stool beside him and presented her ample cleavage to him. He sighed. Anyone he came in contact with was a problem, but this woman might just make him appear as one of the boys.

Coming to this grimy watering hole was to make contact with one of Souza's many fentanyl distributors. He needed to get closer to the man himself, and the intel was that Eduardo Souza hadn't left the state. Traces of him had been detected, including CCTV facial recognition of him, and his known accomplices had been detected in neighboring towns. Souza was on the move and had chosen to hole up in the older small towns, which lacked an abundance of technology. Before Kane arrived, DEA agents had planned on making contact in the guise of a big-time distributor. The team behind Kane had removed every agent from the town, leaving only him and Wolfe to hunt down Souza. Kane didn't want to get involved in the fentanyl distribution. He wanted Souza and would use any means to that end. If he exposed the players in Souza's distribution network, the DEA could mop up after he'd gone. It had taken negotiations at the highest level to risk exposing him again. Others had been suggested to take his place, good men, but Souza was threatening Jenna and Tauri and now it was personal. With permission from POTUS, he'd been sent on a sanctioned mission and wouldn't return home unless he took out Souza or died trying.

"You new in town?" The woman leaned closer. "Me too. Buy me a drink?"

Aware of people causing distractions to enable an accomplice to sucker punch him from behind, Kane kept his gaze on the mirror. The smell of her perfume crawled up his nose, and her long hair brushed his bare forearms. His mind went to Jenna's honeysuckle scent, so subtle and alluring. He sighed, ignored the woman, and continued to sip his beer. *This is all I need.*

"Come on, honey." The woman leaned against him, pressing one leg so hard against him the heat from her body soaked through his jeans. "It's no good crying in your beer. Something brought you here. Talk to me. I'm a good listener and I can make you smile."

Perhaps she was just a sex worker. He lifted his left hand and wiggled his fingers, allowing the gold band to catch the light. He'd never worn a wedding ring on a mission before. Allowing the enemy an edge to use against him would never happen, but Souza already knew about Jenna. The ring was staying on. "I'm married."

"Why would that make a difference?" The woman ran her fingertips over the back of his hand. "She's not here now and you are all on your lonesome. How would she ever know?"

Shaking his head slowly, Kane looked at her from under his lashes. "*I* would know."

"Who would believe that a big tough cowboy like you is scared of his wife?" She spun around her barstool to rest both elbows on the bar. Her attention fixed on him.

Keeping watch on the people moving around behind him, Kane took another sip from his bottle. "It's called respect and it goes both ways."

"I'm sure if she's a liberated woman like most these days,

she wouldn't be too worried about you having a drink with me then, would she?" She smiled like a snake. "I mean, as she can trust you not to stray." She giggled. "Don't you find me the least bit attractive at all?"

Not discounting the fact Souza may have sent a woman to check out the latest acquisition to his distribution team, Kane shrugged. "Maybe." He raised two fingers to the barkeep and two bottles of beer arrived. He flicked her a glance. "What's your name?"

"China." She flicked her hair over one shoulder and took a beer and sipped. "Where are you staying?"

Fully aware "China girl" was the local street name for fentanyl. Kane pointed to the ceiling. Either Souza had sent a woman as a contact or maybe her name really was China. He needed to find out. He scanned the room and then flicked her a glance. "Why the twenty questions? You looking for someone, or something?"

"That depends." China swiveled on her barstool. "What's your name?"

Kane used the code name Wolfe had given him. "Angelo."

"Hmm the 'Angel of Death,' huh? You don't look so tough." China licked her lips and sighed. Maybe one day you'll tell me how you got that name."

Shaking his head, Kane observed her in the mirror. "I doubt it. You wanna do business?"

"That depends on how much you need and how much you've got." China met his eyes in the mirror's reflection. "Why don't you finish your beer and I'll follow you upstairs."

Kane looked at her and snorted. "I don't figure you could hide what I need in that outfit."

"I'm the first step, honey." China gave him a slow smile. "We don't take chances with strangers around these parts."

Nodding, Kane reached for his second bottle of beer. "That's good to know."

Two clicks came over his communication device, and he looked into the mirror as Wolfe walked into the saloon. He would have heard everything and would be watching his back. As Wolfe walked up to one of the men playing pool as if he knew him, Kane slipped from his seat, beer in hand, and headed for the stairs. "Room four."

FORTY-ONE

Shouldering his way through the men surrounding the pool tables, Kane slipped through the door leading to a dimly lit passageway. Flickering light bulbs cast his shadow over the worn wooden walls. Remnants of the saloon's long history hovered in the scent of aged whiskey and stale tobacco tainting the air. His footsteps echoed softly on the creaky floorboards as he made his way toward the narrow staircase at the end of the hall. The staircase groaned under his weight, as if protesting the intrusion. He slid his hand over the cool banister, smooth from years of use. A door behind him creaked, and the muffled sounds of laughter and clinking glasses drifted up from the saloon below. He paused to glance behind him and caught the sight of China's black hair and listened as she pressed her back against the wall and whispered into her phone. He frowned. He assumed her backup or backups would be in the bar. Maybe they believed he'd be a soft touch or vulnerable to her charms. He snorted and, shaking his head, continued up the steps and, scanning the shadows, negotiated the small dimly lit corridor. The musty odor made him crave the clean alpine air of Black Rock Falls. Wallpaper, faded and peeling from years of neglect, revealed patches of the original wood beneath. He wondered why it had been left to rot when business seemed to be doing just fine. He walked past a series of closed doors, each marked with a tarnished brass number, until he reached room four.

He used an old brass key to open the door. Inside the neon lights of the saloon's sign cast a faint glow into the room. Partially obscured by heavy dusty curtains, the window offered a view of the street below. Three men leaned against a pickup shooting the breeze. The old truck he'd driven into town sat beside a variety of vehicles, and across the road, he made out Wolfe's truck outside the general store. Footsteps came along the passageway and China stood at his open door. Kane stared at her, saying nothing. He'd learned over the years that in any negotiation allowing the other party to start the conversation often gave him an advantage.

"I've spoken to the boss." China stepped inside and pushed the door shut behind her.

Kane shrugged, allowing his shirt to fall open to display his shoulder holster. Wearing one wasn't unusual in these parts, but he wanted to see her reaction. If China was a spokesperson for Souza, she wouldn't be concerned about weapons. She'd be able to take care of herself and likely had men stashed all over the hotel. Stepping into an undercover DEA agent's shoes so late in a mission was risky. Although taking down a cartel had been the mission, the man at the top had been a mystery as the meet had been negotiated weeks before Souza escaped from prison. The realization that Souza had been running his empire from a jail cell would cause an overhaul of the prison system. He nodded. "I guess now that he's out of prison, things will go back to normal?"

"That's the plan." China eyed him with suspicion. "How do you know the boss? I figured you were a new kid in town."

Smiling, Kane looked away and then back at her. "You have

me all wrong. One name is all I'm giving you. Mateo. Him and me, we had an understanding."

"It's a whole new ballgame now." China leaned against the door. "You want to play in our game, you'll need to prove your loyalty."

Kane straightened. "How so?"

"You figure I'm stupid?" China glared at him. "Lift up your shirt and drop your pants."

Giving her a long sweeping look, Kane smiled. "You first. I'm not the trusting kind."

"You figure I can hide a wire in this?" China indicated to her shirt and then untied the front and allowed it to fall open. She lifted it and turned slowly, revealing a Glock 22 tucked into the back of her tight jeans. Raising both eyebrows, she met his gaze. "Your turn."

Lifting his T-shirt he gave her a slow smile. "I'm not dropping my pants. If you want to pat me down, be my guest." He pulled down his shirt when she refused. "Now what does the boss need me to do to get this done? I don't have much time."

"He needs you to clean out a rats' nest and collect what's owed him. I'll give you directions. I hope you have a good memory because I'm not writing anything down." China slowly tied her shirt.

Kane shook his head. "Why can't he send his own men to do it? I'm alone without my team and he knows it. It wasn't part of the deal."

"I know Mateo had many side operations. So, fine, you're not a small-time operation. You guys need each other, so cooperate. He needs to know you're not a plant." She moved closer to him and stared into his eyes. "Undercover cops don't kill street scum. You'll be on your own out there because Souza doesn't intend to allow him or his men to walk into another FBI trap."

Sighing, Kane looked at her. "Oh, stop, you'll have me in tears. This is business—period. I'm not loyal to anyone but me.

If he can't supply what I need then I'll find someone else. You need me to do a little test to prove I'm not a cop, to make him feel better. Bring it on but move it along. I have couriers waiting for product and I've been wasting too much time in this dive."

"Listen to me." China lowered her voice to just above a whisper and stepped away from the door. "You don't understand who you're dealing with. Do you believe I want to be here, risking my life? You could have slit my throat."

Unimpressed, Kane stared at her. "True, but why would I when you're the link to meeting the boss?"

"You're just like him." China's eyes blazed. "You use people."

Wondering where this was leading, Kane stared at the ceiling and then lowered his gaze back to her. She wasn't an addict like most he'd dealt with in his career. "Do I? You don't know me at all."

"I want out of this place." She ran a hand down his arm. "You're going places. After I get you to Souza and you do the deal, take me with you."

Shaking his head, Kane glared at her. "I'm married. What makes you think I'd do something crazy like that?" He blew out a breath, frustrated by the delays. "Maybe we should call this off. I have other contacts who won't make me jump through hoops."

"You must do it." She gripped his arm and stared into his eyes. "Souza has my little sister." Her expression turned sorrowful and her eyes filled with unshed tears. "If I can't make you comply, he'll kill her or sell her into slavery. I beg you. Make us part of the deal and take us with you." She pressed against him. "I'll do anything to save my sister. If you don't want me, I could make you good money. I'll do anything you say. Please help me."

Knowing what Souza was capable of, Kane searched her face, but it was the little shudder that made him question his own judgment. Did she see him as a way to escape the cartel? Jenna had been stuck in a family and abused with no chance of escape. If he'd been there to help her...? He cleared his throat. "I'll think on it but I want a long-time business relationship with Souza. Messing with you might jeopardize it and that's never going to happen"—he stared out the window and then swung his gaze back to her—"unless he suggests it to sweeten the deal, but I'm not speaking to one of his boys. It's him and me or no deal. I want his word tonight. I don't have time to mess around. Got it?" He shrugged. "Get my terms and then I'll get you and your sister out of here. Now, give me the details of the rats' nest."

"Okay, listen up."

FORTY-TWO

BLACK ROCK FALLS

It was good to be in Black Rock Falls again, and Beth Katz had a particular serial killer in her sights. It wasn't common knowledge that Carl Romero, known as the Blue Man, had been responsible for murdering her only living relative two weeks prior to her mother's death. She'd found her Aunt Carol beaten, bludgeoned, raped, and strangled. She'd sat beside her, holding her hand as she died. Aunt Carol had uttered a few words before she died, and those words were imprinted in Beth's brain. *The gas man.*

When the cops arrived, they'd taken little notice of her once they knew she dropped by regularly after school, to wait for her mother to collect her on the way home from work. It had been some years later when Beth noticed the headlines on a local newspaper announcing Carl Romero, the Blue Man, had been arrested for the murders of a string of women. The article went on to say that he'd gained access to the victims' homes on the pretense of being a gas man searching for a leak. He'd got his nickname because witnesses had seen a man wearing blue coveralls leaving the premises. Once she'd joined the FBI, Beth had hunted down the files on Romero and discovered that her aunt's murder was never included in his list of crimes. In fact, he was charged with only his last five murders, and rumors had it that he'd boasted in prison to killing over one hundred women. Now he was out and killing again.

Since arriving she'd considered putting her grievances toward him on the back burner and allowing justice to take its course. He'd die or be in prison for life, but when Norrell discovered his DNA all over the quiet librarian Elaine Harper and all three prisoners' DNA on Maya Brooks, things had changed. The Tarot Killer inside her had risen to seek revenge for not only her aunt but the other ninety-seven women he'd murdered. If he did, by some miracle, face trial for the recent murders, it would make no difference. A life sentence without parole was like thirty years, and apart from the death penalty for victim number one, he had received four life sentences for the others. She'd discovered his life in prison was better than most. He had influence and benefactors who made his life inside comfortable. He needed to pay for his crimes, and no one had been executed in Montana since 2016. Although current information signaled this might change, if she had the opportunity, she'd take him down. Although she'd be risking everything, it was a chance she'd be willing to take.

Beth glanced up from her laptop. She'd been watching the facial recognition program run the footage from live CCTV cameras around town. There was something fascinating about watching faces flash like fast-forwarding the TV ads, although they'd slowed in the last hour or so as darkness crept into town along with the mist rising from the river. She dragged her attention away from the screen. If there was a match, she'd hear a loud buzzing sound. She stretched and stared at Styles dozing on a sofa in the conference room, ankles crossed and cowboy hat pulled down low over his eyes. Carter was at the other end and the pair of them looked like bookends. Rio and Rowley were busy writing reports. They'd gone home for three hours rest and were eager to lend a hand in catching the prisoners. Across the long table Jenna sat with her feet propped up and chatting on the phone to her son. The atmosphere was strange and unlike any mission she'd been involved in before. She hated waiting and would rather be out in the thick of it. Standing, she went to refill her coffee cup. She had taken two or three sips, when Bear, Style's K9, whined and sat beside the door.

Placing her cup on the table, she walked over to the sofa and kicked the bottom of Styles' boot. "Wake up, your dog needs to go outside."

"What?" Styles sat up with a start and reached for his Smith & Wesson 357 Magnum, aiming the wide muzzle at her face. "Jeez, Beth, I could have killed you."

Beth grinned. It was the only excitement she'd had all day. "But you didn't. Come on, it's dark outside and Bear wants out." She took her coffee from the desk and handed it to him. "Drink this, and wake yourself up. It's been as quiet as the morgue in here. The facial recognition program is linked to my phone, and if it identifies anyone, I'll know right away."

"I'll go with you." Carter stretched and stood. "We'll have a better chance of locating them tonight. The DOC search parties are coming closer and they won't be able to backtrack." He turned and looked at Jenna as'she disconnected from her call. "We'll take the dogs out and do a recon around town."

"There's not many people on Main tonight. Seems they've been listening to the warnings from the media to stay inside and lock their doors." Jenna looked from one to the other. "I'll wait for Raven to return and then decide what to do." Her phone chimed and she listened intently before disconnecting. She looked at them. "The coordinator of the DOC search is dropping by in the next ten minutes to discuss a search pattern. I'll need to be here." She gave Beth a long considering stare. "There's black woolen caps in the storeroom. You might want to cover your hair."

As they all wore black tactical gear, Beth pulled a hat from her pocket. "Yeah, I'm on it." She looked at Styles and Carter. "You too. Those hats cast recognizable shadows."

They headed downstairs and onto Main. The sidewalk was deserted and swirls of thick mist snaked their way across the blacktop to be sucked into the alleyways. The mist seemed to mute the streetlights stretching out the dark spaces in between. As they walked past the dark storefronts their footsteps seemed to echo across town. Wind howled down from the mountains, cold against Beth's cheeks even as summer approached. She pulled on her gloves and brushed her fingers over her weapon in an unconscious check to make sure it was secure in its holster.

The park loomed out of the darkness and at one end a carousel creaked as it circled slowly in the breeze. The swings moved back and forth as if children had just left them. When Styles pushed the gate open, both dogs vanished into the waist-high mist, only the sounds of them sniffing the grass telling their directions. Beth turned to face Main. Across the road only Aunt Betty's Café remained open, the bright light from inside spilling across the sidewalk. Inside, the usual throng of diners was missing, and a woman she recognized as the assistant manager, Wendy, wiped down tables. Her phone signaled an alert and she pulled it from her jacket. "We have a sighting." She placed the phone on speaker and called Jenna. "Did you get that?"

"Yeah, Callahan is in the old part of town, where the deserted warehouses are being sold. A few made into apartment buildings have residents and some are building sites."

Walking up to Styles, Beth touched his arm. "Send us the coordinates. We'll head there now."

"No, I need you in town. I've had sightings of Romero. I'll confirm ASAP."

"I'll take the warehouses." Carter shrugged as he emerged from the darkness close by. "I'll need backup."

"Rio is on his way back to the office." Jenna issued orders to

Rio. *"Beth, if you see Romero, call it in. Stay on Main. I figure Romero is heading your way. I'll update you when we have the confirmation."* She disconnected.

The thrill of the hunt surged through Beth. She bit back a grin and averted her gaze from Styles. "Game on."

FORTY-THREE
TEN STRIDES

The speed with which Wolfe collected vital intel during missions never ceased to amaze Kane. By the time he'd driven halfway to Ten Strides, a busy little mining town approximately an hour's drive away, he'd received enough information to complete his first mission. The group of dealers worked from a dilapidated building on the edge of town and employed local children to sell their drugs. All of the men in charge had been identified as suspects in vicious murders but had escaped arrest by relocating their operation when conditions became too hot. As the lights of the town came into view, Kane pulled the old truck to the side of the road to read the blueprints of the building Wolfe had just sent him. It had once been a printing factory and had fallen into disrepair when the railroad bypassed the town.

Neglected for thirty years, deserted buildings made up most of Ten Strides, but when the mining companies moved in, the railroad spur to the town had reopened and prosperity reigned. As workers became rich, the lowlifes of society moved in to take their money. This drug distribution area had once belonged to Souza, and in the few months he'd been in prison, a new band of dealers had stepped in. From the information China had given him, the men had once worked for Souza but found a new supplier in his absence. When Souza ordered them to deal only with him, they had refused.

Kane considered all aspects of completing the task Souza had set him to prove his loyalty. He had never been a killer for hire. His job was to protect people from a greater harm, so going into the building and blasting away was not an option. If he took out the main players, which would ingratiate him with Souza, someone would need to come in behind him and get any children involved out of their current situation. Many of the children who worked for drug syndicates were either recruited from local gangs or were runaways. He checked the blueprints on his phone. "Have you had eyes on this building?"

"Someone has." Wolfe cleared his throat. *"What do you need to know?"*

Kane checked the aerial images of the street. "Beside it used to be an old fire station. If I can get onto the roof, I'll be able to jump onto the top of the building and enter through the hatch and take them by surprise. Have you come up with a way to ensure there are no kids there when I arrive?"

"Yeah, it took some doing." Wolfe's truck engine roared. *"The DEA had a guy undercover for the last six months. They're aware of what's happening and the method of delivering the drugs. Addicts call a certain number and use a code to purchase something specific. The kids ride out on bicycles to meet the customers. The DEA has two confidential informants on the payroll, so have everything they need to make a purchase. The only way to get all the kids away at the same time is to call the numbers and get them out on deliveries. When they arrive with the drugs, they'll be taken into custody. We'll need split-second timing to achieve this without any of them alerting the main players."* He drummed his fingers on the steering wheel. *"I'll*

give you the heads-up when the kids are clear. We're getting close. Use the coms from now on."

Relieved that none of the kids would be injured or witness what was about to happen, Kane nodded. He shut down his phone and slid it underneath his seat. From this point on, all he would need was the miniature com in his ear. He tapped the earring. "I suggest you start making the calls when I get onto the roof. Once I see the kids leaving the building, I'll go clean out the rats' nest."

Kane drove through the surprisingly busy little town and parked his truck outside the local bar. He stepped out onto the sidewalk and scanned the street without moving his head. Loud music drifted on the air along with the smell of stale beer. He grabbed his duffel from the passenger seat and slung it over one shoulder. From the map, the local dealers distributed drugs from a building in a street behind Main. As he turned the corner the stark contrast between the middle of town and the backroads was remarkable. Empty buildings stretched out as far as the eye could see. Many had rusty old vehicles parked outside as if people had just walked away and left them. Buildings had been burned and stood as charcoal shells, their blackened insides like rotten teeth in an open mouth.

Kids on bicycles hung out in groups outside a dilapidated building. Graffiti covered the walls, and the windows were boarded up. Senses on high alert, Kane stuck to the shadows and approached with caution. He slid into the firehouse entrance and edged his way along the building to recon the drug den. The sounds of laughter, clinking bottles, and voices came from inside. He moved back into the body of the firehouse. "This might be a setup. I can hear more than three people inside and there are seven kids outside with bicycles, so I guess they're expecting a big night as it's Friday. Orders."

"Proceed with caution." Wolfe's voice had fallen into its usual mission calmness. *"I'm close by on Main."*

With no time to waste, Kane headed straight for the fire-fighters' pole. Designed to be slippery to slide down fast, climbing up hand over hand wasn't easy with a full duffel over one shoulder.

Heaving himself through the hole and onto a dusty floor, Kane waited for his eyes to adjust to the darkness before searching for the steps to the roof. He smiled as his tiny flashlight picked up the signage, faded but still readable on the doors along the wall. Papers, dust, and cobwebs littered the entire area. Scratching noises came from the corners and red eyes blinked back at him. He dragged open the door to the roof and it whined in complaint. It had been so long since someone had opened it that it stuck halfway. Kane slipped through, dragging his duffel behind him and took the stairs to the roof.

The roof appeared to be sound but the gap between the buildings was wider than anticipated. He touched his com. "I'm on the roof. Get the kids out of here."

"*Copy.*"

Kane removed his belt and attached it to the shoulder strap on his duffel. Keeping out of sight, he went to the edge of the roof, spun the duffel above his head, and let it go. It sailed across the gap, landing on the opposite roof with a soft plop. Gauging the width of the gap and noting the rough broken red brick along the edge of the roof, he pulled on gloves. Emptying his mind, he walked backward and took a few deep breaths before sprinting to the edge of the roof. Exhilaration spiked an adrenaline rush as he flew across the gap. The air rushed from his lungs as he landed and rolled, ending up beside the roof hatch. He lay still in a pile of dead moldy leaves for a few seconds, listening, but only the sounds of the music and men's voices came from the dilapidated building. Moving with caution, he crawled to the edge of the roof and peered over. One by one the kids were called inside and then left scurrying away on their bicycles.

Moving silently, Kane tried the roof hatch and he pulled it open. Using his flashlight, he peered inside before risking the steps. Dirt and debris crunched under his boots and the hum of a generator came from close by. He slipped through a side door, moving silently through the darkened passageways. Ahead, light crept from under a door and the throb of music came through his boots. He checked the door for any devices or wires, and confident to proceed, he placed one hand on the doorknob and it turned. Slowly, inch by inch, he opened it and pressed one eye to the crack. He found five men inside. One with his back to him was taking stacks of bills from a counting machine and securing them with rubber bands. The other four chilled on a sofa. On a coffee table lay guns surrounded by takeout and empty beer bottles. On one end sat three piles of drugs in small plastic bags, and all the men held phones, waving them as they spoke, as if waiting for the next order. No kids.

Dropping into the zone, he lowered his duffel to the floor and drew his M18 pistol. How the next few minutes went down depended entirely on the five men. Taking a deep breath, he burst into the room. The men went for their guns, but most people caught by an intruder are slow to react. The moment one raised his gun, Kane took him out. *One down.* As they fumbled to kill him, he moved with precision: single shots, center mass. *Three down.*

A screaming woman bolted from an open doorway and jumped on his back, attempting to rake his face with her fingernails. The startled man left alive on the sofa dropped his pistol and dove over the coffee table to retrieve it. Kane holstered his weapon, spun around with his back to the man counting money, and reached up to grab her by the wrists. In her haste to attack him, she'd become a shield. Two bullets hit her, one passing right through and scraping a path across Kane's shoulder. He tossed her body at the man with the gun as the massive man counting the money lunged at him aiming a wild punch.

Ducking and delivering a swift uppercut to the jaw, Kane sent him staggering. He drew his weapon and spun around as the other dealer tossed the body of the woman to the floor and aimed at him. Two taps and the man slid down the wall, jerked a few times, and died. *Four down.* The fifth man had quickly recovered and was approaching with a chair raised high above his head.

"I'm gonna beat you to death." The massive man brought the chair down.

Dancing away as the breeze from the chair brushed his cheek, Kane shook his head. "Never bring a chair to a gunfight."

As the man came again, eyes bulging with rage, Kane shot him in the throat and spun around to check for others, but the only sound in the room came from a phone on a table beside a bill-counting machine. The gangster rap music fit the carnage alongside the stench of gunpowder, male sweat, beer, and death. He cleared the other rooms and then checked the bodies for ID and found none. Taking from his pocket the phone China had supplied when she set up the meeting, he captured images of the dead. Gritting his teeth, he retrieved his duffel and collected the drugs and the stacks of bills. The thing with fentanyl, it didn't weigh much at all, but the idea of returning it and the cash to Souza gnawed at his guts. He hoisted the duffel over one shoulder and pulled a hand grenade from one of the pockets. This place and all the bodies needed to be destroyed. As he walked from the building, he tossed the grenade and then ran at full pelt into an alleyway as the explosion rocked the night. The blast wave hit him in a wall of heat as shattered glass, metal fragments, and broken bricks rushed along the alleyway. Flying out of the entrance flanked by smoke dust and debris, he hurried back to his truck. Inquisitive people spilled out of the bars as he dropped the duffel on the passenger seat and tapped his com. "Six targets down. Five male, one female. The female wasn't mine. I caught a bullet. It skimmed my shoulder. I'll need a first aid kit."

"*Copy. There's one behind the seat, extra ammo, and spare gloves.*"

Kane turned the truck around and headed back to Jezabel. "Thanks. I insisted on delivering the goods and the images in person or the deal's off, and when China put it to him, he agreed."

"*I heard. Into the lion's den.*" Wolfe started his engine. "*I'll be right behind you.*"

Kane shook his head. "Stay back. Souza is street-smart to the max. He'll have men posted along the way. He'll be expecting me to have backup. When I go in, I'll be unarmed. You know that, right?"

"*Yeah. I do.*" Wolfe blew out a long breath but said nothing.

Kane accelerated, wishing he could hear the purr of the Beast's engine. "Tonight we end this once and for all."

FORTY-FOUR

BLACK ROCK FALLS

Eerily quiet on Main, the mist swirled knee-deep as Beth Katz walked alongside Styles. Walking a little ahead of them, Bear seem to fade in and out and sometimes disappeared altogether between the streetlights. The wind blew directly down from the snowcapped mountains, bringing with it a hint of pine and lush underbrush. The sky above and everywhere in between was pitch black. No moon guided them along the sidewalk, but moving in the shadows was something she was used to and she enjoyed the anonymity. If a serial killer was out there hiding in one of the alleyways, they would be as difficult to see as him. When Styles pulled her arm through the crook of his elbow, she looked up at him in astonishment but didn't pull away. A year or two ago she wouldn't have even been walking along a street with him, but since working together they had accepted each other's eccentricities.

"I've figured if one of the escape prisoners was watching us, it would look more normal for a couple walking their dog to be close." Styles patted her hand. "Do you think they've had the opportunity to watch the news?"

Scanning the sidewalk ahead, Beth shook her head. "Not recently. I figured they would have stuck to the forest. Especially after Romero lost control and committed murder." She glanced at him. "We haven't received any reports of any more people going missing in any of the local cabins in the forest and by now neighbors would be watching out for each other."

When Styles' phone buzzed, Beth stared at the caller ID. It was Jenna. "Give me one of your earbuds."

"What is your location?" Jenna's chair wheels squeaked as she moved it across the floor. *"We've had a sighting of a man fitting Romero's description heading toward Cemetery Lane. The old cemetery goes back over one hundred and fifty years. Families have been buried there since the Gold Rush. It's still used by old families, even though the church fell into disrepair fifty years ago. If he is heading in that direction, you'll need to be very careful. The graves haven't been tended for a long time. Many gravestones have toppled over and there's underbrush and tree roots everywhere."*

"Can you give us directions? We are at the end of the park." Styles turned to look at Beth. "Do we need to return to the office and get the truck?"

"No. Turn right at the intersection of Maple and Main. Cemetery Lane is about twenty yards from the intersection on the left. Both sides of Cemetery Lane are wooded, so watch your backs. We've had a few calls tonight. Right now Rowley and one of the Blackwater deputies are handling them. Nothing from Carter and Rio yet. Maggie has offered to stay behind tonight to man the hotline with me. When Raven comes back, we can take over and send her home. Do you need backup?"

"Nah, we're on it." Styles disconnected and took the earbud back from Beth and stuffed it in his jacket pocket.

Biting her tongue about wishing Jenna would remain in the office, Beth looked at Styles and shrugged. "Do you honestly believe that a serial killer would be hanging around a cemetery at this time of night? He has no idea anyone is hunting him down right now and it's not a good place to find a victim."

"None of them know the town as far as I'm aware." Styles unzipped his jacket so he could easily access his weapon. "Maybe he got turned around. I guess we better go and find out. It's dark but we can't use our flashlights. He'll see us coming. I'm planning on sneaking up on him."

If Romero was in the cemetery, she needed to be alone to deal with him. She'd viewed his prison photographs and the size of him was a threat, but none of that mattered once she'd seen what he'd done to Amy Clark, Elaine Harper, and Maya Brooks. He'd never pay for those horrendous crimes even if they returned him to prison. The death sentence would never eventuate. Maybe they'd tack another few life sentences to his jail time and it would mean nothing to him. Already sentenced to death, he had nothing to lose and could kill indiscriminately for his entire life... unless she stopped him. "That's fine by me, but we'll need to split up and use a pincer movement. If either of us flushes him out the other will catch him."

Beth didn't look at his face. He'd have that flash of concern he quickly smothered anytime they went into a situation. She figured by now he'd know she didn't need his protection. She kept her eyes straight ahead, almost feeling his protest.

"This is potentially Carl Romero we're hunting down. He kills first and asks questions later." Styles glanced at her. "I've read about this place. The cemetery has no lights and it's overgrown and there are a number of open graves. You sure you want to split up?"

She nodded. "Absolutely. I trust you to know the difference between Romero and me. I'll be fine. It's you who needs to be careful. Don't creep up on me."

"I'm not suicidal just yet." Styles wiggled his eyebrows at her. "And I have Bear."

Darkness didn't worry Beth. The only thing that had unnerved her had been suffering abuse from her father and during her time in foster care. She figured that once a person had lived through something like that there wasn't much left on the earth to frighten her. She mimicked Styles by unbuttoning her jacket as they headed along Cemetery Lane. "I'll take the right." She crossed the narrow blacktop and walked along the thin sidewalk. Underfoot, the uneven paving was difficult to negotiate. She tripped numerous times, falling into hanging branches. Spider's webs caught in her hair and she batted them away, and yet Styles hadn't made a sound. She glanced in his direction, only to see a shadow moving along, with a smaller shadow beside it. Bear had slipped into K9 mode, and if Romero was in the cemetery, Bear would find him.

The lane opened up to a fence and rusty cemetery gates that hung open. One gate had come away from the post and fallen sideways. She edged her way around the gate and peered into the darkness. Gravestones stood in rows, the ones at the front appearing now and then through the mist as if floating above the ground. Others once white had brown stains and moss covering them. As she walked, she made out the names of the beloved, but most were illegible and some stones had fallen over. A noise close by made her freeze mid-step. In a flutter of wings an owl dropped onto a gravestone with a mouse hanging from its beak not a foot in front of her. Its head turned slowly, its big eyes staring at her and then dismissing her before swallowing the mouse whole. Trying not to gag as the mouse's tail disappeared down the bird's throat, she slid one foot forward feeling gravel beneath her boots and continued on, following the pathway around the perimeter of the cemetery. Behind her in a flap of wings, the owl rose into the sky. She turned to look when something large loomed out of the darkness. Beth stopped and drew her weapon. She would have sworn something moved directly in front of her, or was the swirling mist distorting reality? No footfalls crunched on the gravel ahead of her. Gripping the handle of her Glock, she moved forward, feeling ahead with each step and ducking the long clawing branches of the over-hanging trees. The next second, Bear barked a warning. Picking up her pace when the footpath opened up and she could see a few yards ahead of her, she made out a figure running across the cemetery. Before they reached the path on the other side, they vanished from sight.

Astonished, Beth blinked. Had she actually seen someone or was it a trick of the light and mist? She'd never believed in ghosts, but had she actually seen one? Goosebumps rose on her flesh. She swallowed hard at the sound of a low moan and glanced across the cemetery but couldn't see Styles anywhere. Suddenly feeling very alone, like the night she'd witnessed a mother being murdered and fled to the forest, the cemetery with all its spookiness seemed to close in around her. Some-where here, a serial killer lurked. Pushing back the wave of unease she'd rarely experienced before, she moved closer to the moaning. Ahead, she spotted an open grave and, with her Glock held out in front of her, edged closer to peer inside.

Heart thundering in her chest, she reached for her penlight and shot a small beam of light into the blackness. The light hit the face of Romero. He blinked up at her. His head was on an unusual angle. He'd likely broken his neck in the fall. Beth considered how many women this man had murdered and whether he deserved a lifetime of being cared for in a prison hospital. What he had done to women repulsed her. She moved her penlight around and through the mist found a border of rocks lining the pathway. First, she pulled a sealed tarot card from a zipped pocket in her jacket and removed the covering, which was difficult in her thin leather gloves, and tossed it down into the grave. She extinguished the penlight, bent and rolled the heavy rock to the edge of the grave, and pushed it over. The sound was like a melon being dropped from a height. She kicked gravel over the slight indents in the pathway and straightened. The sentence of death had been completed. Romero would never hurt another woman or child again. Justice had been served.

Hurrying on, Beth moved past mausoleums built long ago. The mist swirling around the dark entrances would scare anyone and played tricks with her mind. The next moment, Bear came bounding toward her. The dog leaned against her legs and then barked once. "Hello, Bear. Where's Styles? Is he okay?"

Her phone vibrated in her pocket and she pressed it to her ear. "Styles?"

"Yeah. I sent Bear to find you. There's no one here. I'm over tripping over tree roots. Let's get out of this place. We'll come back in daylight and search for tracks, but I figure the call was a hoax." Styles loomed out of the darkness, phone in hand. "There you are. I did a complete circle and found nothing. Bear barked at a cat, is all." He pushed his phone back into his pocket. "This place is creepy, isn't it?"

Beth holstered her weapon and pushed her phone back into her jean's pocket. "You could say it's not my ideal place for a date." She grinned up at him.

"Mine either." He held out his arm for her. "We'll call it in and wait for the next sighting. Aunt Betty's is still open. After all this spooky excitement, I need a strong cup of coffee and a slice of cherry pie."

Laughing, Beth slipped her hand into the crook of his arm. "I didn't figure any of the prisoners would be stupid enough to come here. I needed to fight my way through cobwebs and low branches. The fog played tricks with my mind and had me drawing down on shadows. I'm glad I don't believe in ghosts, although I admit tonight had me guessing."

"Oh, I saw ghostly figures and heard moans but that was likely the wind in the trees. The shadows moving when there's no reason for them to move questions my common sense. I guess it makes me a new believer, but I'm not the only person who sees them." Styles stopped to grin at her. "They say they're here in daytime too. Sightings go back decades but they don't concern me." He chuckled. "Like Kane says, it's not the dead people you need to worry about."

FORTY-FIVE

After checking in with the search parties and then meeting with Rowley, Raven stopped at Aunt Betty's for a couple of milkshakes before heading back to the office. His concern for Jenna was growing by the hour. He understood Kane and Wolfe needed to be involved with catching the escaped prisoners, but if so, why weren't they in town? He snapped his fingers as realization hit him. Kane had said they were chasing down the escaped prisoners, and as they weren't with any of the search parties, he and Wolfe had been asked to hunt down Eduardo Souza. He'd heard all about the consequences Kane and Jenna had suffered due to him giving evidence against the cartel kingpin, so Kane had experience dealing with him. This would account for why Jenna never mentioned Kane's or Wolfe's absence. Dealing with serial killers and everything else, she would be under a great deal of stress. Being close to delivery and with her husband in danger wasn't a good mix, especially if it caused her to deliver early. To take a little of the pressure, he'd decided to be her eyes and go personally to speak to everyone involved rather than wait for the DOC coordinator to check in.

As he stepped into Jenna's office, she disconnected from a

call and looked up at him. Dark circles rimmed her eyes. He handed her a milkshake. "What can I do to make this easier for you?"

"Bring Dave home." She sucked on the straw and sighed. "I feel like I've been sleeping in my clothes. I'd call it a night but the hotline is busy. Beth and Styles just called in. They found nothing at the cemetery. It was probably a hoax." She ran a hand through her hair and yawned. "With three serial killers murdering people right on their doorsteps, you'd figure they'd have more sense." She shook her head. "We had a sighting of Callahan on the CCTV, but Carter and Rio checked in before. If he's out there, the guy is a shadow."

FORTY-SIX

JEZABEL

Blood dripped from Kane's fingers as he walked into the saloon, his duffel hanging on his injured shoulder, but not a soul turned to look at him. He went to the end of the bar, which served snacks and coffee. Surprised to see hot cinnamon buns, he ordered a stack and two cups of to-go coffee. He looked at the man behind the bar. "I need to go out. How do I get back in later?"

"We're open until two. By the time I've cleaned up, it's usually around three before I lock up. After that you're on your own." The barkeep handed him a bag and two to-go cups in a cardboard carrier.

Pushing the bag under one arm and juggling the cups, he headed through the door to the stairs and back to his room. Once inside, he locked the door, pushed a chair under the handle, and then sent the images to the number China had preset on the phone. He took a sip of his coffee, removed his wig and soiled clothes, and headed for the shower. The fake tattoos could only be removed with a special solution, so he soaped up. His eyes were gritty from the explosion, but he didn't carry any of the eye drops he needed to remove and reinsert the contact lenses. The wig, tight by necessity, had given him a headache, and he stood beneath the shower longer than necessary. His mind went to Jenna and Tauri. Being away from them was tearing a hole in his heart but he needed to do this. He'd caused this problem and couldn't expect Jenna to live in constant danger for the rest of her life. It was his mess and he wouldn't go home until he'd cleaned it up. His clean clothes and a few personal items were still on the bed where he left them. Wrapped in a towel, he sat on the edge, ate the cinnamon buns, and finished one cup of coffee. His motto, to eat when he could, had always kept him in good stead. He stood and unpacked the first aid kit. The jagged tear across his bicep looked clean enough, but he used the antiseptic in the kit and pulled the wound together with Steri-Strips before applying a bandage. He finished the second cup of coffee and then spent some time brushing the wig to remove the dust and dirt from the explosion. Reluctantly he pulled it back on, looking in the mirror to make sure it was sitting right. He dressed in clean clothes, put on his shoulder holster, and lay down on the bed. However long it took Souza to get back to him about the meet would give him time to rest up. He placed the phone on the bedside table, and with one hand resting on his M18 pistol, he closed his eyes.

Hammering on the door woke him at five after twelve. Kane's ability to wake immediately and jump into action had saved him many times. He stood and pulled on the trucker's cap before removing the chair and opening the door. He'd expected to see China waiting to take him to the meeting, but two burly men pushed their way inside. Kane didn't offer any resistance. He took a few steps back hands raised. "What's your problem?"

"No problem. The boss wants to see you now." A tall wide Neanderthal of a man tried to stare him down. "Hand over your weapon."

Always reluctant to give up his weapon, Kane shrugged. He had no idea what would happen next. "When we get to the meet, unless one of you wants to try to take it from me?" He reached for his duffel and swung it at one of the men. "Carry this for me. It's a gift for your boss."

The Neanderthal's bald partner gave Kane the stink eye but caught the bag, looked inside, and whistled. Kane nodded. "Yeah, I cleaned out the rats' nest. Now can we leave? I've been waiting long enough in this stinking hole." He looked from one to the other. "I'll follow you in my truck."

"That's not gonna happen." The bald man shook his head. "The boss doesn't want anyone to know the location of his hideout, so you'll be blindfolded. If you don't give up your weapon, the deal's off. You don't figure Souza is stupid enough to allow anyone inside his hideout carrying, do you?"

Kane looked away and chuckled. "Doesn't he trust you to watch his back?"

"He trusts us." The bald man sneered at him. "This is a onetime deal to set the terms. From tonight, you'll be doing business with the local boss. His name is Alan Turner. That's not his real name but it doesn't attract attention, does it? It sounds like every other cowboy in town, right?"

Giving him a stare to freeze Black Rock Falls, Kane lowered his voice. "Names mean nothing to me. They all die the same."

"Tough guy, huh? We'll see." He smiled, showing a gold tooth. "If you're lucky, you'll get to see what happens to traitors. It's always a good incentive for new dealers to see what happens when you screw up."

Not intimidated by the men, Kane shrugged. "Money is the only incentive I need."

Kane picked up a jacket from the bed and shrugged into it. He pushed his keys into his pocket, along with a stick of gum, a pack of cigarettes, and a Zippo he'd left on the bedside table. The small pack of Semtex, a plastic explosive, disguised as gum; the detonators inside the cigarettes; and the Zippo had often come in useful during missions and passed unnoticed. He pulled on thin leather gloves and looked at the men. "What are we waiting for?"

"Why are you wearing gloves?" The Neanderthal man raised both eyebrows, making his broad head wrinkle. "You should be accustomed to our weather if you live around these parts."

Towering over the men, Kane opened the door. "I don't like getting blood under my nails." He waited for a reaction but both men just gave him blank looks, no witty comebacks, nothing. "Can we get out of here?"

They weren't taking any chances with him. Pressed between two men in the back of an SUV he allowed the hood to be placed on his head and had no choice but to relinquish his weapon. It made no real difference to the outcome. In seconds, he had formed a plan to take out and disarm the four men surrounding him if necessary. He didn't need to worry about being taken into oblivion. With the tracker chip under his skin, Wolfe could track him anywhere. He would be aware of what was happening as he had been listening to everything that was said.

His mind went to China. Working alongside Jenna had given him a deep compassion for women and children in danger. He understood the situations women became entangled in to save their families. China's eyes had been so imploring. Had she been telling the truth or was it just a ploy to get his sympathy? He'd need to know before this finished tonight, although taking her with him and rescuing her sister would add more time and be a mission that hadn't been sanctioned. Could he spend another day away from Jenna? He'd left her to deal with three serial killers alone and needed to return home. Maybe he could turn China over to the US Marshals? They'd be able to get her into witness protection.

They drove for approximately half an hour and then bumped over uneven ground for maybe ten minutes or so before the vehicle came to a halt and the door swung open. The men got out, pushing him in front of them. Kane straightened, spreading his feet. His hands hadn't been tied and he dragged the hood from his head before they had a chance to stop him. He spun and glared at the men. "No one puts their hands on me. This is your first and only warning."

"We'll put our hands anywhere we choose." Neanderthal man grabbed him by the front of his shirt. His stinking breath oozed out between a smile.

One upward palm strike to Neanderthal man's fat bulbous nose sent bone straight into the brain. He fell backward, and his legs kicked for a few moments before he went still. Kane swung his gaze to the other men. The bald one held his gun in two hands, aiming it at him. He smiled and as the gun lowered, spun and kicked it from his hand and then followed with a stiff uppercut, knocking him flat on his back. Before the other two had a chance to react, Kane attacked, and in five seconds they lay in crumpled heaps on the ground. He bent over the bald guy and retrieved his M18 pistol from his pocket and slid it back into its holster. He grabbed the man by the throat and hauled him to his feet. He eyeballed him with his nose an inch away from his face. "Don't point a gun at me unless you intend to fire it. Just know, before you get time to pull the trigger, I'll have it stuffed halfway down your throat. Now take me to Souza, I'm over playing games with you." He spun a suppressor on his weapon and pushed it into the man's ribs. "Get them to open the door. Tell them you'll be standing guard. I can take it from here."

"They won't do it." The bald man's eyes flashed with defiance, but he took out a communication device. "My orders were to take you to Souza."

Moving behind him, Kane pressed the gun into the back of the man's head. "Then I guess you'll need to be real convincing."

FORTY-SEVEN
BLACK ROCK FALLS

A single streetlight cast an eerie glow over the line of deserted redbrick industrial buildings as Carter scanned the shadows, pausing at each alleyway to shine his flashlight. The old dumpsters, rusty after decades of neglect, cast shadows stretching like fat fingers across the narrow alleyways. The only sound came from Rio's boots as he searched the opposite side of the road. As Zorro wandered into an alleyway, a stray cat arched its back and spat, mouth open and ears flat against its head, with a tail fluffed out to twice its size. Carter snapped his fingers and Zorro looked up at him as if waiting for an explanation. His relationship with Jenna's cat, Pumpkin, was solid, and he even allowed the black silken arrogance to share his basket and knead his cheeks. He smiled to himself. Man might own a dog and they would obey commands, but a cat, well, they owned their humans, and Pumpkin, all big copper eyes and black silk, ruled Jenna's ranch. He'd seen her refuse to allow the dogs to share the basket and neither of them would dare to eat her food. He rubbed Zorro's head. "It's probably got kittens close by." As if he understood the explanation, the dog sneezed and then continued ahead as directed.

They hadn't seen anyone in this area since arriving. Suddenly Zorro froze mid-stride and a low growl rumbled from his chest. Carter hit his com. "Zorro has something. Stand by."

Pulling his weapon, he eased to the corner of the chipped and moss-covered redbrick building to peer into the alleyway as the clunk and slide of a fire escape slid into place. He aimed his flashlight at the man fleeing up the ladder. The man turned to look at him, screwing up his eyes against the light. Carter recognized him as Callahan. "FBI, come down nice and quiet. You know we have the town surrounded with Department of Correction officers everywhere. No one needs to die today."

Ignoring him, Callahan kept climbing the ladder with remarkable speed. He reached the first story and continued up the steps. Carter had no option but to follow him. He pressed his com. "I've spotted Callahan. He is heading for the roof. Follow on street level. He'll need to come down sometime. Don't mess around with this guy. If he draws down on you, take him out."

"Copy, What about Zorro?"

Keeping his attention on the escaping prisoner, Carter turned into the alleyway. "Don't worry about him. He will follow me along the sidewalk. Don't try and touch him and he will ignore you. Try and get ahead of the prisoner. He could come down anywhere. I'm heading onto the roof now."

After scaling the steps, Carter's attention locked on Callahan as he sprinted away, his silhouette a blur against the night sky. Breathing heavily, he took chase, keeping the rusty water tanks and chimneys between them. He must assume Callahan was armed but had no idea if he would stand his ground and shoot it out. The man had spent many years in prison and had an impressive physique and moved with remarkable speed. Increasing his stride, Carter followed. Obstacles covered the roof of the industrial buildings, along with years of slippery detritus. The next moment, the figure in front of him stopped abruptly, took a few paces backward, and then sprinted toward the edge of the building. He leaped over the gap between buildings, landing with a roll and quickly regaining his footing. Holstering his weapon, Carter followed in his path, leaping the distance with ease and landing on his feet in a run.

Ahead, Callahan moved with great speed, darting across the top of the building as if wearing night-vision goggles. Heart pounding in his chest, Carter pushed harder to keep up as Callahan leapt across the next gap. The dark alleyway approached, and Carter had only a few seconds to increase his speed to negotiate the wider gap. In a rush of adrenaline he cleared it. Landing hard and stumbling forward, he rolled and leapt to his feet. Carter's mind raced, calculating every move, every jump, every step. He chased him across two more buildings and ahead was the end of the block. He drew his weapon. He couldn't let Callahan escape.

Ahead, Callahan reached the edge of the building and skidded to a halt, Carter peered over the edge. Below and all around was a sheer drop, the blacktop below a dark abyss. There was nowhere left to run. He aimed at Callahan and walked slowly toward him. If he had a gun, he'd have drawn it by now. "It's over, Callahan. There's no way out."

"You figure you've won, Agent? You have no idea who you're dealing with." Callahan's lips curled into a twisted smile and a knife glinted in his hand.

Raising his weapon, Carter fixed his gaze on Callahan. "Yeah, I do. Drop the knife and you'll be tucked in bed in a nice warm cell before you know it."

"In your dreams." Callahan lunged at him, knife raised.

Without hesitating, Carter fired to disable, not kill, and the noise bounced off the empty buildings. He moved forward as Callahan dropped the knife and staggered, clutching his side, but he wasn't done yet and ran at him. *Murder by cop* flashed in Carter's mind and that was too easy for the crimes he'd committed. He'd take him in alive and paused a fraction too late to take evasive action. A vicelike grip closed around Carter's wrist and they tumbled to the ground, grappling for control. The maniacally grinning face above him was the last sight many murdered women had seen. Carter's Navy SEAL training was like second nature. He flipped Callahan over, regaining control, but the serial killer was back on his feet. Blood poured down one side of his body, black in the night. "Give it up."

"Go to hell." Callahan, eyes burning with rage came again.

Aiming for a head shot, Carter squeezed the trigger. The killer stumbled back, his foot slipping on the edge of the rooftop. For a moment he froze, balanced on the edge, a dark red spot between his eyes. Then, without a sound, Callahan fell, his body disappearing into the darkness below. Carter sat on a water tank, his chest heaving, the adrenaline slowly ebbing away. At the sound of Rio calling his name, he walked to the crumbling edge and looked down at Callahan's lifeless body.

"He's dead." Rio looked up at him, hands on hips. "You okay?"

Tossing a toothpick into his mouth, Carter nodded. "Dandy." As bricks crumbled underfoot, he stepped away. "Call it in. I'll be right down."

FORTY-EIGHT

JEZABEL

Souza had situated his hideout inside a survivalist's bunker. A sealed entrance with a hatch complete with a handwheel reminded Kane of the waterproof hatches in a submarine. The spinning of the wheel as the hatch opened covered the *pop* of the M18 as Kane dispatched the bald guy and rolled him down an embankment. A face appeared at the entrance to the wide hole and then vanished as the man backed down a set of sturdy steel steps. Kane followed. The guard with an AK-47 slung across his chest led him along a passageway of granite walls. Hewn out of solid rock, a nest of tunnels vanished into darkness. The bunker incorporated a mineshaft, giving numerous escape routes. *Interesting.*

Light bulbs hung along the wall like fairy lights and underfoot a raised wooden floor led to a thick metal door. As they went along, Kane searched for guards but found none directly inside the main entrance. So far, apart from the four dead men outside, the only other guard he'd seen was accompanying him. The prison guard, Amy Clark, had mentioned three men in the chopper—two gunmen and a pilot—so maybe five or six men in total Souza could trust... or all that were left from his original organization. He considered his options as the passageway opened out to display racks of automatic weapons alongside a wooden box containing grenades. He hadn't noticed a power supply but surmised a setup this organized would likely be using solar panels and gas-run generators. No doubt, they'd be concealed in the side of the mountain. They passed by open doors leading to sleeping quarters and a wide closed door with glass above it. Through the window, Kane made out a group of people dressed in hazmat suits involved in pill making and packaging. Strangled cries and begging drifted along the passageway and Kane went on high alert as they paused, and the guard turned to look at him.

"The boss is waiting for you." The man chuckled as someone screamed in agony.

Kane glared at him. "Why in there?"

"He wants to show you his daughter's work." The man smiled, showing yellow stained teeth. "You'll enjoy it. You might say she's an artist."

Nodding, Kane slowed his steps. He needed more information. "So is this a family business?"

"Yeah, six cousins are all he trusts now." The guard frowned. "He must trust you, Angel of Death. He speaks about you often."

Surprised the DEA undercover guy he'd replaced had set down such a great history, Kane stopped walking and stared at him. He knew way too much for a simple heavy. "The feeling is mutual. I don't work with amateurs." He leaned against the wall, nonchalant, like this guy was his best buddy. The guard might be a talker. "So what's the deal with Alan Turner? He sure doesn't sound like a family member."

"He's the pilot and can move deliveries around. No one suspects him. He works out of the airport and never comes here. There's no need for a meet. You message him a code word when you require product, and you'll get a message when the shipment is ready to be collected. You send the payment back with the delivery guy. It's a streamlined service. Eduardo is rebuilding the network, but first we needed product in the quantities guys like you require. All the pills are made here. It's safe and secure."

Frowning, Kane stared at him. "Yeah, so if that's what Alan What's-his-name does, that doesn't mean squat to me. Souza told me it was a family business."

"He is part of the family." The guard grinned. "Alan's mom was Eduardo's sister. She married an outsider but they're both gone now."

Kane nodded. "And the workers? Sisters?"

"Nah." The guard chuckled. "They're the old ones from the brothels. Disposable and replaceable. We have a mineshaft full of them. You should hear them scream when we toss them in. Sometimes they take days to die."

Looking into the face of pure evil, Kane lashed out and punched him in the throat. Under his knuckles bone cracked. The guard fell flat on his back, grabbing his throat, wheezing. Windpipe crushed, he didn't have long to live, and Kane grabbed his feet and dragged him into one of the side rooms. He looked down at him and shook his head in disgust. In seconds, the man's eyes stared into nothing, and Kane slid from the room, closing the door behind him. The screams along the passageway grew louder with each step, and knowing Souza would likely recognize him the moment he stepped inside the room, he slid out his pistol and held it down alongside his thigh. He tapped his com and kept his voice to just above a whisper. "Get someone out to the airport. Don't let him get away. He'll have all the contacts of the latest suppliers. Plus he's a family member. He needs to be buried deep or this will start up again."

"*Already done.*" Wolfe sounded confident as usual.

Kane closed his eyes for a few seconds to picture Jenna's lovely face and Tauri's smile. He took a deep breath and slid deep into the zone. He had no idea how many people were inside the torture chamber or if they were armed with AK-47s. He opened the door and digested the scene before him. Eduardo Souza leaned against a wall, his attention fixed on a blood-covered man tied to a chair with wire. He didn't so much as turn his head to look as Kane walked into the room. Too enthralled by the horrific torture, Souza had fixed his mouth in a satisfied grin. Kane's finger slid to the trigger, but the pistol remained at his side as disgust flowed over him. Wearing a blood-soaked apron, her hair tied back, China looked up from her work and smiled at him before grabbing a handful of her prisoner's hair and drawing the sharp blade across the man's pale white neck.

As blood gushed, Kane stared at her in disbelief.

"Very entertaining." Souza clapped. "Ten days must be a new record."

"Aw, it's because I gave him a few hours in between to imagine what I planned to do to him next." China wiped bloody hands on her apron. "It makes it so exciting." She grinned at Kane. "I saved the best bit for you."

Bile rushed up the back of Kane's throat. To think he'd once had concerns about China. He'd been lied to by a sadistic psychopathic murderer. There was no sister and she was just like her father. Without a second thought, he raised his M18 pistol and shot her between the eyes. As Souza turned to stare at him openmouthed, Kane ripped off the ball cap and wig and smiled at him. "She was as twisted as you, wasn't she?"

"You." Souza went for his weapon.

Before Souza's gun cleared the holster, Kane squeezed the trigger.

FORTY-NINE

BLACK ROCK FALLS

Saturday

Waking in a luxury hotel might be some people's idea of fun, but Jenna had spent a fitful night. She preferred her own bed, but most of all she missed Kane. Not hearing from him for so long and not knowing if he was safe was tearing her apart. Even before they were married, she gained comfort from just knowing he was around. His love for her was a warm glow in her heart. He'd told her once that that's where he'd be if he weren't around, and all she had to do was close her eyes and think of him. She stared into the dawn and pictured him. "Come home to me, Dave. We need you."

Unable to sleep, she called room service and ordered breakfast and then trudged to the shower. Everyone had slept in the Cattleman's Hotel last night, apart from Rio and Rowley, who lived closer to town. Dressed and ready for work, she checked the time. It was coming up to seven, so she called Nanny Raya to give her an update. The nanny was already in the kitchen making breakfast for Tauri. She had been calling her son many times since heading into town yesterday. Not having either parent at home would be stressful for him, but surprisingly he took it in his stride. "I'm glad you're having a good time. I'm sure the bed I slept in last night had lumps in it."

Hearing Tauri giggle lifted her mood. He was indeed a ray of sunshine and every day with him was a blessing. "I hope I'll be home today. We're still hunting down the baddie men."

"I hope so because I miss you and Daddy." Tauri grunted as he climbed into a chair at the kitchen table. He lowered his voice to a stage whisper. *"Nanny Raya's pancakes have lumps in them just like your bed. I like Daddy's pancakes best."*

Jenna smiled. "I do too. Eat your breakfast. I'll call you later. Bye."

"Bye, Mommy."

She hadn't heard Jo in the background. Maybe she was asleep or chatting to her daughter, Jaime. Having Jo at the ranch was good because she always helped with the chores and enjoyed tending to the horses. A knock on the door brought room service along with Raven and Carter. Two carts rolled into her room as the men followed them inside. Carter tipped the servers and smiled at Jenna. She went to rescue her breakfast from the cart and looked at them. "What brings you to my room first light?"

"Norrell called." Carter grabbed plates of food and a large pot of coffee and placed them on the table. "We have a positive ID for Callahan. She did a preliminary autopsy last night and my gunshot went through his head." He shrugged. "I had no choice but to take him down, Jenna. He attacked me with a knife."

Nibbling on a slice of toast, Jenna nodded. She didn't need to know if Carter was coping with killing a man. Like Kane, he managed to separate his feelings. "Good job. I'm glad you took him down. After seeing what he was capable of doing, you only accelerated the death penalty. No doubt many relatives of the victims he killed will sleep better knowing he's dead." The news hadn't affected her appetite, and Kane had drummed into her to eat when possible during a case. She scooped up scrambled eggs on her fork. "I can't see a problem with the shooting. It was self-defense and you have a witness." She leaned back to ease the pain in her back. "I'll sign a report for your superiors."

"How's the back?" Raven's gaze swept over her. "Any cramps overnight?"

Giving her head a shake, Jenna swallowed her food. "I feel better since resting. Although the baby was in a fight last night. It just wouldn't settle. It seems the moment I try to rest it wakes up and starts kicking."

"That's normal." Raven waved a strip of bacon around as he talked. "When you walk around, you're rocking the baby to sleep; when you stop, they wake up and become active. It's good it's active. Usually they go quiet before delivery, so that's a good thing right now with Dave away."

"That's good to know." Carter was demolishing scrambled eggs, bacon, and a stack of pancakes. "I do know how to deliver a baby but it's not something I really want to do."

"I'd deliver it if push came to shove." Raven sipped steaming coffee. "But Jenna has an obstetrician on standby and Norrell if needs be."

Slightly annoyed, Jenna looked from one to the other. "This baby is not coming along unless Dave is here. I'm not taking that pleasure away from him. So I'm not doing anything that might cause an early delivery." She waved at them. "I'll keep strenuous activities to a minimum for a time. You and the rest of the team can continue to hunt down the prisoners. The DOC search parties are close to the Triple Z Roadhouse, so it won't be long before they hit town."

Her phone buzzed and she stared at the caller ID. "What's up, Rio?"

"I'm at the old cemetery. I had a call on the 911 line that someone's dog found a body at the bottom of an open grave. It's *damaged, but from the general description, I figure it's Romero. I processed the scene took photographs and a video. There's no evidence around the gravesite. It rained hard last night, no footprints at all. Norrell and her team are removing the body now. She has Romero's DNA, so she'll run a test ASAP. There is a big problem. The body had a tarot card right on top of it."*

Jenna swallowed hard. "Is it the usual card left by the Tarot Killer? They're distinct."

"Yeah." Rio's boots crunched on gravel. *"The thing is, it's pretty obvious the guy fell into the grave, likely broke his neck due to the fall. It looks broken, but there's a large boulder on his head and it smashed his skull. He didn't do that falling down a hole."*

Sighing, Jenna leaned back in her chair. "Well, if it is Romero, I guess we owe the Tarot Killer a gift of gratitude. Although, how he found Romero when we couldn't is a mystery." She cleared her throat. "Beth and Styles searched that area last night. They walked the entire cemetery and didn't see anyone, but we did have a report of someone there earlier."

"Maybe he'd already fallen into the grave before they arrived?" Rio sounded optimistic. *"I doubt they'd have been checking open graves for him, or maybe even seen the open graves in the dark. There wasn't a moon last night."*

Sipping her coffee, Jenna nodded. "True. Can you call the DOC search party coordinator and tell them? Also, send out an ambiguous media release saying two of the prisoners have been found. Don't mention they're dead. I don't want Margos to know."

"Sure. I'll bring everything into the office and update the server." Rio disconnected.

Jenna looked at Carter and Raven. "Two down." She pushed hair behind her ears and raised her eyebrows. "If we can find Margos, life might return to normal."

By eight-thirty they were all in the conference room. Jenna

looked around the table. "Okay, Mason Margos is still out there. The DOC has its search parties ready to roll, and they'll keep moving toward town, searching local ranches, outbuildings, and any cabins in the forest. We'll make ourselves known. Wear your Kevlar vests and jackets clearly distinguishing you all as law enforcement and be visible. The townsfolk need to know we're on the job."

"Would you suggest we split into three groups and search the more unusual places, empty buildings?" Carter moved a toothpick across his lips. "After chasing down Romero, it's obvious they know about the old warehouses. They'd make a good hideout."

Jenna nodded. "Okay, pick an area to search and we'll meet back here after lunch. Take regular breaks. We have a tab at Aunt Betty's Café. I need you all ready to move out if we get a sighting of Margos. Rio and Rowley, I want you in town."

"I hope you're planning on directing traffic from behind your desk today." Carter pushed to his feet and then held up both hands. "I know it's not my place to tell you to rest up, but if Dave knows we stood by while you overtaxed yourself, there will be hell to pay."

Touched by his concern, but knowing if she gave Carter an inch, he'd take a mile, Jenna nodded slowly. "If you insist. I'll remain here with Raven just in case Margos raids the building, gets past Maggie, and I suddenly forget how to shoot my weapon."

"Good." Carter grinned, ignoring her sarcasm. "I figured you'd see it my way." He pointed to an old industrial area on the outskirts of town. "We'll start there. Jo drove your cruiser into town, so we'll take that."

"I figure Margos will be heading toward Blackwater." Styles stabbed the map. "We know his vehicle, so he'll need to swap it out or change the plate. We're heading to the vehicle recycling yards. There's a good chance he'd drop by and take the opportunity to steal one. They're usually up on the walls, like trophies. There are old factories there as well, a good place to hole up."

"The problem is, out there you won't get any bars." Rowley rubbed his chin. "All the businesses in that black spot use landlines. You'll be out of contact between here and here." He pointed on the map.

"Gotcha." Styles nodded and pointed to a meat processing plant. "So if I make it to here, I can make a call?"

"Yeah." Rowley shrugged. "For some reason that small black-spot area wipes out everything, even satellite phones, GPS. It's like the Bermuda Triangle of Black Rock Falls."

"How wonderfully spooky." Beth grinned at Styles. "Maybe we'll drive through and end up in another time."

"It doesn't wipe out vehicles, does it?" Styles frowned.

"It hasn't yet." Rowley chuckled. "Or we couldn't drive to Blackwater."

Jenna's phone chimed and she waved everyone from the room but placed the phone on speaker for Raven's benefit. "Norrell, how good to speak to you. How are things going? You must be snowed under?"

"You could say that." Norrell's footfalls on tile echoed through the speaker. *"I've prioritized the autopsies, so you'll have the findings ASAP, although Wolfe will want to oversee everything when he gets back, so no bodies will be released until he is satisfied. I called mainly to tell you I have a positive ID for Romero. He has extensive injuries, a broken neck, massive head trauma. His body is so distorted we couldn't fit him into a body bag. He is in a cold room storage area until rigor passes and I can straighten him out. So we have positive IDs on all the victims, even the foot found at the first ranch. I used Serena Lee's DNA to match him as her grandfather."* She swallowed hard. *"Jenna, those pigs, they're not going to be used for human consumption are they?"*

"No." Raven leaned forward in his seat. "Raven here. Rio

organized for them to be collected before Norrell searched the pigpen for body parts. They were taken to a pet-food processing plant."

"Oh, that's good." Norrell cleared her throat. *"Have you heard from Dave?"*

Jenna kept her gaze on the desk. "Not yet. I'm guessing they're busy."

"Okay." Norrell blew out a long sigh. *"Call me if you need me, and remember, it's time to pack your hospital bag."*

Smiling, Jenna nodded. *"Already done and sitting in the Beast. Catch you later."* She disconnected and looked at Raven. "I'm putting on a fresh pot of coffee and then we can update the files."

"Oh, goodie." Raven rubbed his hands together. "I mean about the coffee. I hate filing."

FIFTY

At five after eleven, Jenna's phone chimed a message. Chills ran down her spine as she stared at the screen. "Oh, no! We have a kidnapping." She held out the phone to Raven. "It says: I have Wendy. Leave your office alone and follow instructions or she dies."

"Wendy who?" Raven stared at the phone. "No caller ID."

Panic gripped Jenna. "It must be Wendy from Aunt Betty's Café. She's a friend." She called Wendy and it went to voice-mail. "She's not picking up. I'll call Aunt Betty's. Hi, Susie, is Wendy working today?"

"She was due in at eleven and always comes by early. I'm waiting for her to arrive." Susie Hartwig, the owner-manager of the eatery, sounded alarmed. *"Has something happened to her?"*

Forcing herself to keep calm, Jenna raised both eyebrows and looked at Raven. "I have no reason to believe something has happened to her, but I need to know where she is right now. If she comes in, can you ask her to call me, please?"

"Not a problem."

The moment she disconnected, Jenna's phone chimed again. She stared at it. "No caller ID. Call Kalo to trace the call, and I'll keep them on the line for as long as possible." She put the phone on speaker.

"Now you know who I'm talking about. You have exactly five minutes to leave the building alone. Climb into your vehicle and drive to the convenience store. I'll call you again once you're there. Leave now or Wendy dies."

Stomach clenching, Jenna shook her head. "That's not going to happen. For a start I can't drive the truck. Who is this? If you've kidnapped someone against their will and this is a ransom demand, I need the terms before I leave the building."

"Are you dumb or just plain stupid? You know darn well this is Mason Margos. I'll trade Wendy for you, for a start." In the background she could hear a muffled scream. *"Wendy doesn't like me very much. Go figure."*

Trying to remain calm, Jenna sucked in a deep breath. Margos was unhinged and not thinking straight. "I don't like you either, and what do you want with me? If you figure holding a sheriff hostage will get you out of prison, you're sadly mistaken. I would be collateral damage if it meant getting you back in a cell."

"I'm not going back to a cell." Margos chuckled and Wendy screamed again. *"You care about the people in your town. That much I know about you just by speaking to the townsfolk. You know not one of them recognized me and I've been close by all this time. I'll swap you for Wendy. You're valuable and your deputies will release Callahan and Romero in a trade for you."*

Raven slipped back into the room and nodded. He pushed a slip of paper across the desk with an address scribbled on it. From the area it was one of the dilapidated warehouses alongside the old railroad line.

Nodding, Jenna stood. "No deal. Do you figure if I release them, you'll get out of town alive? I have teams of armed people hunting you down. I'll alert the DOC teams that you're in town. You won't stand a chance if you hurt Wendy. Give yourself up and we'll talk. I'll make sure no one shoots you." The line went dead. She looked at Raven. "I guess that's a *no?*"

The desk phone rang. It was Maggie. "Yes, Maggie."

"Agent Carter called in. Everyone is heading to the industrial area. There was a sighting of Margos ten minutes ago. The owner of a recycling yard chased him off. They'll call in again once they're back in range."

Unable to believe her ears, Jenna stared at Raven. "Okay, Maggie, tell them it's a false lead. Margos just called me. He's holding Wendy hostage." She gave Maggie the details. "I'm on my way now with Raven." She disconnected.

"You should call in the DOC." Raven's face was filled with concern. "You can't possibly handle this alone."

Pulling Kane's Kevlar vest over her head, she rounded on him. "I'm the sheriff. Of course I can handle this and I won't be alone. You'll be with me and we have Ben. It's about time we put that dog through his paces."

"Okay." Raven attached a leash to the K9. "Does Kane have a spare Kevlar vest?"

Nodding, Jenna checked her weapon. "In the supply room." When Raven left the office, Jenna pressed her tracker ring. The moment her deputies, Kane, or Wolfe came into range, they would be alerted. They could also hear every word she said and could track her movements.

Unfortunately, it only worked one way. She would have no idea if the cavalry was coming. She made a call to the DOC command post and gave the person answering the phone the details of where she believed Margos was hiding. For now, this was all she could do. Raven was solid. He could shoot straight but he wasn't Kane. She met him in the passageway. "I know the area. We can go off road and then park the Beast inside one of the warehouses and walk. He won't see us coming. Okay, let's do this."

* * *

The old warehouse's rusted metal roof groaned in the wind as Jenna, Raven, and Ben slipped inside. The smell of oil and decay oozed from the dark interior. Shafts of sunlight fought their way through the broken dirt-covered windows to cast long eerie shadows across the floor. Waiting for her eyes to become adjusted to the dim interior, Jenna slipped behind a large rusty bin the size of a boxcar. The ground, once a solid concrete slab, was cracked and weeds grew up all around the floor, leaning toward the light. A scream followed by threats came from the opposite end of the building. Concern for Wendy gripped Jenna. She kept her voice to just above a whisper. "He must be hiding in the other end of the building that held the offices. It has windows all around. We can't risk using flashlights if we want to get the jump on him."

"Ben will be able to see. He'll lead us to them." Raven leaned closer. "He won't kill her, not yet. She is all he has as a bargaining chip right now."

Jenna nodded and scratched Ben's ears. For a K9, the dog was very sociable. "I don't plan on trying to negotiate with a psychopath. Wendy is the priority here. First chance we have, take him down."

"Ben will attack on command." Raven swiped a hand over his mouth. "There's always a risk he'll be shot, but if he can distract Margos, we'll be able to take him out."

A terrified scream filled the entire warehouse. Margos was starting to enjoy himself, which made him even more danger- ous. When Raven moved off with Ben leading the way, stretching out the leash between them, Jenna followed closely behind, keeping to the shadows and using massive pieces of machinery and old boxcars to conceal their movements. Ahead Margos was muttering as if arguing with himself. It was the ravings of an unhinged mind, and Jenna's hand trembled on her weapon. She'd made Kane a promise to stay safe while he was away, and she never broke her promises—until now, but what other choice did she have? Everyone on her team was out of contact and one of her friends was in deadly peril.

Ahead, a small light shone from a divided area that had once been an office. Inside, Wendy sat on an old rusty metal chair, hands tied behind her. Margos had his fist balled in her hair and was grinning down at her as he twisted it. In that moment, Jenna wanted to raise her weapon and shoot him, but the cop inside her would always make her follow procedure. She didn't have a problem shooting a perpetrator if they drew down on her, but if she shot him in cold blood, she'd be no better than him. Making sure both she and Raven were completely protected by the heavy machinery, she pointed her M18 pistol at Margos. "Sheriff's department, put down your weapon and surrender. You're surrounded."

"That's never gonna happen." Margos dragged Wendy to her feet by her hair, holding her in front of him. He waved a pistol around and then pressed it to her temple. "I'd like to kill her. My fingers are itching to see her bleed out on the floor. Do you know how that feels, Sheriff? I can tell you it feels mighty fine, and once you've done it you want to do it over and over again." He laughed manically. "If one of your men takes me down, I'll take her with me. One for the road, you might say."

Jenna watched Wendy's eyes. Her friend stared to the left. Hoping one of the team had arrived, she nudged Raven. A second later Ben flew out of the shadows like a bullet and sunk his teeth into Margos' thigh. The gun moved away from Wendy's temple, and she dropped like a stone just as a shot rang out. Beside her a millisecond later, Raven fired as well. Margos fell sideways, a gaping hole in his head.

"Clear." Raven darted forward to lift Wendy to her feet as Ben ran around them barking. "Are you okay?"

"I've had better days." Wendy tossed her long blonde hair

over one shoulder and rubbed the top of her head. "Thanks for saving me, Raven."

"It wasn't me." Raven indicated to his left and a smile spread across his lips. "It was him."

Jenna leaned against the machinery suddenly exhausted. The room darkened for a second, as someone climbed through an old brick window frame. She turned as Kane dropped to the floor. Relief rolled over her as he holstered his weapon and walked toward her smiling.

"Honey, I'm home."

EPILOGUE

One week later

Sorting out the murders took time, and Jenna waited for Wolfe to sign off on the deaths of Troy Lee, from the first cabin, and Robert Moore, from the second cabin. The DA ruled in his opinion that Troy Lee had been murdered by Romero and Callahan, on Serena's testimony as Amy Clark hadn't witnessed the shooter in the first murder. All she recalled was that the two men carrying weapons were Romero and Margos, so unless positive evidence could be revealed, Robert Moore's case would remain open. No bullets or casings from either of the men's guns had been found at the scene. However, she had given a compelling eyewitness statement on Margos' stabbing murder of Robert Moore. The case was different for librarian Elaine Harper. Norrell had discovered positive DNA evidence that proved Romero murdered her. Both Romero and Callahan were implicated in the murder of Maya Brooks. Both murders appeared to be opportunistic kills.

Kane and Carter had been cleared of the takedowns of both Callahan and Margos, but Romero's remained a mystery. How he'd ended up at the bottom of an empty grave with a tarot card within minutes of agents Katz and Styles searching the area had everyone baffled. Detailed forensic sweeps of the area found nothing. As usual, the Tarot Killer had taken care of business and then vanished.

Jenna closed the cases and so had the FBI. Three notorious serial killers on death row had wreaked havoc in her town and they'd paid with their lives. The news of their deaths had brought a small modicum of comfort to Amy Clark. She'd never return to the prison service but had engaged a lawyer to fight for compensation. Jenna had spent some time with her before she left with her parents to return to Helena. Amy was a fighter and when back on her feet pledged to help abused women.

Serena Lee and her family returned to Black Rock Falls. Although heartsore about her grandfather's murder, the young girl was improving since the therapy sessions. Her mother, Kaya, had informed Jenna, and they would continue for as long as necessary. With the support of a large loving family, Jenna had confidence that, with time, Serena would put the terrifying experience behind her.

With the local cases solved, Jenna called a meeting before Beth and Styles returned to Rattlesnake Creek. Carter and Jo would stay for the weekend for a break. They'd already filed their reports in Snakeskin Gully, collected Jo's daughter, Jaime, and returned to the ranch.

With everyone around the conference table, Jenna listened with interest as Kane gave an abridged account of his mission. He wouldn't give details of how it happened or who involved, so she found it strange when he'd decided to explain anything at all to the team.

"Kalo tracked the chopper that attacked the prison bus." Kane leaned back in his chair nonchalantly as if hunting down cartel kingpins were a routine job. "Wolfe grabbed me and we jumped into a chopper and followed the flight path." He shrugged. "It was basic surveillance. We watched and noticed movement around what was a survivalist's bunker built inside an old mine." He looked at Jenna and dropped his lashes. "Eduardo Souza was inside and we took him and his men down."

"It was after we discovered that the bunker was his new headquarters." Wolfe folded his hands on the table. "Computers held information about shipments, names of suppliers, and locations. Souza was planning on spreading instant death all over the US. All he needed was a continuous supply of raw material. He was making pills on-site."

"So we'd accidentally discovered his complete distribution center." Kane lifted a cup of coffee and sipped. "He had only a few guards. He believed the bunker was impenetrable. He moved product and cash using the chopper. We notified the DEA and discovered the chopper went down over the ocean, no survivors."

"So our notion that Souza had engineered his escape with the serial killers to take you down was an error?" Carter tossed a toothpick in the garbage. "It seemed to fit."

"Oh yeah." Kane smiled. "Souza wanted to take me down along with you and Jo. We found instructions in a book, coded, but the code was so simple a kid could decipher it. First up, to make sure we were all out of town when the escape went down, Souza had petty criminals watching our ranch and around town. His men were prepared to cause a major wreck, or anything to get us all away from the area of the prison escape. It just happened that Jenna drove out alone. From the two men involved, everything that happened to Jenna was created on the fly. They knew we'd all rush to assist and were prepared to do time to complete their mission, so we gather that Souza made them an offer they couldn't refuse."

Jenna raised both eyebrows. "So they weren't after me and Tauri?"

"Nope, Carter and me, because we brought him down in the sting that put him in prison." Kane blew out a long breath. "Once Souza had everyone in the forest, he was using satellite phones delivered by a drone to give the escapees instructions. They wanted us in the cabin so they could burn us alive. When that didn't work, and we left the forest, we figure Souza turned his back on the prisoners. He was using them, and I doubt he ever planned to get them away."

"We believe Souza intended to rebuild his empire and then send in his goons to take down Dave and Carter." Wolfe shrugged. "The DEA will be searching his files and there are thousands. This guy had files on everyone. He was a danger to the country. When the DEA director spoke to us before we left, he told us drugs were only the tip of the iceberg. We knew about the arms deals, but there was much more. The poor addicted souls they had working like slaves in the old mine gave up a ton of information." He held up both hands like a traffic cop. "Don't ask, because they didn't give us details. It's classified, and to be honest, we wanted to get out of there as soon as possible." He glanced around the table. "I put eight stitches in Dave's arm." He held up a thumb and finger an inch apart. "He came that close to taking one in the head. Trust me, none of us needs to deal with cartels again."

Impressed, Jenna leaned forward in her chair. "Well, we won't need to worry about Souza any longer." She stood and looked at her watch. It was five after twelve. "It's been a long couple of weeks. Great job everyone. Go home and enjoy your weekend—before anything else happens."

She noticed Wolfe hanging back and sat back down. Kane had called Raven to one side, and they were chatting about motorcycles. She looked at Wolfe, who was frowning at her. Shaking her head, she waited for him to insist she rest. "I'm fine. Honestly. Raven cared for me very well. He has great bedside manner and never frowns at me like you do."

"I frown at you because I care." Wolfe narrowed his gaze at her. "I've seen the latest ultrasounds, and everyone agrees the baby is ready to come. Your blood pressure is a little elevated, so I must insist you rest until delivery." He cleared his throat in his doctor way when he's deadly serious. "It's not easy giving birth, Jenna. It might take hours and you need to be in good shape, not exhausted from working twelve and fourteen hours a day." He shot a glance at Kane. "Dave, if you want everything to go smoothly, you must insist Jenna rests."

"I couldn't insist Jenna does anything." Kane smiled at him. "I could refuse to drive her to work, but that's the best I can do."

Jenna glared at him. "Don't you dare. Give me one time when I've been reckless. I'm the sheriff, and being weak isn't an option."

"Okay. Why did you figure you could take down Margos with Raven alone?" Kane stared at her, but his expression was soft not condemning. "Being stubborn could have gotten you killed."

Shaking her head, Jenna blew out a long breath. "I had Raven *and* Ben. We got the job done."

"That's not the point." Kane walked around the table as Jenna stood. "Agreed, Raven took the shot and hit center mass, but if Wendy hadn't followed my orders and pretended to faint, it might have been a different story." He looked at Raven. "You did an excellent job caring for my wife and I appreciate it. Your K9, Ben, is something else. He gave us the edge."

"It was your shot that took him down." Raven shook his head. "Do you ever miss?"

"Nope." Kane slid an arm around Jenna and pulled her close. "But you had him. It all worked out okay. Come over tomorrow. I'm making ribs. I've gotten together some of the motorcycle parts you brought over. You mentioned finding other parts and frames in some of your cabins. We could take an afternoon and go and pick them up? I need more parts to bring one or two of them back to life."

"I'll look forward to it." Raven indicated with his chin to Wolfe. "Will the entire gang be there?"

"Yeah, apart from Beth and Styles. They have a new case." Kane rubbed Jenna's back. "People usually start dropping by around ten." He looked at Wolfe. "I've restocked my wine cellar, so get Norrell to drive you home."

"See you there." Wolfe headed for the door.

"Hey, wait up." Raven hurried after him. "I want to talk to you about Emily."

Jenna wanted to chase after them to hear what was being said. Instead, she melted into Kane's arms. Being without his solid strength for what felt like a lifetime had been difficult. Her mind went back to the confrontation with Margos. "I know I promised to stay at home until you came back, but things happened so fast. I was needed here and, in any case, I could have taken Margos."

"I know, but I took the shot. It was safer from my angle with Wendy there and all." Kane turned her to face him. "I don't intend to make any demands on what you do, Jenna, but I hate it when you put yourself in danger."

Nodding, Jenna read the trouble in his eyes. He'd been closer to death than she'd realized and he'd never divulge what really happened. "That's not the entire story is it, about Eduardo Souza?"

"Nope, he was worse than I imagined, and it turns out his daughter was a psychopathic killer just like her dad." He frowned. "She almost fooled me." A shudder went through him and he sighed. "I'd like to lock those memories up and throw away the key." He looked into her eyes. "So let's go home. Are you ready to buy things for the nursery? I know you want the baby in our room for a time, and that's fine, but he or she will need their own space before you know it. I'm glad we added extensions to the house along with Nanny Raya's rooms. I figure we'll be needing more bedrooms." He smiled at her. "What do you say? We can furnish the other rooms as well. It will be fun."

Jenna smiled. "Yes, I should buy furniture. I know I've held off on buying furniture for the baby for a long time, but I've been afraid something might happen. If I don't do something soon, our baby won't have a place to sleep. Not that I'll want to put it down for a second."

"I think that's normal, especially when we've waited so long, but now you're ready, we'll do some online shopping, and when you're taking a nap, I'll take Tauri out for a ride. He is anxious to ride Firebird more and I kinda promised. Carter can come along. Seagull needs exercising. He mentioned taking Jo and Jaime to supper at the Cattleman's Hotel, so I'll be cooking just for us tonight."

Having people around for days meant their time together was limited. She put her arms around his neck and looked into his deep blue eyes. A surge of love engulfed her and she figured that would never change. Her reaction to him was so great that her knees had gone weak when he'd dropped through the window in that grimy warehouse. Her once almost robotic, in the zone, sniper husband had a big loving heart, and to think he trusted her with it. She swallowed a rush of emotion. "Oh, that's good. Not that I don't like having them around but I miss our alone time together. Snuggling on the sofa and watching a good movie would be bliss."

"Me too. Let's head off home right away." He kissed the end of her nose and grinned. "Once Tauri is settled for the night, you choose the movie and I'll pop some corn."

Sighing with delight, Jenna grinned. "Perfect."

A LETTER FROM D.K. HOOD

Dear Readers,

Thank so much for choosing my novel and coming with me on another thrilling adventure with Kane and Alton in *Fear for Her Life*.

If you'd like to keep up to date with all my latest releases, just sign up at the website link below. Your details will not be shared and you can unsubscribe at any time.

www.bookouture.com/dk-hood

You'll be able to download a free copy of my short thriller *In the Dead of the Night*.

I enjoy writing the stories of Jenna Alton and Dave Kane and having you along. This story in particular, with every member of the team involved, was particularly exciting for me to write. Keeping Jenna involved proved quite a challenge so late in her pregnancy. Don't worry, she will be right in the middle of the action in Book 26, and when I get to Book 27, we'll leap forward six months, so the entire team will be together fighting crime.

Until next time, stay safe, and I'll look forward to you joining me soon in Black Rock Falls for our next adventure.

If you enjoyed my story, I would be very grateful if you could leave a review and recommend my book to your friends and family. I really enjoy hearing from readers, so feel free to ask me questions at any time. You can get in touch on my Facebook page, my Facebook Reader's Group, or my website.

Thank you so much for your support.

D.K. Hood

www.dkhood.com

 facebook.com/dkhoodauthor
x.com/DKHood_Author

ACKNOWLEDGMENTS

To all those people who support me in so many different ways: the team working tirelessly behind each book, my wonderful husband, my grandsons, who make me laugh, the reviewers and the readers who comment on my posts, and the people who stop me for a chat or just give me a smile. Thank you!

PUBLISHING TEAM

Turning a manuscript into a book requires the efforts of many people. The publishing team at Bookouture would like to acknowledge everyone who contributed to this publication.

Audio
Alba Proko
Sinead O'Connor
Melissa Tran

Commercial
Lauren Morrissette
Hannah Richmond
Imogen Allport

Cover design
Blacksheep

Data and analysis
Mark Alder
Mohamed Bussuri

Editorial
Helen Jenner
Ria Clare

Made in United States
Orlando, FL
24 March 2025

59780017R00169